THE BALACLAVIAN SOCIETY ONLY RECRUITED THE TOWN'S SNOBS, BUT WAS SOMETHING ROTTEN IN THE UPPER CRUST?

RUTH SMUTH—Bouncy, blonde social butterfly of Balaclava Junction. Had she taken a dangerous tumble into blackmail and a politician's bed?

WILLIAM TWERKS—The wealthy squire of Twerks Hall. Beneath his taste for tartan plaid and furniture made of animal horns, is he suppressing an appetite for murder?

HENRY HODGER—Aging attorney crippled with arthritis. Why does his walking stick look like the perfect murder weapon?

MR. AND MRS. POMMELL—The pompous town bank president and his pampered wife. They may know that a rich man won't get to heaven, but would they push someone else in that direction for a price?

Professor Shandy suspects that someone in Balaclava Junction's high society has stooped low enough to murder. And with the help of Police Chief Fred Ottermole (who trained with reruns of "Barney Miller") and Edmund, Betsy Lomax's feckless feline, he's out to collect the clues that will catch a killer.

Other Avon Books by
Charlotte MacLeod

Something The Cat Dragged In

CHARLOTTE MACLEOD

AVON
PUBLISHERS OF BARD, CAMELOT, DISCUS AND FLARE BOOKS

Some readers wonder what actual area and institution Balaclava County and its college are drawn from. The fact is, neither exists except in a space warp somewhere between the writer's imagination and her typewriter. No similarity to any actual person or place is intended. The characters and situations are only as real as you want them to be.

AVON BOOKS
A division of
The Hearst Corporation
1790 Broadway
New York, New York 10019

Copyright © 1983 by Charlotte Macleod
Published by arrangement with Doubleday & Company, Inc. Library of Congress Catalog Card Number: 83-45024
ISBN: 0-380-69096-9

The Doubleday & Company, Inc., edition contains the following Library of Congress Cataloging in Publication Data:
MacLeod, Charlotte.
Something the Cat Dragged In.
I. Title.
PS3563.A31865S6   1983   813'.54

First Avon Printing, September, 1984

For Maggie Curran

Something The Cat Dragged In

Chapter One

"Edmund! You know better than that. Dragging in some poor, dead creature just as I've finished mopping the floor."

Like Eliza navigating the ice floes, Mrs. Betsy Lomax stepped from one to another of the newspapers she'd put down to protect her clean, wet linoleum. Edmund was a well brought up cat, as cats go, but males were tomcats the world over.

"Never seen one yet, feline, human, or otherwise, that could pass up a chance to trail his muddy feet through a fresh-scrubbed kitchen," she grumbled. "I've a good mind to slosh you right between the whiskers with this mop."

But what would be the use? Edmund's memory for punishments that conflicted with his hunting instincts was conveniently short. Besides, Betsy Lomax was deeply attached to Edmund. Furthermore, much as she deplored wanton slaughter, she had to admit chipmunks were not an endangered species. This had to be a chipmunk. The lump of ruddy fur clamped between Edmund's jaws was too big for a field mouse.

No, it wasn't a chipmunk. It wasn't a red squirrel, either. It wasn't a mole or a vole or anything recognizably four-legged. It was only a scrap of fur. Wrong again, it wasn't even fur. It was hair. Human hair, from the look of it. Mrs. Lomax wasn't a squeamish woman, but she gulped once or twice and folded the hem of her apron over her fingers before she reached down to pry Edmund's mouth open.

"I do declare!" she gasped, when she'd got the prey away from him. "Edmund, have you been sneaking into Professor Ungley's bedroom again? He's going to have seventeen kitten fits in one straight row if he ever finds out you've taken this. Now what in tarnation am I going to do?"

Betsy Lomax had reason to ponder. Professor Emeritus Herbert Ungley was touchy about a great many things,

9

but most particularly on the subject of his hairpiece. He'd managed to delude himself into believing there wasn't a soul in Balaclava Junction who knew he wore one; even though the toupee was the same ginger color it had been when he'd sneaked into Boston some forty years back and bought it, while the few hairs that still managed to straggle out of his scalp emerged an unpleasant yellowish white.

Ungley was an unpleasant old man altogether, if it came to that. He was also a careful tenant who'd been paying on the dot for more years than Mrs. Lomax cared to remember. A widow without a great deal to sustain her except her own two hands and the rent of her downstairs flat had to consider both sides of the situation. One way or another, she'd better get that hairpiece back to him before he missed it and threw a conniption.

Mrs. Lomax pondered her strategy. Professor Ungley wasn't up yet, most likely. He'd never been one to bestir himself at first crack of dawn. Or second crack, either, if there was such a thing. Last night he'd been at the monthly meeting of that foolish Balaclavian Society, so he'd have got to bed later than usual. She nodded briskly to Edmund, cut a slice of fresh-baked coffee cake, laid it on a plate, and wrapped a paper napkin around it. Then she slipped the by now somewhat mangled hairpiece into her apron pocket, picked up the cake plate, and went down the back stairway.

She had a key to her tenant's door, of course. She was used to going in and out, cleaning for the old man once a week and doing other chores as occasion required. Sometimes she'd leave him a little treat, not that she ever got thanked for it. The cake would make a plausible excuse if he should happen to be up and catch her coming in. Mrs. Lomax tapped gently, got no answer as she'd hoped she wouldn't, unlocked the door, and went in. She'd just sneak the toupee into the bathroom and Ungley would never be the wiser. At least he'd act as if he wasn't, which would amount to the same thing for practical purposes. She started for the connecting door, then stopped in her tracks.

"Well, did you ever?"

She was too astonished not to make the remark out loud to Edmund, who'd tagged along hoping to get the toupee back. There on the kitchen sink stood the professor's milk, untasted.

As Betsy Lomax well knew, for there was precious little about anything in Balaclava Junction she didn't know, it was Herbert Ungley's invariable habit to pour himself a glass of milk every afternoon at half-past four and leave it standing on the drainboard until he was ready for bed. By that time the chill would be off and he wouldn't have to bother heating the milk. No two ways about it, Professor Ungley was a lazy man.

The old coot wasn't too lazy to attend to his personal comforts, though. Why hadn't he drunk that milk? Mrs. Lomax began to feel uneasy. Why hadn't Edmund, if it came to that? He must have got in here somehow to find the toupee, and it wasn't like him to pass up a chance at some free grub.

Professor Ungley had turned eighty on his last birthday. Mrs. Lomax knew that for a solemn fact because she'd been politely invited to bake him a birthday cake, though she hadn't got asked to share it. Her own father had died at eighty. She sidled along toward the bedroom, listening for snores and not hearing any.

Her tenant was not in his room. Moreover, the bed hadn't been slept in. She could tell; she'd changed the sheets and made it up fresh only yesterday, and it was just the way she'd left it.

Betsy Lomax was too sensible a woman to panic, but after she'd searched every inch of the flat to no avail, she found herself walking out the front door still wearing her apron and clutching the plate of coffee cake. The nippy autumn air brought her to her senses fast enough. She went back upstairs to put on a coat and cap.

"He could have fallen and twisted his ankle or something, I suppose," she remarked to Edmund, who'd given up hope of the toupee and retired to sulk among the wax begonias on the window seat. "One of them," she meant the Balaclavian Society members, "might have taken him home for the night and not bothered to let me know. Why should they? 'Tisn't as if he was anything to me."

Still, you couldn't do for a man all these years without feeling some concern. If Ungley had hurt himself or got sick at the meeting, it was more likely his fellow members would have brought him back here and expected his landlady to take care of him. Unless he'd had to be rushed to the hospital. No, in that case she'd have heard by now, early as it was. A second cousin by marriage was sister-in-law to the admissions nurse who'd been on duty last night at the Hoddersville Hospital, which was the only one close by. Surely Priscilla'd have passed the word to Marge, and Marge would never have been mean enough to keep back a piece of news like that about Betsy's own tenant.

Maybe she'd better phone Henry Hodger or one of the others. Maybe she'd better forget the phone and stir her stumps over toward the clubhouse. If Professor Ungley had fallen in the dark on his way home and lain out all night with a heavy frost—she pulled on her knitted gloves, tucked her door key into her palm, and went out.

Chapter Two

Like most New England main streets, Balaclava Junction's had some pleasant old buildings. The Balaclavian Society's clubhouse was not one of them. It was old, true enough, but not pleasant; just a sparse little box with too little paint on its clapboards, too many weeds in its yard. Out back was where she found him, lying hatless and of course wigless among the frost-blackened dock and plantain. Mrs. Lomax took one long, thoughtful look, then turned and walked down the main street to the police station.

Nobody could call Chief Fred Ottermole lazy. Though the station clock said not yet half-past eight, the chief was already behind his desk, diligently polishing his badge on the sleeve of his uniform.

"Fred," said Betsy Lomax without regard to rank or protocol, "you hoist yourself right straight out of that chair and hike on over to the Balaclavian Society."

"What for?" He blew on the badge, gave it one last rub, then pinned it on and stood up. "Somebody busted in and stole all their mothballs?"

"Don't you smart-aleck me, young man. Professor Ungley's out back in the weeds."

"So what? That's no crime, far's I know."

"Depends on who put him there, doesn't it?"

"Huh? Oh, cripes! Not another murder?"

"I wouldn't want to say, but I daresay I can tell a dead man when I see one. Furthermore, suppose you tell me what would possess a person his age to go wandering around back lots in the pitch dark on an October night with frost on the punkin and no rubbers on his feet. You're going to look an awful fool if somebody else finds him before you do, Fred. Take a blanket or something with you in case old Mrs. Pearworthy happens along and gets the daylights scared out of her. I'll stay here and call Dr. Melchett. He won't have left for the hospital yet. Well, don't stand there gawking. Move, can't you? The body's beside that old harrow they've always been going to do something about and never got around to."

"Name me one thing they ever did get around to," Ottermole grunted.

He'd already taken a gray blanket out of the first-aid locker, though, and was heading for the door. Nobody argued with Betsy Lomax, at least not successfully. Ottermole tried to tell himself a body behind the museum would be an interesting change from issuing stern warnings to youngsters throwing candy wrappers around the sidewalks, but he couldn't make himself believe it. What he'd have preferred was a nice, uncomplicated traffic violation. His wife had given him a genuine gold-plated ball-point pen for his birthday and he was itching to write some duly impressed miscreant a ticket in grand style.

Besides, there'd been too many mysterious deaths around Balaclava of late. Fred Ottermole did not like mysterious deaths. Therefore, when he got to the scene of the alleged crime, he was disinclined to see anything remarkable about Professor Ungley's demise.

"Plain as the nose on your face," was his official verdict. "Tripped in the dark and fell against that old harrow. Hit one of the pegs. See all that blood on the back of his head?"

"I don't see any on the harrow," said Mrs. Lomax, who'd passed the word to Dr. Melchett as promised and then hustled back to where the action was. She wasn't about to miss a trick if she could help it.

"You can't tell with all that rust," Ottermole argued.

"Who says you can't?" she snapped back. "Blood's darker than rust."

"Well anyway, he'd have had his hairpiece on when he fell. That might have mopped it up, sort of. Say, where is it?"

"Right here."

Mrs. Lomax unbuttoned enough of her coat to get at her apron pocket. "Oh, hello, Dr. Melchett. I was just showing Fred the professor's toupee. Edmund brought it into the house this morning, I'm ashamed to say. He thought it was something to play with. Can't blame him for not knowing any better," she added defensively.

"Edmund?" Dr. Melchett, who didn't like bodies in odd places any better than Fred Ottermole did, eyed the hairpiece suspiciously. "Who's Edmund?"

"Her cat," the police chief explained. Fred and Edmund were rather good friends, as it happened. Edmund often dropped in at the station during his morning stroll for a rest and a bite of Fred's coffee-break doughnut, which he could easily have done without. Those visits were the one thing in town Betsy Lomax didn't know about.

"Anyway, that's how I happened to come looking for Professor Ungley," Mrs. Lomax told them. "You know how touchy he always was about not wanting anybody to know it wasn't his own hair, as if this thing would fool a blind man. When I caught Edmund with the hairpiece, I couldn't imagine how he'd got hold of it. Then I figured Professor Ungley must have left his door open, so I'd better go down and close it."

That was close enough to the truth as made no matter. "So anyway, I went and there was his glass of milk that he always drank before he went to bed, sitting on the sink still full. I began to get worried and went looking around. I saw the bed and knew he hadn't been in it because I'd made it up fresh yesterday and it wasn't even wrinkled. So I thought I'd better come over this way and take a look, and here he was."

"You didn't try to move him?" Dr. Melchett asked her.

"I never so much as laid a finger on him. At my time of life, I've been to enough funerals to know a corpse when I see one. To tell you the truth, it was no more than I expected, an old man like him out here on the bare ground all night."

"What made you think of coming here?" Ottermole wanted to know.

"Where else would he be? They had the Balaclavian Society meeting last night, didn't they? For whatever that might be worth."

There was meaning behind Mrs. Lomax's sniff. The Balaclavian Society was an organization neither she nor her late husband had ever been invited to join, notwithstanding the fact that one Perkin Lomax was well-known to have been among the founders of Balaclava Junction and she herself had been a Swope from Lumpkin Upper Mills. Why any group claiming to be "dedicated to the preservation of our heritage" had passed up its chance to take in both a Lomax and a Swope at one swoop was something she'd never understand to her dying day, not that she'd ever demean herself by letting them think she gave a hoot.

"Besides," she went on, "my house is no great distance from here if you cut through the back yards, as you well know. I didn't think Edmund would have drug that hairpiece any great distance. Edmund's not one to strain himself, any more than Professor Ungley used to be. What gets me is how the professor got out here, unless somebody brought him. If he left the meeting under his own steam, you'd think he'd have gone out the front way to the sidewalk, where there'd be plenty of light and easy walking. There's no other way out except the service door around on the far side, and that's overgrown with weeds and the sill rotted away. They haven't opened it in a month of Sundays, far's I know. Why should he risk breaking his neck on those broken steps last night of all nights?"

"She's got something there, Ottermole," the doctor admitted. "I had to be out on a late call myself, and I can tell you it was no time for a man his age to go prowling through the back yards. The sky was overcast and there was some ground fog in spots. I don't see any path he could have followed. Ungley was weak in the eyes and none too steady on his legs the last time I examined him. Where's that silver-headed cane he always carried, by the way?"

"Stolen, most likely," said Mrs. Lomax.

"Now, just a minute," Ottermole protested. "Are you trying to make out he was mugged and robbed? Don't you think I've got brains enough to think of that myself? Well, he wasn't, see." Fred held out the old man's wallet so they could see the bills inside. "There's fifteen bucks and change in there. The cane fell down, that's all. It must be here somewhere."

He began pawing among the weeds. After a moment, he

straightened up waving something around. "See, what did I tell you?"

Dr. Melchett reached for the cane Ottermole was brandishing. "Mind if I take a look? Lord, this thing is heavy. I'd hate to get whacked over the head with it, myself."

He fished out his reading glasses and put them on to take a close look at the cane's handle. Then he bent down to peer at the harrow.

"There's blood on that peg his head's resting against," he pointed out. "Not much, considering the way a scalp wound bleeds, but some. See it?"

Ottermole and Mrs. Lomax both admitted they could see the stain, now that Melchett had pointed it out. Nevertheless, the doctor kept on turning the cane over and over in his hands. Though worn at the ferrule and scarred on the shaft from much use, it was still a handsome thing of its kind. Its silver handle was not the usual knob or hook, but went straight back at a right angle to the blackthorn staff. It was carved in the shape of a running fox, with the forepaws bent to make the joint with the staff and the tail and back legs molded together into a rather formidably pointed end.

"Professor Ungley set a lot of store by that cane," Mrs. Lomax remarked. "He always claimed the fox was solid silver."

"Maybe so," the doctor grunted, "but I'd be more likely to believe it's been made hollow and filled with melted lead, myself. Strange thing for a respectable retired professor to be carrying, but then Ungley was a strange man in some ways. If that harrow hadn't been right there for him to fall against, one might have wondered—"

Melchett said no more. He himself was not a strange man but a most discreet man who knew only too well how much havoc an ill-judged remark by a reputable doctor could create among his practice.

Fred Ottermole took the cane back. "There's no blood on the fox," he insisted, "and there is on the harrow peg. Seems to me all that fancy carving would have collected stains fast enough. Let's have a look at that hairpiece."

"There's not a speck to be seen," Mrs. Lomax told him. "I've already looked. And don't try to claim Edmund licked it clean because he wouldn't have been able to. It would still be matted up, which it isn't. Anyway, Edmund's mighty particular about what he puts into his stomach."

"Huh," said Ottermole, who knew better but wasn't about to rat on a pal. "Okay, so the hairpiece fell off when Professor Ungley tripped on the harrow, that's all."

"You'd have thought his hat would keep it on," Mrs. Lomax argued.

"The hat fell off, too, for Pete's sake. See, here it is."

And there it was, clutched in Professor Ungley's right hand as if by some miracle he'd managed to catch it in mid-air a moment before his death. Mrs. Lomax said that looked mighty peculiar to her, but Dr. Melchett riposted with some learned reference to cadaveric spasm and she changed her tack.

"I wonder how he happened to fall backward instead of forward. Any time I stub my toe, it seems to me I always go straight down on my knees and ruin a good pair of stockings."

"Maybe he caught his leg in a vine and it threw him on his—"

Ottermole's attempt to think up a genteel synonym for backside was spoiled by Betsy Lomax's snort.

"Maybe pigs can fly. You still haven't come up with any reason why Professor Ungley would have been out here in the first place."

"Oh. Well, heck, that should be pretty obvious, shouldn't it? I mean," Fred hesitated again, for Mrs. Lomax had once been his Sunday school teacher, "an old man like him, his kidneys might not be—you know what I mean."

"If you mean a man who stood as much on his dignity as Professor Ungley did would sneak around behind a building right on the main street to relieve himself like a common drunk out of the gutter, you'd better rack that so-called brain of yours a little harder, Fred Ottermole. There's a water closet in the museum as I know to my certain knowledge because they had to get my cousin Fred Swope to fix it the time the boiler went off and all the pipes froze and busted. Being a proper gentleman, Professor Ungley would have used it before he left the building."

"But what if he'd suddenly felt the urge, if you don't

mind me saying so, after the rest had gone on ahead and he didn't have a key to get back in?"

"He did so have a key. He was curator, wasn't he, or supposed to be. Why don't you take a look in his pockets instead of standing around shooting your mouth off?"

Fred Ottermole glowered, but obeyed. To his unconcealed satisfaction, no keys were to be found either on Professor Ungley's person or anywhere in the vicinity of his body.

"Well, that's that. Anybody got any more bright ideas, or can I turn him over to Harry Goulson?" Goulson was the local undertaker.

Dr. Melchett shrugged. "He's all Goulson's, as far as I'm concerned. I'll wait here while you fetch him, if you like. Tell him to bring a death certificate form along, if he's got one."

Mrs. Lomax wasn't asked to stay, but she did. Her neighbors had begun drifting down Main Street on their morning errands. It was not to be supposed that any show of activity around the generally quiet museum could go unobserved, or that people wouldn't come to see what was up. By the time the police chief got back with the undertaker, Professor Ungley had gathered quite a crowd.

Chapter Three

"Oh, how dreadful!"

That was Mrs. Pommell, the banker's wife, got up regardless in kid gloves and a felt hat to go and buy a pound of scrod at Carey's Fish Market. The hat was year before last's, but it was too dressy for Carey's nevertheless. Betsy Lomax didn't have much time for people who gave themselves airs, though she did have to admit Mrs. Pommell was looking decently upset instead of just standing there gawking like the rest of them.

"And to think he was alive and well only last night," the banker's wife observed to the admiring multitudes.

"This was at the Balaclavian Society meeting?" Fred Ottermole asked her, whipping out his notebook and handsome new gold pen.

"Yes." Mrs. Pommell took out a tissue and sniffled into it in a dainty and ladylike manner. "My husband and I were also among those present."

"Did you both stay till the end?"

"Certainly." She appeared surprised at the question. "After our business meeting, Professor Ungley gave us a most interesting talk about penknives. They were originally used, you know, to shape the ends of feathers that were used as pens. Goose quills, turkey quills, crow quills for fine drawing—they still sell pens called crowquills at art supply shops, or did when I was taking my fine arts courses at boarding school."

She would have to get that in, Mrs. Lomax thought. Ottermole showed no interest in Mrs. Pommell's school days, but the professor's choice of topic appeared to ring a professional bell.

"Penknives, eh? How big would they be? Big enough to hurt a person with, I mean?"

Mrs. Pommell shook her hat. "Mercy, no. They were tiny things, many of them, small enough to carry on a watch chain or fit into a lady's writing desk. After all, the tip end of a wing feather, even a turkey's, isn't very—surely you're not thinking—that is, Professor Ungley wasn't *stabbed*, was he?"

"Far as we can tell from the evidence, he fell and hit his head on this old harrow," Ottermole had to admit. "That's right, isn't it, Dr. Melchett?"

"I see nothing inconsistent with your findings, Chief Ottermole," the doctor replied.

Naturally he wouldn't. Mrs. Lomax knew Dr. Melchett of old. He was a good enough medical practitioner, but he was a better politician. Catch him giving the wrong answer in front of the banker's wife!

"What a dreadful pity." Mrs. Pommell plied her tissue again as an example to the gapers. "I wonder what he was doing back here? Taking a shortcut, do you think?"

Melchett shrugged. "You knew Ungley better than I did. Was he in the habit of taking shortcuts?"

"Professor Ungley was something of a law unto himself, as you'd surely realized. We did have our car," a vast and opulent Lincoln (the Pommells lived fully a quarter of a mile away), "but we wouldn't have dreamed of offering him a lift. We'd suggested it several times previously and he used to get quite huffy. One must respect our senior citizens' wishes to be independent, mustn't one?"

Senior citizens, for crying out loud! As if that old hen hadn't been graduated from her fancy boarding school while the then Betsy Swope was still struggling through her first reader. Mrs. Lomax straightened the fingers of her woolen gloves in a way that let everybody know she understood perfectly what was what, but was too much of a lady to say so. Mrs. Pommell made a point of not noticing, and Chief Ottermole again was not interested.

"Did Professor Ungley leave the clubhouse before or after you did?" he asked.

Mrs. Pommell reflected. "It seems to me we all left at pretty much the same time. I have a vague idea it was Mr. Lutt who locked the door behind us, but I couldn't say for sure."

"Mr. Lutt's the guy who has the key, is he?"

"As a matter of fact, we all have keys. That is, I personally don't have one, but my husband does and somehow it's managed to wind up on my key ring. Mr. Pommell has so many keys to carry around in the way of business that I always get stuck with the leftovers. You know how it is with bankers."

And if they didn't, she'd certainly be the one to tell them. Betsy Lomax buttoned her lips tighter and straightened her gloves again.

"What about Professor Ungley?" Ottermole persisted. "Would he normally have a key on him?"

"Why, I should suppose so. That is—oh dear, I remember now. He took out his key ring to show us a charming little gold penknife he carried on it. Then he laid the ring out with the other knives on the table. I'm wondering now whether he forgot to pick it up before he left. If you'll wait just one moment—"

Mrs. Pommell fumbled in her impressive handbag and brought out a key chain of her own with fancy plastic bobbles at the ends. "Let's see, this—no, that's the garage. Here we are. Do you want to come in with me, Chief Ottermole? It's against the rules for non-members to enter except on visiting days, but in a situation like this—"

"Aw, that's okay," said Ottermole, which was just as well since Mrs. Pommell had already darted inside, closing the door behind her with an air of absentmindedness that didn't fool Betsy Lomax one iota.

"I've found them," she called out, "right where I thought they'd be."

The clubhouse wasn't much bigger than a bread box anyway. She was back outside before she'd finished talking, the keys in her hand and the gold penknife sticking out from the bunch.

"You see, that's the knife he was showing us. It belonged to a great-uncle of his, so I don't suppose the heirs will care to donate it to our museum collection, though this is hardly the time to be thinking of such things, is it? Poor, dear Professor Ungley. How we shall miss him!"

As she reached for another tissue, Fred Ottermole held out his hand for the keys. "I'll take those for the time being, Mrs. Pommell. I expect his lawyer will want them."

"What about the cane?" said Dr. Melchett, who still appeared to be intrigued by that silver fox.

"Why don't I take it along and leave it in his flat?" Mrs.

Lomax suggested. "That way, all his things will be together and the heirs, whoever they may be, won't have
anything to squawk about when it comes time to settle
up."

"Good idea." Fred Ottermole handed it over to her and
that, as far as he was concerned, was that.

Maybe the old geezer had got caught short as originally
theorized and found he didn't have his keys to get back in
and use the facilities. Maybe he simply happened to
remember a few seconds too late that he'd left his door
keys, plus that nice gold penknife, inside and started
around the building hoping to find a window open or
something so that he could climb in and get them. It was
six of one and half a dozen of the other. He gave it as his
official verdict that Dr. Melchett might as well issue a
certificate of death by misadventure and Harry Goulson
might as well get on with the laying-out.

Mrs. Pommell thought it was all too sad for words but
there was nothing else to be done, was there? Dr.
Melchett, conscious of the fact that his own wife was about
to give a hospital volunteers' luncheon at which Mrs.
Pommell was slated to be guest of honor, agreed there
wasn't.

Mrs. Lomax officially turned the hairpiece over to
Harry Goulson, knowing Professor Ungley would have
hated to be caught dead without it whatever the circumstances. Then she went home to wash up her breakfast
dishes and brood.

She didn't brood long. There was the cane to be returned
to the downstairs flat, and that glass of milk still on the
drainboard going sour, like as not. The now tenantless
landlady took her own keys and went to redd the place up.
The professor had never once had a relative to call while
he was alive, to the best of her knowledge, but Betsy
Lomax knew human nature. Once news of his death got
around, they'd come scampering out of the woodwork to
see whether there might be anything in it for them. She
was not about to have any long-lost Ungleys claiming
Elizabeth Swope Lomax hadn't known enough to take
proper care of her tenant.

As she puttered around wiping off a speck of dust here
and twitching a slipcover there, she gradually realized

things were not precisely as they ought to have been. Professor Ungley, indolent as he was, had been persnickety about his flat. For instance, he'd always wanted the sofa pillows, three rock-hard squares of a particularly bilious green, arranged just so: two at the ends and one in the exact middle, all balanced diagonally on their points instead of sitting flat on their bottoms.

Mrs. Lomax had never been able to see that it mattered how she left them, since he hardly ever set foot in the parlor except to find fault on cleaning day, but she'd always heard about her dereliction in that tiresome, yappy old voice of his if she hadn't put them back just right after she'd vacuumed the furniture, so she'd learned to humor the man and avoid the lecture. Today, the pillows were sitting flat. The middle one was off-center and the seat cushion pushed forward a trifle, as if somebody had been rummaging behind it.

People did rummage behind sofa cushions, of course. She did herself, often enough. Edmund was wont to amuse himself by batting her thimble, her reading glasses, or whatever other small object she happened to be most urgently in need of at any given moment into some such hidey-hole. But why should Professor Ungley go dropping things there? She doubted if he'd ever sat on that sofa since he'd moved into the flat. He never entertained, so there'd been no occasion for a guest to come mussing the place up. Not an invited one, anyway.

Where the professor had spent most of his time was in the room he'd called his study, lolling in one of those patent reclining chairs with a back that went down and a footrest that came up. That was the real place to look. Mrs. Lomax got no farther than the door before her trained eye caught the signs. "Sticks out like a sore thumb," she told Edmund, who'd come along to be sociable. "Somebody's been."

Books that had been lined up on the shelves as if with a ruler and probably never taken down since Professor Ungley stopped professing were now noticeably out of alignment. One desk drawer wasn't quite shut. When she slid it all the way open, reaching from underneath and shielding her hand with the apron she was still wearing, for Mrs. Lomax had taken to reading detective stories lately, she found its contents in what both she and its late owner would have considered a complete welter.

"He never did this," she informed Edmund.

Even if the old man had been hunting for those foolish penknives, and a more boring subject for an evening's entertainment she personally couldn't imagine; even if he'd put off the looking till the last minute, which was entirely possible because procrastinating was what he'd always done best, not to speak evil of the dead, but facts were facts; he still wouldn't have mussed up the drawer like this because then he'd have had the nuisance of putting it right again.

Besides, Professor Ungley would have known exactly where his penknives were and spent weeks before the meeting fiddling around with them and planning out the talk hardly anybody was going to hear. And trotting them out to bore his landlady with, no doubt, if he'd got the chance, which he hadn't because they'd had the church rummage sale this week and Mrs. Lomax hadn't been around much. She ought to be over at the vestry now, making sure the cleanup committee was doing a halfway decent job, which it probably wasn't. Instead, she went back upstairs and picked up the telephone.

Chapter Four

"Hello, Mrs. Shandy? I expect the professor's busy teaching or grading papers or suchlike, but I was wondering if he'd have time to drop down to my place for a minute."

"You mean right away?" gasped Helen Shandy, a petite blonde who could have been the sort of Helen whom E. A. Poe had in mind when he alluded to Psyche and possibly even to those Nicean barks of yore, though the latter point is debatable.

"Sooner the better." Mrs. Lomax wasn't on a party line any more, but she remained laconic on the phone from force of habit. "I wouldn't ask if it wasn't important."

"Of course you wouldn't."

Helen was startled at the mere fact of Mrs. Lomax's calling, let alone her request. The woman had been showing up faithfully every week to clean the little red-brick house on the Crescent since Peter Shandy's marriage just as she'd done when he was a bachelor. She was chatty enough when she came to work and ready to stop and pass the time of day if Helen and Peter happened to bump into her at the drugstore or the supermarket, but she had old-fashioned ideas about town and gown. If she said it was important, it was.

"Peter's up at school right now," Helen replied, "but I'll get hold of him as fast as I can. Will you be at home for a while?"

"I'll be here."

Mrs. Lomax hung up feeling a trifle easier. Helen, on the other hand, was in a state by the time she caught Peter at his office.

"Oh, I'm so glad you're there! Do you have a student with you, or a class in two minutes or anything?"

"Neither and nothing, mine own. I'm just pondering on how do I love thee. Let me count the ways. It may help to

26

get my mind off the most moronic set of test papers I've ever had the misfortune to grade. Would you believe at least three quarters of my freshman agronomy class don't know how to spell fungicide?" -

"Certainly I would. Furthermore, they can't look it up in the dictionary because nobody ever made them learn the alphabet. Darling, could we shelve the fungicide for the moment? Mrs. Lomax wants to talk with you."

"If it's about a new mop, I flatly refuse. That woman has a mania for mops. She'll mop us out of house and home."

"It's not mops. She wants you to go down right away."

"Down where?"

"To her place. It's all uphill from there, isn't it?"

"I'm sure she finds it so. What in Sam Hill for?"

"I don't know, but you'd better go. She said it was important."

"Good God! Then I'm off in a puff of smoke. These young ignorami will have to sweat for their test results. Do 'em good."

Peter grabbed the mackinaw he'd slung over the back of his office chair, shoved his arms into the sleeves, and took the stairs of the century-old building at a pretty nippy pace for a man of fifty-six and a bit. Peter wasn't particularly tall, nor was he short. He wasn't thin and he wasn't fat. Helen honestly believed him to be the handsomest man alive. Most people would have said Professor Shandy wasn't bad-looking, all things considered, and wasn't it a shame his hair was getting so thin on top.

If there is truth in the agricultural homily that grass can't grow on a busy street, then Shandy's hiatal hirsuteness was only natural. During the past year, he'd revealed a new talent and acquired an unexpected reputation. To be sure, he'd already been world-famous, or at least well-known among turnip growers in those parts of the world where turnip growing is taken seriously. It was one thing to be known as codeveloper of that super rutabaga, *Brassica napobrassica balaclaviensis,* or Balaclava Buster. It was something else to have become Balaclava's replacement for Philo Vance. In short, the locals had found out he was good at solving mysteries.

Mrs. Lomax, after he'd ascended the stairs to her tidy

flat and paid his respects to Edmund, lost not a moment in letting him know why she wanted him.

"I don't care what Fred Ottermole says, nor Dr. Melchett neither. Professor Ungley would never on the face of this earth have gone traipsing around behind the clubhouse in the dark, no matter what. He was kind of a coward, between you and me and the lamppost. He used to run on about crime in the streets and all that stuff he got out of the Boston papers till you wondered why he didn't quit taking 'em if they scared him so. You mark my words, either he took somebody with him or else he was made to go. And it amounted to the same thing in the long run."

"M'yes," said Shandy, who'd been buttonholed by Ungley on the subject of general perfidy a few times himself. "I'm inclined to your point of view, Mrs. Lomax. And your theory is that his own cane may have been used to kill him?"

"Well, it's heavy enough. Dr. Melchett said he judged the handle was filled with lead, though why Professor Ungley would carry a thing like that when he'd barely lift a hand to tie his own shoes is beyond me. And it's got a pointy end that could have punched a hole in his skull, which is what killed him. And there was a powerful lot of dried blood all over the back of his head and next to none at all on that harrow peg he's supposed to have tripped and fell on. I don't know if he was killed outright or just stunned and left out there to die, but it wouldn't have mattered much, would it? I mean to say, he wasn't a strong, vigorous person like Mrs. Ames."

Jemima Ames, the village's most recent bludgeoning victim until now, had been found dead in Peter Shandy's own living room. Mrs. Lomax must have realized she could have been more tactful than to bring that up, for she hurried on.

"An old man like him, out there where nobody'd be apt to see him, on a night like that—the weatherman said it was going to freeze again, which it did because those weeds were all black and slimy like they get after a frost—and there was the cane, right beside him. I don't believe that harrow yarn for one second. I think he was hit first and then propped up there beside the harrow and some of his blood daubed on the peg. Fred fell for the trick because Fred's got about as much sense as a good-sized louse, and Dr. Melchett went along with him because the doctor's got about as much backbone as Fred has brains."

Shandy thought Mrs. Lomax's estimate was a pretty fair one, but refrained from saying so. "Still, neither of them could find any bloodstains on the cane?"

"A little soap and water would fix that up soon enough, wouldn't it?"

"I don't know." Shandy took the cane she'd brought back from Professor Ungley's apartment, hefted it, and regarded the intricately carved fox with a good deal of interest. "It might take a fair amount of scrubbing to get all the blood out of those deep grooves. And where would the alleged murderer have got the soap and water?"

"In the clubhouse, of course. They've got indoor plumbing, though you might not think so. What if Professor Ungley didn't forget his keys after all? The person that killed him could have found them in his pocket, gone in and washed the cane off, then left the keys on the table where Mrs. Pommell found them, couldn't he?"

"But didn't you say Mrs. Pommell claimed Ungley had left them there after his lecture?"

"She thought he must have when Fred couldn't find the keys in his pocket," Mrs. Lomax amended. "Then she went in and there they were, so she figured she'd been right, but that doesn't prove she was."

"True enough. And how did Mrs. Pommell get in?"

"She used her own key, or rather her husband's. She carries it for him because he has all those bank keys to tote around, as she took pains to let us know."

"But why would her husband have a key to the clubhouse?"

"She says all the members do. All the men, that is. Women don't count, apparently. Anyway, I don't know if there's another woman but herself who goes to the meetings these days. She probably wouldn't either, if it wasn't so darned exclusive."

"Um. Just for the sake of argument, Mrs. Lomax, can you think offhand of anybody who might possibly have a reason to kill Professor Ungley?"

"I might myself, if I'd got stuck for a whole evening having to listen to him maunder on about penknives," she confessed. "Being as how I never got asked to join, though—"

"Penknives?" Shandy interrupted. "What in Sam Hill did he want to talk about penknives for?"

"It's not so much why he wanted to do it as why the rest of 'em let him that flummoxes me. No wonder they can't get any new members. Not that they don't do everything they can think of to keep people out."

"Keep people out? What do you mean by that, Mrs. Lomax?"

"You ever tried to join the Balaclavian Society?"

"Er—no, I can't say I have."

In fact, Shandy couldn't have said for a certainty that he'd ever been aware until today that the group existed. He'd noticed the clubhouse because he was a noticing man, and wondered why it was never open at a time when he might conceivably have wandered in to see what it was all about. He'd also noticed a general flavor of mild decay similar to that so aptly described by Oliver Wendell Holmes in *The Deacon's Masterpiece,* and thought it rather surprising that nobody ever did anything to spruce the place up a bit, but he couldn't recall ever having tried to find out why.

Since Mrs. Lomax was clearly waiting for him to ask what a person had to do to get in, he obliged. "How do you join?"

"Beats me," she replied. "Most of the clubs in town want new members so bad they're practically yanking 'em in off the street with meathooks, but to my sure and certain knowledge, the Balaclavian Society hasn't let in a single, solitary one for the past sixteen years. Even Harry Goulson doesn't belong."

"Good gad!" Shandy had been under the impression that the popular local mortician belonged to just about every organization in the county, even one or two of the women's clubs. "And what about Jim Feldster?" Professor Feldster, who taught Fundamentals of Dairy Management, was an even more inveterate joiner than Goulson.

"Turned him down flat as a pancake," Mrs. Lomax replied, "though some said it was on account of that wife of his. Meaning no offense, her being your next-door neighbor."

"None taken."

Shandy would have blackballed Mirelle Feldster himself, if he'd ever got the chance. She'd been a continuing pain in his neck ever since he'd got his appointment to Balaclava Agricultural College. "They must have fantastically strict membership requirements, then?"

"Fantastic isn't the word for it, Professor. First you have to mail in a formal letter of application, along with your birth certificate—or a copy of it, anyway—and character references from your minister and two members of the church."

"What if you don't go to church?"

"Then you might as well forget it because you're licked before you start. And, of course, if you happen not to be a Protestant, that puts the kibosh on you, too, though they don't come straight out and say so. Then Mrs. Pommell invites you to tea so the members can look you over and ask you a lot of embarrassing questions. If you haven't folded up and quit by then, you're supposed to submit an essay on 'Why I am dedicated to the preservation of our heritage.'"

"Good Lord!"

"And after all that, they take a secret vote on whether to let you in. One single nay and that's the end. No second chances."

"Considering the requirements, I'm surprised they have any members to vote," said Shandy. "Who does belong to this august assemblage?"

"Well, there's Mr. and Mrs. Pommell, as I mentioned. He's head of the First Balaclava County Guaranteed National Trust, Savings, and Loan. You know him, I expect, seeing as how you folks have an account there."

That could have gone without saying. The Guaranteed was the only bank in town. "I believe I've met Mrs. Pommell, too," Shandy agreed.

"I shouldn't be surprised. She's president of the Garden Club and a few more things, as she'd be first to tell you if you gave her half a chance. And there's Henry Hodger the lawyer, and Congressman Sill who served one term in the state legislature back when Alvan T. Fuller was governor.

He's still active in politics, or claims he is. Goes to Boston and hangs around the State House. Making a pest of himself, most likely."

This observation was also redundant. Shandy'd had the misfortune to hear Sill orate on far too many occasions. "Does Mrs. Sill belong?" he asked.

"She used to, but she's been bedridden ever since she had that stroke about ten years ago, poor soul. Just lies there staring at the ceiling, though if I had to choose between that and old Sill's face, I daresay I'd take the ceiling, too. And there's Lot Lutt who used to be on the board of directors over at the soap factory. He's a widower. And William Twerks, who's never done a hand's turn at anything in his life, to the best of my knowledge."

"Twerks is the hulking chap who lives in that brown-and-yellow house with the fancy trimmings isn't he?" Shandy remarked. "I've had a few encounters with him."

Twerks had, in fact, wandered over to the campus on various occasions for the purpose of ogling female students doing fieldwork in their sawed-off jeans, and been dealt with by them in various imaginative and interesting ways.

Mrs. Lomax's lips twitched. She knew, of course. "Yes, Twerks is quite a one for the ladies, they say, though he's never stuck to one long enough to matter. Anyway, he goes to the meetings alone. And that's the lot, as far as I know, except for Professor Ungley, and I guess you can't count him any more. He claimed to be curator of that museum they've talked about starting for the past forty years or so, but never get around to. He'd gas along about how much work it was trying to get the place organized, but he never did anything as far as I could make out. Though he did keep a lot of records and papers in that big filing cabinet down in his study, so maybe he was working on those when I used to think he was just snoozing in his chair. Serve me right for judging if he was."

"He never showed you any—er—plans or documents or whatever that he was working on?"

"No, and I never looked to see."

"Naturally not, but don't you think we might have a glance now?"

"Seeing as how that's what I got you down here for."

Mrs. Lomax picked up her keys. "The thing is, Professor, somebody's been in his place. You follow me and I'll show you what I mean. I haven't touched anything."

She paused to unlock Ungley's door. "I'd meant to clean up, after I got back home from the to-do down behind the clubhouse. I figured the heirs would be nosing around, and I wouldn't want them thinking I didn't keep the place decent."

"You don't know who they are?"

"Nary a notion, unless he left everything to the college, which would be sensible, or to the Balaclavian Society that doesn't need it and wouldn't use it, which would be more like him. I suppose there must be a relative or two somewhere because there always are, but he never mentioned any and they never came to see him. As for who his friends were, I expect you'd know better than I. He must have had his old cronies up at the college."

"Well—er—actually, no," Shandy confessed. "Most faculty members of his—er—vintage aren't around any longer, and those who are, like John Enderble, have their—er—sundry occupations. I myself hardly knew Professor Ungley, except to nod to in the faculty dining room when we happened to be there at the same times."

Mrs. Lomax nodded. "Then it looks as if he only had that lot from the club. They're all well-heeled themselves, so they wouldn't need any inheritance from him. Though I suppose he might have left 'em his penknives out of sentiment." Mrs. Lomax could be pretty funny at times, though nobody was ever sure whether or not she was doing it on purpose. "That's assuming he ever bestirred himself to make a will. If he did, he'd have got Henry Hodger to write it up for him, and you can bet Henry won't lose any time coming forward if he smells another fee in it for him."

Shandy was willing to take Mrs. Lomax's word for that. However, Henry Hodger's hypothetical fee was not the matter uppermost in his mind at the moment. "You say the place has been broken into? How can you tell? It looks perfectly tidy to me."

"Oh, it's neat enough as far as that goes," said Mrs. Lomax, "but there's little things I can see that you wouldn't ever notice. Nor would anybody else except

Professor Ungley if he was alive. And he'd have come jawing at me about 'em if it meant dragging me out of my warm bed at three o'clock in the morning."

"So you're saying it happened after he was dead."

"No I'm not, because I don't know when he died. That mush-brained Fred Ottermole never thought to ask Mrs. Pommell when the meeting broke up, for one thing. I'd guess they must have called it quits sometime around eleven because that was when the professor usually got back here, though don't ask me what he found worth staying for in the first place. If he left with the rest of 'em, which he must have or she wouldn't have said so with five other people in a position to call her a liar, then I'd say he was probably waylaid a few minutes later. After he'd turned the corner off Main Street, like as not. Unless he hung around down there by himself in the cold, which doesn't seem likely, does it?"

"Most unlikely, I should think," Shandy agreed. "We might be safe in assuming whoever broke in here knew it was safe to do so because Ungley wouldn't be coming back. Otherwise, there'd have been the risk of his making a row, which you'd have heard."

"I certainly would. Nothing wrong with my ears so far, knock wood. Furthermore, I sat up late reading some foolish book I got from the library"—it was a detective story but she wasn't about to confess that to Professor Shandy—"and Edmund was asleep in my lap the whole time. He'd have hopped up and made a fuss the way he always does if a stranger so much as sets foot on the doorstep. It was about twenty minutes to twelve when I let him out for the night. Come to think of it, I noticed then that the light over the front steps was still on."

"Wouldn't that have told you Ungley wasn't in yet?"

"Yes, but I didn't think anything of it at the time. I knew he was giving the talk, see, and not to speak ill of the dead, once Professor Ungley got started, he wasn't easy to stop. I figured he must still be down there chewing the fat with those other old gaffers. Now, there's a funny thing."

"What is?"

"The light was off when I came down this morning. I'd have noticed if it wasn't. That proves somebody was here, because I know I left it on."

"There's no chance Ungley—er—came in and went out again?"

"Him? Make the trip twice? I might have believed it if I'd seen it, but I didn't, so I won't. Besides, he'd still have left the light on, wouldn't he, because he'd expect to be coming back and have to see his way in again."

"True enough," said Shandy. "So you got to bed around midnight, would you say?"

"Six minutes before, on the dot. I'd got my night things on before I sat down to read, so all I had to do was wash my face and put my teeth to soak. I noticed the time because I keep a clock beside the bed, for company mostly. Anyway, I turned out the lamp and went to sleep on the dot, as is my habit, and never woke up till half-past six this morning. And it wasn't till I'd had my breakfast and done the floor, this being Thursday, that Edmund came caterwauling through the cathole with that hairpiece in his mouth. Soon as I made out what it was, I decided I'd better sneak it back to Professor Ungley's flat before he woke up, and that's how it all started."

"I'd say you've behaved with remarkable perspicacity, Mrs. Lomax. Now could you point out those—er—discrepancies that aren't apparent to the untrained eye?"

"Well, the first thing I noticed was the sofa cushions."

Mrs. Lomax explained the cushion situation in detail, and threw in a few dark hints about the antimacassars for good measure. Then she led Shandy into the study. "See that?" She was pointing to Ungley's reclining chair. "That's where he always sat."

"It—er—appears a trifle elongated for sitting," Shandy ventured.

"That's my point. The chair's built on some kind of balancing spring. When you sit down and want to lean back, the back goes down and the footrest comes up. When you want to get up again, you sort of scrooch forward and the chair comes up straight so you don't have to dislocate your sciatica trying to get out of the pesky thing."

Mrs. Lomax gave the chair a gentle nudge by way of demonstration. Sure enough, the back popped up and the footrest flattened itself demurely between the front legs. Gone was the recliner. In its place sat the sort of ordinary club chair one might find in any well-appointed home whose owners didn't object too strenuously to plastic upholstery in tobacco-spit brown.

"M'yes. That's significant."

Shandy wasn't sure what the significance was. The intruder might have happened to brush against the chair in passing and been too preoccupied to notice its antic behavior, or in too big a hurry to bother putting it back upright, or too ignorant in the ways of reclining chairs to know how. On the other hand, somebody might have pushed it back in order to search more easily under the cushions.

The most logical person would have been Ungley himself, searching for the eyeglasses, the penknife, or the lecture notes he might have dropped during his premeeting siesta. Thinking back to his own bachelor days, though, Peter was inclined to side with Mrs. Lomax. He recalled how seldom he himself had been wont to enter the front room Helen had lately turned into a hotbed of social activity. No doubt his own sofa pillows had remained in whatever position Mrs. Lomax had chosen to leave them after she'd cleaned, and no doubt he'd guiltily sneaked them back to that position if he'd been so unchancy as to disturb one.

As to the recliner, supposing Ungley had been the one to shove it flat, wouldn't he have flicked it upright again, if only to help straighten himself up? Ungley had, after all, been an old man, and that silver cane he'd toted around must have been more than a status symbol.

It was odd about that weighted handle. It was odd Shandy hadn't thought of doing what should have been done before he started horsing around with reclining chairs. Blasting himself for an idiot, he asked, "Mrs. Lomax, may I use your telephone?"

"Why not use Professor Ungley's?" she replied, thinking perhaps of her clean kitchen floor.

Why not, indeed? It was unlikely the now more than hypothetical intruder would have rung up a pal for a chat. And if he had, being adroit enough to get in and out without waking Mrs. Lomax or falling over Edmund, he'd no doubt have had sense enough not to plaster the place with fingerprints. Shandy picked up the phone that was on Ungley's desk, and called Harry Goulson.

"Goulson? This is Peter Shandy. Have you begun your Ptolemaic rites on Professor Ungley's body yet? Then don't. I'd like to see it first. I'll be over in a few minutes. And—er—mummy's the word."

Mrs. Lomax gave him a look and he was ashamed, but it was too late now. He hung up and put on an air of brisk efficiency. "Now what about that file cabinet you spoke of?"

"It's right here behind the desk."

"Ah yes, the desk. Perhaps we might just have a look in here while we're about it."

This was where Ungley had allegedly spent so many hours toiling at the History of Balaclava County he'd claimed to have been at work on for the past quarter-century. According to the notes Shandy found, though, he'd only got as far as 1832, a year in which nothing of any particular significance appeared to have happened.

The drawers were unlocked and held only trifles: some Balaclavian Society stationery yellowed around the edges, a few stub pens and small bottles encrusted with long-dried ink, notes for lectures that hadn't been delivered at the college since Thorkjeld Svenson had summarily emeritized Ungley on his accession to power in 1952. There was also a copy of the commencement exercises for that year at which Ungley had been singled out for special recognition since the president had a heart as big as his feet and seldom lopped off a head without some twinge of remorse.

There were a fair number of other things, but none of the clutter usually found in people's desks. Mrs. Lomax had been right about Ungley's finicking ways. Anybody who'd take the trouble to stack forty-eight paper clips in neat rows of six apiece within their little box would not be apt to leave the sofa pillows askew. Shandy swiveled the desk chair around to face the files.

"I just hope you can get into 'em," Mrs. Lomax observed. "The professor was always fussier about those files than anything else. He'd hardly let me dust the cabinet, and he always kept the drawers locked. Fred Ottermole's got the keys down at the station. Do you think maybe we'd better go ask him for them?"

"Not if you don't object to another spot of burglary." Shandy took out his multi-bladed jackknife.

"I don't care what you do with that thing, just so's you don't expect me to listen to a lecture about it."

"I don't, but would you mind handing me that reading glass off the desk? Before I tackle this lock, I want to make sure there aren't any fresh nicks or scratches on it."

"Why should there be?" Mrs. Lomax asked, peering over his shoulder as he scanned the brass keyholes on the varnished oak drawers.

"There would be, most likely, if the drawers had been forced. I don't see any, so we can take it they weren't. Until now."

Shandy applied his blade with judicious pressure. The locks yielded. The drawers opened without protest. Every single one of them was empty.

Chapter Five

"Why, that old fraud," cried Mrs. Lomax. "All these years, making me think—"

Shandy held up a shushing hand. "Don't judge him too hastily, Mrs. Lomax. Notice those scraps of paper and whatnot at the bottoms of the drawers?"

"Dust and litter," she sniffed.

"Exactly, and Ungley was a tidy man. If these files had in fact been empty for any length of time, wouldn't you have expected he'd make some effort to clean them out? I'd say they were full enough until last night, and that your nocturnal visitor took whatever was in them because he hadn't found whatever he was looking for anywhere else and assumed it must therefore be in among the stuff in the drawers."

"But why go to the bother? Couldn't he have leafed through them right here?"

"Certainly he could, but it takes a long time to go through four drawers full of God knows what. Now, I'm no expert on housekeeping like you, but I think I'm safe in saying it's a lot faster to be messy than neat. This search was carried out so discreetly that it would have fooled anybody except yourself, most likely. Therefore, it would have taken a fair amount of the night, and we know from your and—er—Edmund's testimony that it couldn't have been started until sometime after midnight. By six o'clock at the latest, there'd be people stirring around the neighborhood, so my guess is that by the time the searcher got around to the files, he felt he couldn't take the chance on staying, but decided it would be wiser to carry them off and examine them at leisure. Would there have been any cartons or whatever around to pack them in?"

"Plastic trash bags." Mrs. Lomax was brisk and collected again. "There's a box of 'em in the kitchen. I don't hold with the dratted things myself, but the professor always used 'em because he was too lazy to empty his garbage every day. He'd keep it tied up in one of those bags so's it wouldn't get too smelly. I'd drag it out to put with my own trash on the days I cleaned for him, and wash out the wastebasket and line it with a fresh bag. And air out the kitchen, as you can well imagine," she added with a sniff.

"That's not the way I'd have managed if it was left to me, but that's what the professor wanted and that was the way it stayed. Terrible set in his ways, Professor Ungley was. I'm just glad I didn't have to cook for him. He'd get his own breakfast, mostly boiled eggs and toast and jam and instant coffee, far as I could make out from his garbage. Then he'd mosey on up to the college dining room around five o'clock and eat an early supper, then he'd have his glass of milk and maybe a cracker or something at bedtime. That was plenty for a man his age. Mrs. Mouzouka puts on a fairly decent meal as a rule. I've eaten there a few times, myself."

Shandy nodded. Since Mrs. Lomax cleaned for about half the faculty, she claimed certain faculty privileges which nobody begrudged her. He'd seen her in the dining room often enough himself, tucking into one of Mrs. Mouzouka's invariably superb meals for all she was worth, but he'd never seen her eating with Ungley. He'd never seen anybody else at Ungley's table, come to think of it, except once or twice kind old John Enderble, who was also emeritus but still taught his course on Local Fauna and would set off a student riot, no doubt, if he ever decided to retire in earnest.

As far as Shandy knew, there'd been no protest about dropping Ungley's course on Early Political History of Balaclava County; only a gentle wonder as to why he'd ever been allowed to teach it in the first place. Somebody had once suggested Ungley had been related to the previous president's in-laws, and that seemed as reasonable an explanation as any. Still, he'd been a relic of an earlier time and Shandy supposed he himself ought to feel a twinge at Ungley's passing, but he didn't.

Ungley had been either sullen or tedious, according to his mood. He'd contributed nothing of significance to the college and hadn't even raised a finger on behalf of the Buggins Collection during all the years those precious books had lain neglected in the back room at the library. God alone knew what he'd been allowing to moulder away down there at the Balaclavian Society.

Now, there was a thought. Maybe Ungley himself had recently decided to transfer those vanished files to the clubhouse. Shandy mentioned the possibility to Mrs. Lomax and was promptly shot down.

"Him? When he wouldn't even transfer his own garbage to the woodshed? He's never transferred anything except maybe a bag of groceries or his shirts from the laundry in or out of this house since the day he moved in, which would be twenty-nine years ago this past July when they tore down those old flats up behind the college barns to make room for the power plant. They say there used to be rats over there big as woodchucks. Never saw any myself, and I certainly wouldn't want to."

Shandy said he wouldn't either and was Mrs. Lomax absolutely positive about those files? After all, she was away at work most days, wasn't she? Couldn't they have been moved in her absence?

Mrs. Lomax snorted at the mere notion. "If they'd been taken out in the daytime decent and proper, I'd have heard about it plenty. Been pestered to help on my busiest day, like as not. Furthermore, they'd have gone cabinet and all, wouldn't they? The easiest way would have been to get Charlie Ross up here with his truck and load the whole shebang aboard at once, and if there was an easiest way to do anything, you can bet your bottom dollar Professor Ungley would have been the man to find it. Let me go get those plastic bags. I noticed yesterday he'd bought a new box because I busted a fingernail trying to open it."

She hustled out to the kitchen and Shandy followed her. The box of bags was neatly disposed in a cupboard beside the sink.

"See there, Professor? I took out the first one yesterday, and you know how the rest bulge out to fill the gap and make the box look as if it's still full? Well, maybe you don't, but they do. And look at it now."

Mrs. Lomax had a point. The box certainly did not look full. When Shandy counted the bags, he found only seven instead of the dozen it was alleged to have contained. Five gone then, one for the wastebasket, one for each of the four file drawers. Half-filled sacks would be easy enough to drag out to a car, over to the clubhouse by that back route Edmund must have taken with Ungley's hairpiece, or to any number of other places. Down here in the village, houses were crammed tight together. If Ottermole persisted in calling Ungley's death an accident, it was going to be one hell of a job tracking down whatever had come out of that cabinet.

If only the old man had been killed on campus instead of down in the village, Shandy'd have got President Svenson to call in the state police like a shot. But what jurisdiction could Svenson have now over a dead professor whom he'd got rid of thirty years ago as soon as he'd had time to see what Ungley was, or rather wasn't up to?

Shandy supposed he might have a go at Svenson anyway, but first he'd better make that projected trip over to Goulson's and fully satisfy himself that they did in fact have a case of murder on their hands. Mrs. Lomax was already champing at the bit to be gone, she having an urgent appointment up at the Crescent with the Ameses' vacuum cleaner.

"Go right ahead, Mrs. Lomax," he told her. "I've got to be back for my eleven o'clock class myself, but I want to see Goulson first. I don't know whether Mrs. Shandy's gone over to the library yet, but if you should happen to see her, you might give her a brief rundown about Ungley. If you don't mind."

Mrs. Lomax assured him she wouldn't mind a bit, and sped Crescentward. Shandy took the path Edmund must have used over to the clubhouse. He could see a few people still hanging around telling each other how Professor Ungley's head had been impaled on that very peg right there and pointing to the wrong one more often than not.

Anyway, from what Mrs. Lomax said, Professor Ungley hadn't been impaled at all, but merely slumped against the harrow when she found him. There was no particular reason to suppose she hadn't been first on the scene after his death, and still less to imagine anybody would have gone to the bother of lifting him free, then dumping him and running off.

The scant amount of blood on the harrow peg would seem to rule out impalement or anything else but a hope of fooling some of the people some of the time. To the delight of the onlookers, though, Shandy took out his jackknife again, found a used envelope in his pocket, and scraped a little of the bloodstained rust into it.

"Hey, Prof," yelled an urchin of eleven or so, "you goin' to investigate?"

"I'm going to investigate what you're doing out of school on a weekday morning," Shandy snapped back. "Does your mother know where you are?"

The youngster muttered a scathing reference to Shandy's own parentage, then wriggled his way backward out of the gathering and disappeared. Shandy pocketed his sample and went on to Goulson's. The undertaker was waiting for him, wearing his second-best black coat and an expression of kindly concern.

"Right this way, Professor. I've got the deceased all laid out on the embalming table, with a sheet over him so you won't have to look any more than you want to, though I don't suppose a corpse means much more to you these days than it does to me. Still, we mustn't forget it's been a human being that meant something to somebody," he added, for Goulson was a good man withal.

"Um," said Shandy. "I wonder what Ungley meant, and to whom. Would you mind rolling him over, Goulson? I want to get a look at that head wound."

"Glad to." The undertaker obliged with professional dexterity. "Want me to wash off the blood? The back of his skull's kind of messy."

"That's a polite understatement." Shandy shook his own head. "How in Sam Hill could he have bled so much without getting more of it on that harrow? Goulson, you wouldn't happen to have a camera handy?"

"One of the tools of the trade, Professor. Some folks still like to have a picture of the dear departed after we've got 'em fixed up and laid out in the casket, you know. In my father's time, it was more the custom than the exception. Pop used one of those big old box cameras on a tripod that he'd put his head in a black velvet bag to focus. Took a glass plate and you either had to use a magnesium flare or take a time exposure. Not that the exposure was any problem. One thing about our subjects, you'd never have to worry about 'em wiggling around and blurring the image. I've still got Pop's camera and I can do it according to tradition if you'd like, but seeing as how you want it for detecting purposes, I'd better use my new instant-developing color camera. Bought it last year when the wife and I went to Hawaii on our trip. I was going to take pictures of the hula-hula girls, but she wouldn't let me. Hold on a second."

While Goulson went to get the camera, Shandy stood and pondered. Last night there'd been a person inside that framework of flesh and bone. Now there was only a problem, to be disposed of one way and another. Goulson could handle the physical remains. It looked as if Shandy was stuck with the rest.

He still couldn't feel anything about Professor Ungley. Could anybody? Mrs. Lomax hadn't shown more than a decent concern despite her long years' association with the dead man, and she was by no means a cold-hearted woman. Maybe Ungley's old cronies at the Balaclavian Society would miss him. Shandy hoped they would, at least a little; but his own concern was still with that disparity between the thick rivulets of dried blood on that bald skull and the tiny dab he'd found on the harrow.

Ungley might well have been killed somewhere else altogether and brought to where Mrs. Lomax found him. Shandy bent over the embalming table and hefted the body experimentally. It didn't weigh all that much for so tall a man and dragging him over that frosty, slippery yard wouldn't be hard. Dumping him beside the harrow and daubing the peg with enough of his blood to fool Fred Ottermole would be a cinch.

Shandy had searched among the weeds around the harrow for bloodstains and signs of dragging while he was down there, but of course by then so many people had tramped over the area that there was no hope of a significant find. Edmund the cat might have seen something, but Edmund wasn't talking. He decided to ponder about something else. For instance, why did Ungley carry a loaded cane when he'd led so sedentary and circumscribed a life? Why had his rooms been so neatly but thoroughly rifled and all his files removed? How could a dull old man who gave boring talks on trivial subjects to a handful of people who had nothing better to do than sit around and let him pontificate have managed to get bumped off in so dramatic a way?

The obvious explanation was that Ungley had been in possession of something that somebody else wanted desperately to get hold of. It must have been small and easily hidden; otherwise the searcher wouldn't have bothered messing around behind the sofa cushions. Ungley must have known he was in danger because he had it; otherwise he wouldn't have carried that secret weapon for protection. Shandy supposed a lead-stuffed silver fox could count as a secret weapon. Unless the old goat just had the lead put in to add weight and make people think the fox was in fact solid silver.

And if Ungley did have anything small and valuable, why didn't he put it in a safety deposit box at the bank? He must have had it a long time.

No, that didn't necessarily follow. Because Ungley himself was old and everything in his flat had been old, one could too easily assume this hidden thing was old, too, but it needn't be. He was, after all, in daily contact with the world, or a little bit of it. He went up to the college dining room, he visited the shops, he brought home bags that presumably contained only things like groceries and shaving cream, but what if they didn't? What if this coveted object was something he had in his possession sometimes but not always?

Narcotics came instantly to mind, but how in thunderation could old Ungley have carried on any sort of drug dealing right under Mrs. Betsy Lomax's hunting-hound nose without ever letting her get a whiff of what he was up to?

That Ungley himself might have been a drug user was not outside the bounds of possibility. He'd been born during the era when mothers swigged patent medicines that were mostly port wine and laudanum, when babies were dosed with paregoric for everything from diaper rash to cradle cap, when morphine pills were kept in big jars on drugstore counters and sold by the handful to anybody who walked in and asked for them. He might have acquired a narcotics habit early in life without even realizing he had one. That could have accounted for his habitual indolence.

But times had changed. You couldn't even buy paregoric now without a prescription. Ungley couldn't have been getting drugs on campus because Thorkjeld Svenson would have discovered and personally annihilated any pusher who dared to come within miles of the college. It was more than doubtful he'd be able to buy them around the village. While Fred Ottermole might be a trifle dense in some directions, he wasn't that kind of fool.

As for the Balaclavian Society and its crazy rules that seemed expressly designed to keep anybody from joining, that could conceivably be a horse of another color. But Banker Pommell and Lawyer Hodger and Congressman Sill and Lutt the former soap tycoon? The mind boggled.

Goulson interrupted Shandy's musings by appearing with a modern camera that bristled with automatic exposers and focusers. "She's all loaded and rarin' to go," he explained. "And I brought my wife's Instamatic, too, just in case. She'll have convulsions when she gets the film developed. It's supposed to be the Garden Club's Autumn Flower Festival, but she's got a couple of shots left on the roll, so I figured what the heck?"

Inspired perhaps by memories of his father, he proceeded to take a number of exposures, from various artistic angles, of the unlovely spectacle on the embalming table.

"Save some film," Shandy told him. "We ought to get a shot or two of the wound after we wash the blood off. Got a basin or something?"

"Leave that to me. It's all in the day's work, as we say in the trade."

Goulson brought hot water and a sponge, and deftly cleaned the back of Ungley's head. "Say, Professor, you think there's something peculiar about the way he died, don't you?"

"Well, Goulson, you've seen a lot more cadavers than I have. What do you yourself think?"

"I think Fred Ottermole's going to find himself wishing he hadn't been in such an all-fired hurry to write this one off as an accident, since you ask me. I'm also wondering why Dr. Melchett was ready to swallow that yarn about the harrow without doing a complete examination."

Goulson stripped the covering sheet partly away, leaving Ungley's body bare to the waist. "See what I mean? Now, you've seen that harrow and so have I. It's nothing special, just an oldtime what they call a peg harrow that some blacksmith slung together out of a heavy roller and a bunch of iron spikes. I shouldn't be surprised if it was one of the Flackleys out at Forgery Point who made it, but that's neither here nor there. What I'm getting at is, those spikes are fairly close together. Now, I'm not saying Professor Ungley couldn't have tripped and fallen backward like Fred claims, and bashed that hole in his skull on one of the pegs. What I do say is, how come we don't see any bruising any place else? How did he manage to fall that hard and hit that one peg and none of the others?"

"That's an astute observation, Goulson. I'm also wondering why the hole made by a straight, round spike wouldn't be somewhat smaller and neater than this," Shandy replied, thinking of that loaded fox and what it might do with plenty of muscle behind it. "What I'm mainly thinking is that we'd better get both Melchett and Ottermole back here and find out whether they might not care to reconsider their assumptions. Sorry to put you out like this, Goulson, but that's your penalty for being more intelligent than your neighbors."

"Shucks, Professor, it's no trouble to me. Makes a break in the daily routine, as you might say. Embalming can be lonesome work. I'll see if I can raise Doc Melchett on the phone right now."

He had no luck. Dr. Melchett was at the hospital seeing patients and wouldn't be available till after lunch.

"Then we'll just have to wait," said Shandy. "No sense in getting Ottermole over here by himself."

"In that case, I'd better slide the departed into the refrigerator, to keep him nice and fresh. Can I offer you a cup of coffee, Professor?"

"Thanks," Shandy told him, "but I have a class in about three minutes. See you later, Goulson."

Chapter Six

Shandy could move fast enough in a pinch. He even managed to stop at the chemistry lab and leave his envelope of rust scrapings with Professor Joad before getting to class on the dot. No doubt he taught well enough, but when a couple of students came to ask questions afterward, he had some trouble fishing his brain for relevant answers. The only thing really on his mind was, "What the hell shall I do next?"

As soon as he could decently escape from the classroom, he went. Rather, he started. He'd barely got one foot over the threshold when he was confronted by what the less discerning might have mistaken for a rampaging *Tyrannosaurus Rex.* Shandy didn't even flinch, but merely remarked, "Hello, President. What's eating you?"

Thorkjeld Svenson merely jerked his massive head in the direction of his own sanctum. "Office."

Shandy followed. The presidential reception room was empty, the secretary having gone to lunch. Nevertheless, Svenson closed and locked his inner door before he ordered, "Sit."

"If it's about Ungley," Shandy began.

Svenson barked, "No." There followed a brief silence, during which the president appeared to be mentally damping the fires under his interior lava dome. Then he uttered again.

"Claude."

"Claude who?"

"Not Claude who. Who Claude. Bastard. Congress."

"I understand, do I not, that you're referring to State Representative Bertram G. Claude, that smarmy son-of-a-bitch who's tried to vote down every pro-agriculture bill that's been presented since he managed to buy his way into the State House."

"Urrgh."

"What about him?"

"Wants to campaign here."

"Is he crazy? Our students would rotten-egg him straight out of the auditorium."

"No."

"But drat it, President—"

"Can't let it happen."

Thorkjeld Svenson fumed in silence a moment longer, then waxed, for him, loquacious. "Claude's running against Peters."

"For U.S. Congress. I know that. He must be out of his mind. Peters is a good man. Claude couldn't beat him. Nobody could. Peters has been Balaclava's man in the House of Representatives ever since Hector was a pup."

"Longer. Lacks charisma."

"What the flaming perdition do farmers need with charisma? Peters always votes on our side, doesn't he? He's introduced more sound farm legislation than anybody else there, hasn't he? He fought like a tiger to get that agricultural aid program for small farmers through Congress, didn't he? And he got it passed over the President's veto, moreover. Peters may lack charisma, but he sure as hell doesn't lack intelligence, integrity, or guts. Claude's a yammering idiot, and a vicious one at that."

"Yes."

"Then what's your problem? President, Balaclava Agricultural College stands for something in this congressional district. If we come out one hundred percent solid for Peters as we've always done before—"

"We'll lose the election for him. We've been suckered, Shandy."

"What?"

"That goddamn silo. Only time we ever accepted donations. Big fund drive. Public-spirited citizens of Balaclava County. Money pouring in from all directions. Pictures in *Balaclava County Weekly Fane and Pennon.* In one of 'em myself. With that blasted woman who started it all."

"I know," said Shandy.

How could one forget? The spectacle of Thorkjeld Svenson beside that dainty slip of femininity had looked like King Kong posing for a casual family photograph with Fay Wray. Shandy and his crony Timothy Ames had

laughed themselves sick over it. "She was a Mrs. Somebody. Smith? Smythe? Smath?"

"Smuth. Ruth Smuth. One of those women who head
committees. Urrgh! Sieglinde never heads committees."

Sieglinde Svenson had a big enough job on her hands
heading Thorkjeld, but Shandy didn't say so. "Well, what
about Ruth Smuth? She doesn't come into the suckering,
does she?"

"Hell she doesn't. She's Claude's campaign manager."

"Christ! But she wasn't when we built the silo. Damn it,
that was five years ago. She wasn't involved with Claude
then."

"No. I checked her out, damn it. Checked the whole
blasted committee. Not a smell of politics about one of
'em."

"So where's your problem?"

"She claims she was. Claims she told me at the time.
Damn liar. If I'd ever so much as suspected Claude was
behind that silo, I'd have ripped it off its foundation and
bashed him over the head with it."

"M'well, that might still be a solution."

"Too late," croaked Svenson. "Goddamn it, Shandy,
she's put me in the same pants-down position as one of
those poor slobs who picks up some respectable-looking
woman along the road with a sob-story about car trouble,
and then gets nailed for blackmail when she rips off her
clothes and starts yelling rape. If we give Claude the
horselaugh and come out swinging for Peters, she threat-
ens to plaster that silo all over the papers. CORRUPTION ON
CAMPUS. TURNCOAT SVENSON SECRETLY TAKES CLAUDE
FUNDS WHILE ENDORSING PETERS. By the time they get
through spreading that kind of muck around, poor old
Sam Peters will look like something the Mafia dragged
in."

Shandy nodded. "I hate to say it, President, but I'm
afraid you could be right."

"I'm always right," Svenson replied with his accustomed
modesty, "except when I pull a blooper, and then it's a
lulu. Damn it, Shandy, you've got to get us out of this. I'm
not asking for myself. I don't care if they make me look
like a horse's crupper, but if Sam Peters loses his seat in
Congress to a twerp like Claude, the country's whole

damn agricultural situation could be in even worse trouble than it is now. The fate of the nation is in your hands, and what the hell are you going to do about it?"

Shandy scratched the thin spot on the back of his head. "Good question. When's this son-of-a-bitch Claude clamoring to pollute our atmosphere?"

"Tomorrow night. This Smuth woman just sprung it on me half an hour ago. Think fast, Shandy."

"Jesus, President!" Shandy shook his head, then obediently plunged into thought.

"As far as sabotaging Claude's speech is concerned," he said at last, "that would be a cinch. It's the repercussions we have to worry about. Now, don't start yelling. I don't mean we can't do it, I just mean it has to be done right. There's also the matter of Ungley. That could be whipped up into another juicy scandal unless I go along with Ottermole and Melchett, and let it get swept under the carpet."

"Ungh? What about Ungley?"

"Unless I'm farther off base than I think I am, Ungley was murdered somewhere in the general vicinity of the Balaclavian Society's clubhouse sometime after eleven o'clock last night."

Shandy explained what he'd learned so far, while Svenson sat looking like an iceberg formed of frozen gloom. At last the president heaved a sigh that blew a Webster's Unabridged Dictionary halfway across his office, and shook his iron-gray mane.

"Ungley was one of ours, Shandy. We didn't want him, but we can't disclaim him. If we go along with a cover-up, the Claude bunch will be at our throats. If we make a stink, they'll turn it into a worse one. We'll do what's right and the hell with 'em. Come on, let's eat."

They walked down to the faculty dining room in silence, Svenson glowering sideways at Shandy every few steps to make sure he was thinking. It was an enormous relief to the smaller man when they walked in and spotted Helen Shandy sitting at a table by herself, seeking surcease from her duties as assistant librarian for the Buggins Collection. Peter kissed his wife with a shade more enthusiasm than was appropriate in so public a place and took the chair beside her. Svenson flung himself into the one opposite. To everyone's surprise, it didn't shatter under the impact.

Helen noticed the tension and tried a spot of light conversation. "Peter, how did you make out with Mrs. Lomax? Or have I phrased the question indelicately? One never knows nowadays."

"You haven't or I didn't, as the case may be. I'll give you a full report later. What's new at the library?"

"Poor Dr. Porble's in grave danger of spraining his upper lip from trying not to look smug."

"What's he got not to be smug about?"

"According to scuttlebutt among the stacks, Dr. Porble's tried on several occasions to join the Balaclavian Society because he thinks he ought to, and has been blackballed each time for reasons nobody can fathom. You'd think they'd positively leap at the chance to have the college librarian as a member."

"And no reason was ever advanced for their failure to pounce?"

"None. Dr. Porble always thought Professor Ungley was keeping him out. He came in as librarian shortly before Professor Ungley retired, and found the professor had some books he'd been keeping out for ages and ages. Being a new broom, Dr. Porble went out on the sweep and made Professor Ungley bring the books back. They say Ungley never set foot inside the library again, and kept Dr. Porble out of the Balaclavian Society as a form of revenge. It all sounds like a plot for Donizetti to me, but you know how people are."

"Urrgh," said Svenson.

"Indeed we do," Shandy interposed before catastrophe could ensue. "So now Porble thinks he can join that moribund mélange of malingerers. Why in Sam Hill would he want to?"

"Don't ask me, but you know Dr. Porble. He's not one to back down when he's set his mind on something."

That was most disturbingly true. Shandy liked and respected Porble, but he'd found out long ago that the librarian was a remarkably stubborn man. Furthermore, a temper of surprising proportions was concealed behind his scholar's manner. Shandy sat and scowled at the menu until the student waiter got tired of waiting and ventured to remark, albeit in a somewhat frightened tone, that the chicken croquettes were very good today.

"I'll have a club sandwich," he replied perversely.

Helen prattled on like a good hostess, clearly wondering why Peter was so abstracted and Thorkjeld so gloomy, but clearly realizing this was no time to ask. Svenson at least managed to perk himself up a degree or so by eating three helpings of the chicken croquettes which he wouldn't have got had Sieglinde been there to stop him. They did look good and Shandy was sorry he hadn't chosen them after all; but he reflected that his own error in judgment was a bagatelle compared to that of Thorkjeld Svenson in accepting a concrete silo, three stories high and costing some amount his overstrained mind boggled at remembering, from what had now turned out to be a hostile political pressure group.

But how had Svenson made such an egregious blooper? If he said he'd checked, he'd most assuredly done so, backward, forward, and sideways. It was simply not credible there had been any discoverable connection at that time between Bertram G. Claude and the Silo Supporters, as they'd called themselves, though God and Ruth Smuth only knew why. So that meant either that Ruth Smuth had got involved with Claude later on and realized she was in a position to do him some good by doing the college in the eye, or else that the whole Silo Supporters' affair had been part of some long-planned and fantastically well-covered-up ruse.

Raising that kind of money had been no jolly task of a few amateurs spending a few hours here and there putting the bite on their neighbors. The drive had gone on for months. Shandy couldn't recall how many, but he did remember all too clearly that the late Jemima Ames, then a flaming spearhead of all good works, had been pretty miffed about Ruth Smuth's having grabbed the initiative away from her. There had been hot words between the two women as to which of them was going to furnish the scissors to cut open the first bag of cement at the dedication ceremonies.

The entire fund-raising project had, in fact, taken on

such a low comedy turn that even as the concrete was being poured, nobody had quite believed the Silo Supporters had actually pulled it off. Was it humanly possible that, during all those farce-crammed weeks so long ago, Ruth Smuth and Bertram Claude had been secretly conniving toward the seat that Claude was surely going to get beaten out of on the upcoming first Tuesday in November?

Claude had been spending a lot of money on his campaign. Shandy hadn't been paying much attention, but now that he thought of it, it did seem he'd been turning off a lot of television commercials, throwing away a lot of pamphlets, and wadding up for fireplace kindling a lot of newspaper advertisements from which Claude's sexy smirk flashed out at him. Sam Peters had sent out one of his usual lackluster, fact-filled newsletters at a net cost of about thirty-seven dollars, probably. That would be it for this go-round, as it had been for all the others at which Sam had beaten the pants off opponents whose names Shandy couldn't even remember.

Where did Bertram G. Claude hail from, anyway? He'd manifested himself in Hoddersville about eight years ago, started shooting his mouth off to anybody who could be prevailed upon to listen, and managed to glad-hand himself into the State House on the strength of some expensive dentistry, a fine taste in neckties, and a voice that would have made his fortune as a television revivalist.

Once in office, Claude had committed every iniquity in Shandy's glossary, voting straight down the line in favor of big money against the independent farmer, the small businessman, against the old, the small, the weak, the sick, against anybody who hadn't a hefty wad to contribute to a rising man's next campaign. Claude's record on open-land preservation, on toxic-waste control, on clean air, clean water, clean anything proved that as far as he was concerned, politics was indeed a dirty game.

Even Professor Daniel Stott of the Animal Husbandry Department, a man not easily aroused to wrath, had waxed hot in defense of the genus *Sus* when somebody had been so injudicious as to call Claude a swine. In Stott's considered opinion, the district would have been far better advised to elect a sensible, well-disposed, right-thinking sow or boar to the seat Claude now occupied. The local

Plowmen's Political Action Committee was said to be taking Stott's recommendation under advisement.

And this was the oaf who was clamoring to address the student body at Balaclava. In a way, Shandy thought it mightn't be a bad idea. For one thing, there was the doctrine of free speech to consider. Claude was as entitled to spout his slimy rhetoric as anybody else. What they really ought to do was set up a debate with Sam Peters and invite the public. It would be interesting to see what happened.

Claude would make mincemeat of Peters, that was what would happen. He'd flash that come-hither smile and toss his curls and finger his fancy tie and talk a lot of garbage that people who couldn't listen and think at the same time would swallow hook, line, and sinker. On election day, there'd be good old Sam flat on his unhandsome face and Bertie packing his bags for Washington. Sam's best and maybe his only hope was for the college to come out swinging on his side as they'd always done before. And how could they, with that silo ready to explode in their faces?

Shandy was trying to recall precisely how the Silo Supporters' idea had got started in the first place. The college had needed the silo, no question about that. There'd been money enough in the coffers at the time to build a new one, and the plans were already drawn up. The builders were ready to roll when, for some reason not even the bankers could explain, farmers around Balaclava County began having a hard time borrowing money. Families that had been managing nicely found themselves caught in a squeeze with sound credit but no cash to finance their spring plantings. Naturally they appealed to the college's Endowment Fund, and naturally they got the help they needed.

Shelling out so much so unexpectedly left the college pinched for cash, too. Svenson and the Board of Trustees had decided it would be foolhardy to embark on any new major expenditure until after the fall harvest when, God and the elements willing, the farmers would be solvent again and the loans paid back. By then, however, it would be too late to build the silo in time for it to house that year's crop of ensilage. That raised the question of how the

flaming hell they were going to winter over their newly
augmented herds and flocks without putting the college in
hock.

Everybody in Balaclava County knew what was happening. Those who hadn't been required to nick Svenson
for a loan knew somebody who had, and those who'd been
hoping to get short-term jobs working on the building of
the new silo were loud in their disappointment. The
trustees hadn't even thought of appealing to the citizenry
for help because it was a fundamental tenet laid down by
Balaclava Buggins himself on that long-ago founding day
that Balaclava Agricultural College wasn't never going to
ask nothing from nobody, but that didn't prevent the
aforesaid citizens themselves from volunteering.

And volunteer they had. As soon as the word got
around, a group of concerned neighbors, or so they'd
described themselves, had clubbed together to form the
Silo Supporters. Since the college was doing so much for
the farmers, they clamored, it was no more than right the
county should do something for the college. They'd seemed
a well-meaning though somewhat bumble-headed lot.
Even so, Shandy remembered, Thorkjeld Svenson had
demurred until the Board of Trustees had decided what
the hell, this bunch would never raise the price of a binful
of concrete anyway and they might as well be given free
rein.

So the Silo Supporters, spearheaded by fluffy little Ruth
Smuth, had started holding bake sales, barn sales, plant
sales, book sales, all the different kinds of sales by which
well-meaning volunteers raise a few hundred dollars, if
they're lucky, for a worthy cause.

At first it had been rather touching and mildly amusing
to watch the self-appointed do-gooders out on the lawns
and commons peddling their homemade zucchini bread
and hand-embroidered needle books. Shandy himself had
contributed flats of seedlings and pots of geraniums to the
plant sale. Every faculty family had cleaned out its attic,
donated an armload of books, done something or other to
further the cause, merely to show appreciation and not
because they really expected anything to come of the
project.

But then, by George, the money had started piling up.

Those amateurish little fund-raising events were bringing in sums that left everybody gasping, notably Ruth Smuth and the Silo Supporters. Serendipity ran rampant. For instance, some family moving out of town contributed a pile of stuff to a rummage sale. Most of it was junk, but among the heap were a pair of genuine Chippendale side tables. The donors had left no forwarding address and in the general confusion nobody could exactly recall who they were. There really hadn't been a thing the sellers could do except regard the tables as manna from heaven and price them accordingly.

That was no doubt the time somebody should have begun to smell a rat. Instead, the alleged windfall had served to turn enthusiasm into euphoria. After that, all Balaclava County was silo-happy. Ruth Smuth was everywhere, getting her picture plastered all over the *Fane and Pennon* as she tacked up yet another poster, sold yet another loaf of zucchini bread, or paid yet another tribute to the marvelous, fabulous, just too utterly darling folk of Balaclava.

Jemima Ames had, to be sure, taken a dark view. Along with everybody else, Shandy had at the time put her waspish utterances down to pique at the fact that she herself hadn't been quick enough to grasp the reins of command. To make a long story short, the college had got its money, got its silo, and was now getting the shaft. And how in thunderation was Peter Shandy going to bail out Thorkjeld Svenson and defuse Ruth Smuth?

Chapter Seven

They finished their meal and dispersed; Helen to observe developments with regard to Dr. Porble's stiff upper lip, Peter to keep his appointment with Harry Goulson. He phoned down first to make sure Ottermole and Melchett would be on deck as scheduled, found they were even then closing in on the funeral parlor, and turned to Svenson.

"Care to come to the private viewing?"

"Ungh," said Svenson, so they went. On the way down, Shandy filled the president in on what he and Mrs. Lomax had found out so far. Svenson listened without so much as a grunt until he'd run out of things to tell, then nodded.

"Files. Had 'em."

Shandy was used to interpreting his superior's gnomic utterances. "You mean you know for a definite fact Ungley kept things in that filing cabinet of his. How?"

"Saw 'em."

Svenson took a few more giant steps, then condescended to utter. "Happened along the day Ungley was moving out of those old flats. Last one to leave, naturally. Demolition people standing around waiting. Movers bringing stuff out. Couldn't manage that filing cabinet. Bunch of pantywaists. Took out the drawers and carried 'em one by one. Ungley having fits because it was raining a few drops and his blasted archives were getting wet. I went in and got the cabinet, shoved the drawers back in, and carried the damn thing down to Mrs. Lomax's over my shoulder."

"The very model of a modern college president," Shandy murmured. "All four of the drawers were more or less filled, would you say?"

"Ungh."

"Old papers and stuff, I suppose?"

"Don't know. Didn't notice. Wasn't interested. Too damn glad to get rid of the old bastard. Pest. Bore. Expensive."

"Expensive?" That surprised Shandy. Svenson wasn't

58

one to toss words around lightly, if at all. Nor was he a skinflint about paying decent wages to his faculty members, much less coughing up a respectable pension for a superannuated professor. "What do you mean, expensive?"

"Highest-paid man on the staff, God knows why. Wasn't worth a plugged nickel. Squawked like hell at the size of his pension, too. Told him to take it or leave it. He took it. Too damn much as it was, damn it. What did Ungley need with all that money? No family, no house to keep up, not even a blasted goldfish to feed. No travel, no hobbies, no goddamn anything. Wouldn't even buy his own books. Pinched 'em from the library till Porble got after him."

"M'yes, so Helen told us. Surely Ungley hadn't really held a grudge against Porble all these years?"

"Why not? Held everything else he could get his grabby mitts on. Still be holding on to his job if I hadn't kicked him out. Did you know not one single student had enrolled in his course for three solid years before I retired him?"

"Er—no, I didn't. Ungley was out before I ever got here, you know."

"Show you in the records."

"I'll take your word for it. Yet you say Ungley was the highest-paid teacher on the faculty. That doesn't make any sense, President."

"No. Damn it, Engberg was no fool."

Dr. Engberg had been Thorkjeld Svenson's predecessor, though not for long. He'd been killed in an accident of some sort only a short time after he'd taken office. Shandy wasn't sure of the details, since that, too, had occurred before he'd come to Balaclava. So it must have been the president before Engberg, old Dr. Trunk, who'd hired Ungley in the first place.

"Was it Engberg or Trunk who gave Ungley so much money?" he asked.

"Trunk. Signed a crazy yearly increment contract. Couldn't be broken. Engberg tried. No go. Hodger."

"Do you mean Henry Hodger couldn't break the contract, or that he drew it up?"

"Drew. Tighter'n a bull's crupper in fly time."

"That's interesting. Hodger's also a member of the Balaclavian Society, which appears to have been the only—er—meaningful relationship Ungley ever formed around these parts. So it's dollars to doughnuts Hodger also drew up Ungley's will, if he ever got around to making one. I think we'd better go and call on him, President."

"Now?"

Svenson began veering leftward, toward the tomblike edifice of red brick and gray Quincy granite in which Hodger had maintained both his office and his living quarters since the beginning of recorded time. Shandy managed to head him off.

"Not yet. There's Melchett's car pulling into Goulson's driveway. No doubt he's in a swivet to get back to his giblets and gallstones, so let's not keep him waiting. Besides, I'm curious to see how he weasels out of his original willingness to pretend Ungley's death was accidental."

They were almost to the funeral home when Fred Ottermole clanked up in the village's only police cruiser, practicing his tough-cop expression en route. Catching sight of President Svenson, he came to a rubber-burning halt. His features contorted into those of one who has just caught sight of some unnameable horror in a lonely graveyard at the final stroke of midnight.

But Ottermole was no poltroon. Drawing on hidden resources of valor, he managed to get his jaw under control and accompany them more or less unflinchingly into the handsome white clapboard house to which Harry Goulson's grandfather had added the wing not long after the great influenza epidemic of 1919. Harry's own son and heir, who'd been hastily summoned home from morticians' school for this history-making event, greeted the party in hushed tones appropriate to his destined calling.

"I'm not sure if I should ask you to sign the book or not," he confessed artlessly. "I've never before assisted at a—at this kind of viewing."

"I'm not clear on the etiquette myself," Shandy told him, "so why don't we just—er—get on with it?"

Having given the boy his moment of glory, Goulson himself now appeared to take the party in tow. He was wearing his very best black coat now.

"This way, gentlemen, if you please. We're honored to

have you along, President Svenson. Of course, Professor Ungley was one of your own, so to speak."

"Ur," said Svenson.

Shandy decided they'd better get off that topic fast. "Ottermole, Melchett, good of you to come. I want you to understand that I have no quarrel with the—er— preliminary findings you made this morning," he began diplomatically. "However, certain facts have since come to light that I thought you should be apprised of before you arrive at any—er—final decision."

"Huh?" Ottermole was clearly under the impression they'd already made a final decision. Then he took a reflective look at the set of Thorkjeld Svenson's jaw and appeared to remember they hadn't.

"To begin with," Shandy went on, "you were no doubt struck by the—er—disproportionately small amount of blood you found on the harrow peg, in contrast with the copious bleeding from the victim's head wound."

Dr. Melchett averred that he'd called it to Ottermole's attention at the time of discovery. Ottermole said he had the fact down in his notebook for further study.

"Since then," Shandy went on, "I've had additional testimony from Mrs. Elizabeth Lomax. She was, as you know, Ungley's landlady."

"How come she gave it to you instead of me?" Ottermole demanded.

"Perhaps because she's been keeping house for me ever since I came to Balaclava. Mrs. Lomax is somewhat—er—feudal in her ways as you may have noticed."

"I'll say she is." Ottermole wasn't sure what feudal meant, but he knew Betsy Lomax. "Okay, so what did she tell you?"

"That Ungley's flat had been searched. She took me in there and showed me various indications of disturbance that would have been imperceptible to the—er—untrained eye. Being myself so familiar with Mrs. Lomax's housekeeping methods, I had no doubt she knew whereof she spoke. Furthermore, we found evidence that Professor Ungley's filing cabinet had been cleaned out last night, presumably by the person or persons who burgled the flat."

He explained about the missing plastic bags. "Lastly,

President Svenson has some information, which I'll let him give you himself."

Svenson could be articulate enough when he had to be. He imparted what he knew so forcefully that Ottermole was left insisting he'd known all along there was something fishy about Ungley's death. Melchett was calling attention to the fact that he hadn't yet signed the certificate; mainly because he hadn't got around to it, but that was beside the point. And Goulson was feeling a parental glow, knowing he hadn't hauled his son so abruptly out of Embalming II in vain. Here, not in some stuffy classroom with an articulated plastic figure stretched out on the table, was the real nitty-gritty of undertaking. He could see the heir apparent to the Goulson dynasty gazing at him with reverence, seeing Dad as a true mover and shaker, a veritable Batman among morticians. And the boy, he thought indulgently, would be picturing himself as a valiant young Robin, and not so far out at that.

"About that hole in the skull." Dr. Melchett must have decided Shandy had been hogging the floor long enough. "Ottermole, you remember I said it was an unusual wound to have been made by a harrow peg."

There was in fact no reason why Ottermole should remember since Melchett hadn't actually said so; but he'd been on the verge of thinking so. He avoided the chief's eyes and cleared his throat.

"I also remarked that the head of Ungley's cane was surprisingly heavy and might be filled with lead. On reflection, I think we ought to get that cane tested for possible traces of human blood."

"I couldn't agree with you more, Doctor," Shandy replied, since he was already having it done anyway. "Why don't we have the tests run in the college's Chemistry Department so that if the finding is negative there won't be any—er—"

"Great idea," Ottermole interrupted. "You go right ahead and do that, Professor. How soon can you get me a report?"

"Quite soon, I should think. It's a simple enough test."

"Good. We'll handle this one ourselves. No calling in the state police, huh?"

Ottermole's tone was jocular, but his glare was baleful.

Shandy looked at Svenson. Svenson looked at Melchett. Melchett looked at his watch and said he must get back to his patients. Goulson asked if they'd be wanting any more photographs of the deceased.

"Why don't you take one of Chief Ottermole with the corpse?" Shandy suggested to restore the atmosphere of bonhomie. "Covered, of course. I expect the *Fane and Pennon* will ask for it when he holds his press conference. Though that will have to wait on the results of our findings. There's still plenty of time to catch next week's edition," he added when Ottermole's face began to fall.

Goulson was only too happy to oblige. He took one of President Svenson and Shandy with the corpse, the chief, and the boy for good measure, because this was a day he wanted his son to remember. When the film was all used up, they thanked him profusely, granted permission for him and the boy to start their customary duties to the deceased, and left.

Once outside, Melchett immediately got into his car and sped officeward. Ottermole said briskly, "Well, I better get on with the investigation," then sneaked a hopeful glance at Shandy, who nodded.

"Strike while the iron's hot. President Svenson and I were saying on the way down here that somebody ought to pay a call on Henry Hodger the lawyer. He'd be most apt to have Ungley's will, if there is one. That might give us a lead."

"Worth trying," Ottermole agreed. "I've been thinking about that, myself."

Which was a lie, or he'd already have been over to hound the lawyer, but Shandy didn't mind about that. What counted was having Ottermole along. The chief's presence might make Hodger less unwilling to disgorge any information he might have. They went.

Hodger was in his office. In fact, he gave the impression of having taken root to his desk chair. That wasn't strange, considering how many years he must have spent sitting in it. He didn't rise when they entered.

"Figured you'd be around sooner or later, Ottermole. I know about Ungley, if that's what you're here to tell me."

He didn't appear to notice either Shandy or the president, and overlooking Thorkjeld Svenson was quite a feat.

Shandy became more interested in the lawyer than he'd expected to be, although Hodger was by no means an intriguing man to look at.

He had a strangely blank face for a man of his years, as though he'd trained himself so rigorously in the discretion required by his profession that he'd ended by shutting out expression entirely. Yet he wasn't beyond feeling. He was being deliberately rude to Svenson and Shandy, unless he was either blind or close to it. Even Ottermole noticed the slight, and did his clumsy best to smooth it over.

"You know President Svenson from the college? And this is Professor Shandy."

Hodger didn't even turn his head in their direction. "What do you want out of me, Fred? A statement about last night?"

"Yeah, that's right. About last night. You had a meeting of the Balaclavian Society?"

"We did."

"And Professor Ungley gave you a talk about penknives?"

"He did."

"Was he okay during the talk?"

"That would depend on what you mean by okay. If you refer to his physical condition, I suppose I'd have to say that to the best of my knowledge, not being a registered physician and not having examined Ungley more closely than one member of a fraternal organization might reasonably be expected to observe another during the course of a meeting, he appeared to be neither better nor worse than usual. If you're asking whether he presented an interesting topic in an organized and informative manner, I prefer to reserve any statement on the grounds of *de mortuis nil nisi bonum.*"

"Huh?"

"No doubt your learned companions can translate for you. What else do you want to ask me?"

"Well, uh, did Professor Ungley leave with you, or did he stay behind?"

"It is my impression that we all left more or less in a group. I recall that I held open the door for Mrs. Pommell, then said good night and came directly across the street to my own quarters here. Ungley would have stayed on the museum side of the street, which is to say the opposite side from this to make myself perfectly clear. Assuming he meant to go back to his own dwelling place, he would then have walked right as far as the corner, then turned left."

"You didn't turn around to watch him?"

"No. Why should I have? It was late, and I wanted to get to bed."

"Can you think of any reason why Professor Ungley might have gone around behind the museum?"

"I'm not in the habit of thinking up reasons, Ottermole. The law concerns itself with facts."

"Yeah, well, uh—"

"I believe," Shandy prompted, "you meant to ask Mr. Hodger about Professor Ungley's will."

Ottermole brightened. "That's right. I was just going to mention it. We figured you'd be the one to know."

"To know what?" asked that infuriating old man.

"Whether Ungley made a will, like Professor Shandy just said. Did he?"

"He did."

"Then how about giving us a gander at it?"

"Whom do you mean by us?"

"He means himself, President Svenson, and me," said Shandy, who'd decided Hodger had been allowed to play cute long enough. "We're assisting Ottermole in his investigation of Ungley's death. Unless you have some reason to continue being obstructive, we assume you'll wish to do the same."

"Is that supposed to be a threat?"

"I don't see how it can be construed as one, unless you know of some reason why you ought to feel threatened."

The lawyer's face was, after all, capable of expression. Hodger performed a superb dramatic rendering of malignancy before he reached into his top desk drawer and fished out a document covered in faded blue paper.

"Ungley's will is a very simple one and will be filed for probate as soon as the necessary formalities are completed. Since it will then become available to the public, I see no reason why I cannot with propriety give you a summary of its contents now. Myself and Henry Pommell, president of the First Balaclava County Guaranteed National Trust, Savings and Loan, are the executors. One-third of whatever assets Ungley possessed at the time of his death is left to the college, to be used in setting up a department of Local History, a subject Ungley considered to have been grossly neglected during recent years. One-third goes to the Balaclavian Society, of which he was a past president and perpetual curator. The remaining third is left to his sole surviving relative, one Alonzo Bulfinch who is, if I am not mistaken, currently in the employ of Balaclava Agricultural College."

Hodger refolded the sheaf of papers and put it back in the drawer. "Now if you'll excuse me, I have to get over to the county courthouse."

He began struggling out of his chair. Shandy hadn't realized until then how badly the lawyer was crippled with arthritis. Seeing Hodger's cane hooked over the edge of the desk, he reached to hand it over. Then he noticed its handle was of carved silver in the shape of a running fox and as disproportionately heavy as Ungley's.

"Would you happen to have another cane, Mr. Hodger?" he asked.

"What business is it of yours?" the lawyer barked.

"Well, you see, I think Chief Ottermole is about to impound this one as possible evidence, and I'm sure he wouldn't want to leave you with—er—no visible means of support."

Chapter Eight

Oddly enough, Hodger didn't make any great fuss over the cane. He did have another one, and got Ottermole to fetch it for him out of the umbrella stand beside the door. He then demanded a receipt and asked, not unreasonably, how soon his property might be returned to him.

"That depends on what we find when we analyze the handle," Shandy took it upon himself to answer.

"Analyze the handle? For what, if I'm not out of order in asking?"

"Not at all. We're looking for bloodstains, bone slivers, fragments of brain matter, that sort of thing."

"Good God! And why should you expect to find them on my cane?"

"Simply because yours happens to be identical with the cane found beside Ungley. That one is already being tested as the possible murder weapon. There's the outside chance yours and his may have been switched."

"Why should they have been?"

"That takes us into the realm of speculation, Mr. Hodger. Since you deal only in facts, any reply I could make at this time would not be germane to the issue."

"Umph. Have you then established what the issue is?"

"Oh yes. The issue is that Ungley's death was no accident as was at first supposed, but deliberate murder."

"Murder? That's ridiculous. Who'd want to murder Ungley?"

"You're asking another question we can't answer at this time. The murderer's identity will be established on the basis of the evidence."

"What evidence?"

"The evidence that will be presented at the trial. Thank you for your cooperation, Mr. Hodger. We'll take great care of your cane." Hodger himself did, obviously. His was in far better condition than Ungley's. Another tidy man, drat it. "Er—would it be out of order to ask how yours and Ungley's came to be just alike?"

"They *came* to be identical because they were *made* that way. As to how I obtained mine, which I gather is what you're attempting to ask, the answer is simple. I admired Ungley's and he presented me with a mate to it. Where he got them, I am unable to say. As you leave, please tell my clerk I'm on my way out and to bring the car around. I don't like to be kept standing."

Having been so adroitly given the bum's rush, the oddly assorted posse could do nothing more than pass on Hodger's message to the harried law clerk at the front desk—nobody ever knew who these wights were because he got them fresh out of law school and wore them out in no time flat—and go away. Once they were out on the sidewalk, Shandy turned to Svenson.

"Who the hell," he demanded, "is Alonzo Bulfinch?"

"Security guard," Svenson replied. "Just hired. Never said he was related to Ungley."

"Seemed like a nice enough guy when I met him," Ottermole put in. "Just goes to show you never know, do you?"

"Never know what?" said Shandy. "Where did you meet him?"

"He's an old army buddy of Silvester Lomax. They were in the MP's together. Silvester's wife had me and the missus and a few other people over night before last to meet him. He's staying with her and Silvester till he can find a place."

Finding a place to live was no mean feat in Balaclava Junction. Most of the students lived in the dorms, but rooms and apartments were still at a premium because of the many comings and goings among staff and faculty, and because there weren't many of them to start with. Mrs. Lomax probably had six or seven prospects already camped on her doorstep trying to rent Ungley's flat.

The logical person to have it would be Ungley's heir, and maybe Alonzo Bulfinch had already thought of that. Surely, though, the new security guard hadn't bumped off his uncle just to get himself a place to sleep.

Ottermole was champing at the bit to do some more detecting. "Now what, Professor?"

"We may as well take this cane of Hodger's on up to Professor Joad, and let him test it along with Ungley's," said Shandy. "After that, it mightn't be a bad idea to have a chat with Bulfinch, if we can find him."

"Yeah, we better nail that guy before he decides to skip town. Say, I wonder how much he stands to inherit."

"Plenty," snarled Thorkjeld Svenson.

The memory of that outrageous salary Ungley had milked from the college for so many years must still be rankling.

Shandy decided a precise answer to Ottermole's question mightn't be such a bad idea, at that. "I expect Pommell will know how much Ungley had in the sock. Let's go ask him. If he won't tell, Ottermole can flash his badge and threaten to run him in for obstructing justice. I'd be surprised, though, if Hodger didn't take time to give Pommell a fast phone call before going off to keep that urgent appointment."

"Come on," said Ottermole. "Let's move. Chemistry Department first, right?"

The bank was only a few doors away, but they stuck to their original itinerary. Svenson was happy at getting to ride in the police cruiser. "Where's the siren, Ottermole?" he demanded. "I'll work it."

"Better not, President," Shandy warned. "The students will think Ottermole's running you in for disturbing the peace."

Svenson growled but subsided, perhaps reflecting on what Sieglinde would say if she found out. They got to the chemistry building without attracting undue notice. When Joad saw them coming, though, he ran to meet them, waving a full test tube with reckless abandon.

"It's blood, all right. Human, type AB negative. Minute traces definitely present on the cane handle, also in that iron rust you scraped off the harrow peg."

"What about the sample Goulson sent over?"

"AB negative. I have to say also human, though coming from Ungley I must say I was rather surprised. I'll break down the factors more precisely to remove all shadow of doubt, but I'd say you've got yourselves a murder weapon."

"Drat," said Shandy, handing him the other cane. "I was

rather hoping we might pin the killing on Henry Hodger. Test this one anyway, will you?"

"Delighted. What happens to the evidence when I'm finished?"

"I'll impound it," said Ottermole masterfully. "And I want a written report of what you just said. If you don't mind," he added in a meeker tone when he noticed Svenson's eye boring at him.

"Don't mind in the least. Glad to oblige. We don't get one like this every day."

Like Harry Goulson, Joad was relishing his part in the affair and making no bones about it. Well, why not? Ungley had afforded Balaclava little enough diversion during his lifetime. Maybe he was atoning by departing in a fashion so much more dramatic than his lectures could ever have been.

That was a sobering thought. Shandy began to wonder if he might put a spot more zip and dash into his own classroom technique. He thanked Joad, watched with interest while the various exhibits-to-be were marked and wrapped, then followed Svenson and Ottermole back to the cruiser.

"We got to pick up this Bulfinch, don't forget," Ottermole reminded them.

"I never forget," said Svenson. "Security office. Next left."

Ottermole didn't have to be told where the security guards hung out. They were, so to speak, brothers under the badge although the campus police were a totally independent force from Ottermole's; considerably larger, busier, and better managed now that Silvester Lomax and his brother Clarence were jointly in charge, neither of them being willing to assume precedence over the other.

Being cousins-in-law of Betsy Lomax and both owning cats from the same litter as Edmund, they were of course in full command of the particulars by the time Ottermole and his distinguished escort arrived to inform them. They were, however, surprised to learn that Alonzo Bulfinch was Ungley's relative and heir.

"Lonz never said nothin' to us," Clarence grunted.

"No reason why he should," said Silvester, sticking up for his friend. "Still an' all, a person might o' thought—"

"He never visited Professor Ungley since he got here?" Ottermole cut in.

"Nope."

"You sure?"

Both the Lomaxes gave him a look. How could they not be sure? The old man had been Betsy's tenant, hadn't he? And Lonz was staying at Silvester's, wasn't he? Fred Ottermole ought to know damn well by this time you couldn't get much past the Lomaxes.

The chief gave them a sheepish grin in return. "Yeah, well, where's this Bulfinch guy now?"

"Home asleep in our spare room bed, most likely," said Silvester. "He was on duty last night."

"You don't say? Now we're gettin' somewhere."

Ottermole didn't exactly rub his hands and chuckle, but he did zip up his black leather jacket in a grim and purposeful manner. "So Bulfinch was roaming around up here on his lonesome. What were his hours?"

"Ha' past ten last evenin' to ha' past five this mornin'."

"And the meeting broke up around eleven. It's a perfect setup. Bulfinch meets Ungley down at the museum so's Mrs. Lomax won't know they've been together, takes him around back on some pretext or other, whangs him over the head with his own cane, cleans up the handle, or thinks he does, then hightails it back up here to get on his rounds and punch the clock like he's s'posed to."

"Having managed to search Ungley's rooms very tidily and take away the contents of four file drawers en route?" said Shandy. "That would have taken some adroit footwork, Ottermole."

"He went back an' did the searching later, that's all. Hell, he had the whole night, didn't he?"

"Not so's you'd notice it," Silvester Lomax contradicted. "Look here, Fred, we don't sit around on our backsides up here like you do down at the station. We're on the go all the time, specially at night. The two guards on outside duty have their routes laid out crossways, kind of, so's they can keep tabs on each other in case one of 'em runs into trouble. Besides, we got the signals rigged so the man in the office will know if they don't punch in on the dot. That's another safety measure. The guards carry them walkie-talkies, but if a man was grabbed from behind, say, he might not get a chance to use it. Purvis Mink was on with Lonz last night, an' you know Purve. Nobody's goin' to try pullin' nothin' with Purve around. Not that Lonz would anyways."

"How do you know he wouldn't?"

"'Cause he's a friend of Silvester's," said Clarence.

Both Lomax brothers folded their sinewy arms over the chests of their neat green uniforms and stood there, firm as the bedrock under their feet and just about as persuadable. Ottermole gave up and took out his car keys again.

"Okay, boys. Thanks. We better get movin'. You coming, President?"

Thorkjeld Svenson regretfully excused himself on the grounds that he had a goddamn meeting to attend. Shandy thought of that pile of test papers still waiting for the slash of his tutorial pencil, of the seedling flats in the greenhouse he'd meant to have a look at, of seventeen other odd jobs he'd planned to get around to on this allegedly free afternoon, and said, "I'm coming."

"I figured there was no sense in us wasting any more time on that pair," Ottermole grunted as he and Shandy got back into the cruiser. "They're stubborn as mules, both of 'em. Naturally they're not going to admit Silvester made a mistake hiring Bulfinch. Hell, you can't trust a man just because you had a few beers with him in the PX thirty or forty years ago."

Shandy made a noncommittal noise. Ottermole didn't say any more. They drove out the back road to Silvester Lomax's neat two-story Cape Cod house and hauled up in front of the driveway, blocking off an elderly but well-kept blue Chevvie.

"That's so if he tries to make a run for it, he won't be able to get his car out of the driveway," Ottermole explained.

Shandy refrained from pointing out that it would be easy enough for the Chevvie to cut across the lawn, assuming it did in fact belong to Alonzo Bulfinch and not to Mrs. Silvester Lomax, who was even now emerging from the house dressed up and carrying a pie basket. He waited for the fur to fly, and was not disappointed.

"Fred Ottermole, as I live and breathe! Come to pick up

a few tips on how to do your job, have you? Too bad
Silvester isn't home just now. He could have told you for
one thing that a grown man ought to know better than to
block a person's driveway. I'm due at the Churchwomen's
Tea, and I've got to be there early because I'm the one that
has to start the water boiling, so you just move that tin
lizzie fast or you'll soon wish you had. Clarence's wife,
Maude, was saying just the other day you didn't have the
brains of a good-sized hen, but I stuck up for you. I said
you did, just about. Now do I go over you or through you?
Take your pick and make it snappy. Maude's waiting for
me to pick her up and I'm late already."

Growling, Ottermole went to move the cruiser. Shandy
took the pie basket and walked Mrs. Lomax to her
Chevvie, seizing his chance to tell her, "We really came to
talk to Mr. Bulfinch."

"Lonz? Whatever for?"

"Well—er—I expect you've heard about Professor
Ungley?"

"Betsy called me."

"But perhaps you didn't know Bulfinch is one of the
heirs?"

"Well—I—never!" Mrs. Lomax automatically stowed
her pie basket in the car, laid her pocketbook on the seat,
and slid behind the wheel. Then she whirled the window
down and stuck out her head. "Did Betsy know that?" she
demanded in a voice of thunder.

"No. I don't believe anyone knew, except Henry Hodger
the lawyer."

"Oh, that old—"

She slammed her foot down on the gas pedal and backed
the car out in a cloud of dust. It was as well Ottermole had
moved his cruiser.

The chief appeared to bear Mrs. Silvester no grudge. He
merely grinned after her and remarked, "Ought to be a
lively meeting down at the Churchwomen's today. Well, I
guess I better go wake up the sleeping beauty."

He made sure he had his handcuffs at the ready and
started toward the house. Then he paused. "Say, how
about you going around to the back door so's you can stop
him if he bolts."

"Why should he?" Shandy objected. "He doesn't know what you're here for. Anyway, you have no grounds to charge him with anything."

"What do you mean, no grounds? He had motive and opportunity, didn't he?"

"So did a number of other people."

"Who, for instance?"

"Anybody who had to sit through that lecture on penknives, according to Mrs. Lomax. Furthermore, don't forget the Historical Society gets as much of the estate as Bulfinch does."

So did the college, but Shandy thought perhaps he wouldn't mention that. Thorkjeld Svenson had troubles enough already.

Chapter Nine

Ottermole wasn't interested in other suspects. He was wondering, "I wonder if I should knock first, or just barge in?"

"Why don't you see if the door's unlocked?" Shandy suggested.

They did and it was, so they barged. The staircase being dead ahead, they continued to barge until they found themselves in a dazzlingly clean upper hallway with one door closed. From behind it came the peaceful sound of low, rhythmical snoring. Ottermole whipped out his service revolver and was about to bang the panels with the butt when Shandy stopped him.

"If you dent that woodwork, you'll catch a double dose of hell from the Lomaxes."

"Huh," said Ottermole, but he used his knuckles instead.

Immediately the snoring stopped, a voice called out, "Just a second," and they heard sounds as of scuffling for slippers and bathrobe. Almost within the appointed second, the door was opened by a shortish, thinnish man with his sparse gray hair neatly combed and his bathrobe cord neatly tied.

"Sorry I didn't hear the doorbell," he apologized. "Evelyn must have gone on to her meeting. Say, you're Fred Ottermole. What's up? Do they need me over at Security?"

"No, I need you right here."

"Then I'm at your disposal. Come right in."

Bulfinch backed away from the door. "Sorry the bed isn't made, but I was on the night shift and I helped Evelyn around the place a little when I got off. Figured I'd grab my sack time after the house quieted down. Oh, sorry, didn't realize you had company, Fred. It's Professor

75

Shandy, isn't it? This is an unexpected honor, sir. Maybe we'd better go down to the parlor. Evelyn won't mind."

"This is fine." Shandy seated himself on the unmade bed. "We're sorry to get you up, but the fact is, we've had a murder."

"On campus?"

"No, downtown. Behind the museum. It was Professor Ungley."

"Ungley?" For some reason, Bulfinch sounded more excited than dismayed. "You don't mean to tell me you've got Ungleys right here in Balaclava Junction?"

"Come on, Bulfinch," said Ottermole, "don't try to play cute with us."

"I don't understand, Fred." Bulfinch looked as if he really didn't. "What is there to play cute about?"

"We know he was related to you."

"No kidding? I knew I had some Ungley connections around these parts and I meant to look them up once I got settled, but what with breaking in on a new job and trying to find a place to live, I hadn't got around to it. You sure we were connected, Fred?"

"He's got you down in his will. Alonzo Bulfinch. That's you, isn't it?"

"Says so on my birth certificate. But how come he mentioned me in his will when he didn't even know me?"

"He knew about you. Claimed you were his only surviving relative."

Bulfinch rubbed his open left palm across his sleek gray head. "I don't know but what I might be, come to think of it. Seems to me my mother said the Ungleys had pretty much died out. She was an Ungley herself, and glad enough to swap a name like that for Bulfinch, though she didn't get to keep it long, poor soul. Mother died when I was nine. I've always been closer to the Bulfinch side, naturally. She did have a brother, but I thought he must have gone long ago. He was a lot older than my mother, if I'm not mistaken."

Ottermole's eyes narrowed. "How come you're giving us all this family stuff? Don't you want to know how much he had you down for?"

Bulfinch shrugged. "Stands to reason it wouldn't be much, seeing as how he never so much as passed the time of day with me in his life. Some relics he didn't want to go outside the family, I suppose. I've never been one to go looking for handouts anyway. It just galls me to think I could have got to meet him any time this past week, and now I'll never have the chance. Did he know I was in town, I wonder?"

If Hodger knew, it was quite possible Ungley did, too, but Shandy was kind enough not to say so. "How should he? He was, as you say, an old man and—er—somewhat reclusive in his habits." He tried to visualize Ungley in the role of long-lost uncle, and failed. "How did you happen to come here, Mr. Bulfinch?"

"Silvester invited me, is the long and short of it. He and I were in the service together, as you may have heard, and we always kept in touch after the war. I'd been living in Detroit—my wife was from there—but you know what it's like in the automotive industry these days. When jobs got tight, they asked some of us old-timers to take early retirement and make way for the young guys with families to support. I wasn't ready to hang up my hat by a long shot, but I had to say I would. So I mentioned getting laid off in my next letter to Silvester, naturally, and he wrote back saying he and Clarence had an opening and how'd I like to come back East? I had nothing to keep me in Detroit—wife's gone and all the kids married and moved away—so I said sure and here I am."

"You never mentioned your Ungley connection to the Lomaxes?"

"If I had, they'd have told me there was a Professor Ungley at the college, wouldn't they? Look, you did say my uncle was murdered? I was still kind of half asleep when you came, and I'm not sure I took it all in. How did it happen?"

"He was struck over the head with the handle of his own cane."

"That's one for the book. You wouldn't think a cane could kill a man."

"This one could. The handle was in the shape of a running fox, made of silver and filled with lead. Traces of blood matching your uncle's type have been found on it by our college Chemistry Department."

"How come you didn't use the police labs? Sorry, Fred, I

keep forgetting I'm not in the big city any more. But how could a thing like that happen? I wouldn't have thought you'd get muggings in a quiet little village like this."

"We don't," said Ottermole. "Put your clothes on, Bulfinch. I'm taking you down to the station."

Alonzo Bulfinch shook his head. "Sorry, Fred. I'd sure like to help you out, but I promised Evelyn I'd stick around and let in the man to fix the washing machine, if he ever shows up. She's been waiting since Monday."

"You trying to resist an officer in the performance of his duty?"

Ottermole started to reach for his handcuffs, but Shandy intervened. "I believe Mr. Bulfinch means he'd prefer to make his statement here rather than inconvenience his hostess. If you'd care to borrow my pen—"

Shandy didn't know it, but he'd said the magic word. Ottermole pulled out his new gold ball point and flourished it for the others to see and envy.

"I've got my own. Now let's start from the beginning. You're Alonzo Bulfinch, right?"

"Sure, Fred, you know that. You met me night before last at the party Evelyn and Silvester gave. Alonzo Persifer Bulfinch, if you want the whole of it."

"Address?"

"Right here, till I find a place of my own. You wouldn't happen to know of an empty flat anywhere?"

"There's Professor Ungley's," Shandy couldn't resist suggesting.

"You mean my uncle's?"

"Why not? You've probably inherited the furniture anyway."

"Look, would you let me get on with the questioning?" snapped Ottermole, waving his gold pen some more in case they hadn't noticed. "You've been a security guard at the college for how long?"

"One week today. Unpacked a clean shirt and went to work as soon as I'd parked my suitcase. Silvester and Clarence were shorthanded."

"And you've been house hunting in your spare time, you say? So you know your way around the village pretty much by now."

"I wouldn't go so far as to say that, Fred. I know the campus like the palm of my hand because it's my business to, but I'm none too sure about the rest of the country around here. See, I gave my car to my son before I came on here. He needed one, and I didn't care to drive all that way by my lonesome. I figured Silvester would know where I'd be able to pick up a pretty good one secondhand, but that's another thing I haven't got around to yet. Haven't needed it so far. The other guards have been great about picking me up and bringing me home, and Evelyn and Maude drive me around some when I'm off duty."

"Taken you downtown, haven't they?"

"Oh yes, I was down with Maude just yesterday. She had some errands and so did I. Went into the bank and cashed some travelers' checks, bought stamps at the post office so I could let the folks back in Detroit know I got here all right—"

"If you went to the post office, you were right next door to the clubhouse."

"Was I? I can't say I noticed."

"Tell that to the Marines. You couldn't have helped noticing."

"I think he could, Ottermole," Shandy objected. "That clubhouse isn't much to look at, you know."

"Say, you're not talking about that dinky little old clapboard building with the weeds growing up around it?" Bulfinch exclaimed. "I was meaning to ask Evelyn why they didn't either fix it up or tear it down. When you said clubhouse, I thought of—oh, something kind of classy, I guess. Don't tell me that's where my uncle got killed? How did he get in?"

"He was a member and he had a key," snarled Ottermole. "Don't try to kid me you didn't know anything about him. Anyway, he wasn't killed inside, as you also know."

"Excuse me, Ottermole," Shandy murmured, "but we don't know that ourselves. Perhaps we ought to reserve judgment until we've checked the interior."

"Yeah, and don't think we won't. I'm going over that place with a fine-tooth comb."

Ottermole unzipped his leather jacket in the tough-guy manner he'd been practicing. It was getting pretty warm with the three of them crammed into that one small bedroom. "Okay, Bulfinch, I want you to account for every second of your time last night."

"Let's see. I had supper here with the folks about half-past six when Silvester came off duty. Then we sat around swapping yarns and watching television till it was time for me to leave. Purvis Mink was on with me last night, so he and Clarence picked me up. We drove to the office together, signed in at Security, then Purve and I got our keys to the time clocks and our routes for the night. See, we don't stick to any single routine. We cover the campus in a different pattern every night. That's so if anybody happened to get the bright notion of following the guards around one night to find out where they'd be the next, he'd be letting himself in for a surprise. Silvester says Clarence thought up the system; Clarence says it was Silvester. Anyway, what we do is pick a number when we get there. We don't even know ourselves what route we'll be on till just before we start out."

"Okay, so which route were you on last night?"

"Three. That's mostly the back part of the campus, out around the barns and the power plant."

"Farthest away from town, in short," said Shandy.

"That's right. See, we have to punch the clocks every five hundred yards or so right on the dot. You've seen 'em, they're in those little blue cast-iron boxes all over the place. If we don't punch in, a buzzer goes off in the security office and whoever's on duty there tries to raise us on the walkie-talkie. If he can't, he knows which box we're supposed to be nearest to, and he comes out to see what's up. I don't say I couldn't have snuck off on a bicycle, if I'd had one, and committed a murder maybe two miles from where I was supposed to be, and got back in time to punch my next clock on time, but it would have taken some pretty fancy footwork."

Ottermole started to say, "Clarence might have covered—" then stopped. Clarence Lomax wouldn't do a cover-up for his own brother or his mother or the Angel Gabriel, much less Alonzo Bulfinch.

As the chief was floundering for a way to finish the sentence without getting egg on his face, the front door burst open and confusion filled the hallway. "Ma! Ma, are you home?"

"Excuse me, I'd better go see who that is," said Bulfinch.

But Ottermole was ahead of him. "Hey, what's up down there?"

"Oh, Fred!" cried a distraught woman's voice. "Am I glad to see you! How come you're here, though? Anything wrong with the folks?"

"No, your mother's just gone to the church."

"Where's Pa?"

"Working, I guess. What's the matter, Mary Ellen?"

"Fred, you won't believe it. I don't, myself. A helicopter from the air base flew over the house and dropped a bolt or something right down our kitchen skylight. I was frying doughnuts. Whatever it was hit the kettle of fat and sent it all over the hot stove. That started a fire, and it went so fast I—" She caught her breath.

"Luckily I happened to be over by the door putting the cat out because he'd got up on the counter and was trying to walk through the dough. The baby was on the porch in her carriage, so I just rushed out and grabbed her and ran over to the neighbors' and called the fire department. They got the fire out, but the house is such a mess we can't stay in it. Smoke and water all over everything, and my lovely new kitchen gutted—oh, Fred!"

Mary Ellen sniffed a bit, then tried to pull herself together. "Anyway, I managed to salvage a few things for us to wear and picked up the boys from school and came on here. Ma and Pa will have to bed us down somehow till we can get the house fit to live in again. Would you mind helping me get the stuff out of the car? I've got to change the baby, and I'm worn to a frazzle. Jim doesn't even know yet. He's on the road with his rig and the dispatcher says he's not due to call in till five o'clock."

"Who's taking care of the cat?" asked Bulfinch.

"The neighbors. I told them to give him a steak and I'd pay for it. Oh, my goodness, Mr. Bulfinch! I completely forgot you were staying here."

"Don't fret yourself about putting me out, Mary Ellen. I've found a place. In fact, I was just packing my bags. Fred and his friend here were going to give me a lift. I'll have the room cleared for you in two shakes of a lamb's tail."

Fred Ottermole, looking bemused, went to give Mary Ellen a hand. Shandy decided he might as well pitch in, too. He lugged a few armloads of clothes and playthings, all reeking of smoke, and gave a six-year-old a piggyback to stop its crying. By the time they'd emptied the car and quieted the children, Bulfinch was dressed and downstairs with his luggage.

"You want to open the trunk, Fred? I made the bed up fresh, Mary Ellen, and phoned your dad at the security office. He's sending your cousin Sally to baby-sit and says for you to lie down and take it easy till your mother gets home."

Ottermole opened the trunk, still looking as if he too had been hit by an unexpected flying object. Bulfinch stowed his gear, then climbed into the back seat of the cruiser. A teenager in a blue down-filled jacket biked frantically into the yard. It was time to go.

"Hope you don't mind, Fred," said Bulfinch. "You can pinch me as a suspect and bed me down in the lockup, can't you? I couldn't hang around there getting underfoot. That poor young woman's had just about all she can take, from the look of her. Darn good thing she kept her head and got the baby away."

Ottermole shook his own head to get his brains back in gear. "Yeah, Mary Ellen was always smart in school. Jeez, I can't believe it! I helped Jim put that skylight in myself, one weekend last summer. He and I were in Boy Scouts together. Then we played on the football team. Hell, we used to double-date, him and Mary Ellen and me and the wife. Before we got married, I mean. Two raspberry-lime rickeys, four straws, and a spare dime for the juke box. Look, Bulfinch, how about if I drop you at your uncle's place? No sense in letting it sit idle. You see any objection, Professor?"

"None whatever," said Shandy. "Good thinking, Ottermole."

Those were words he'd once thought he would never have occasion to utter. This was indeed a day of strange happenings.

Chapter Ten

"What the hell, I didn't have anything to hold him on, did I?"

They'd got Alonzo Bulfinch stowed in Professor Ungley's flat. Ottermole appeared to be having second thoughts, but Shandy reassured him.

"Not a thing, as far as I can see. You'll check his time sheets with Security, I expect, as a matter of routine, but I have no doubt you'll find they're perfectly in order. In any event, you'll know where to find him if you need him again, and we do have all those other Balaclavian Society people we haven't talked with yet. Suppose we tackle Mr. Pommell at the bank for starters. He's nearest."

Ottermole, perhaps thinking of his own mortgage, demurred. "I already spoke to his wife this morning."

"He may have something of his own to add. Anyway, we owe him the courtesy of a personal call."

Ottermole couldn't see why. Neither, in fact, could Shandy, but they went anyway. Pommell was in his office out behind the tellers' booths and seemed willing enough to grant them audience. He was what Shandy's grandmother would have called a fine figure of a man, though somewhat on the portly side for cholesterol-conscious modern taste. Pommell ought to have a heavy gold watch chain stretched across his front with an elk's tooth dangling from it, Shandy thought as they shook hands.

"Come in, come in. I've been expecting you. All well down at the station, Ottermole? Professor Shandy, I understand you're trying to help us clear up this dreadful business about Professor Ungley. I want you to know, sir, that you have my fullest cooperation. We townsfolk value the prestige of the college just as much as you people up on the hill do. As they say, one rotten apple in the barrel—"

"Huh?" Ottermole was lost again. "You're calling Ungley a rotten apple?"

Pommell froze him with a look as only the man who holds the mortgage can freeze. "Certainly not. Professor Ungley was a scholar and a gentleman. I'm referring to the college students, whom I should have thought you'd be investigating right now. Our local residents don't go in for assault and robbery, I'm relieved to say, but with all those young who-knows-whats from here, there, and everywhere—"

"At least fifty percent of them from right here in Balaclava County," Shandy interrupted rather testily, "and all of them too damned busy trying to learn how to run their family farms so you won't foreclose on their parents to have time for any shenanigans in the village. Furthermore, Ungley wasn't robbed. Chief Ottermole can testify to that."

"I can," said Ottermole, relieved to have a piece of evidence to fall back on. "I searched the body in accordance with regulation police procedure, and found his wallet in his hip pocket with his money still in it."

"How much money?" asked Pommell.

"Fifteen dollars and thirty-two cents."

"Ah, there's your answer. Who but a college student would have been clever enough to leave enough cash to disguise the true nature of the crime?"

"What makes you think Professor Ungley had any more than that?" Ottermole was shocked into asking.

"Because he withdrew five hundred dollars in cash only yesterday afternoon," Pommell replied, with a one-up smile. "I can show you the slip, if you like. Now, since Ungley told me he was going straight back to his rooms, to rest up for the meeting last night, he would have had no opportunity to spend the money on the way. If he didn't have that remaining four hundred and eighty-five dollars on him, suppose you tell me what happened to it, eh?"

"You mean to tell me he was wandering around town with that much dough in his pocket?" Ottermole demanded. "What the heck for?"

"Ungley had the old-fashioned habit of paying his bills in cash. To the best of my knowledge, he never had a checking account in his life. If it were my business to wonder what my depositors do with their own money once it leaves the bank, I'd have assumed Ungley was planning to pay his rent and settle whatever other bills he might have outstanding. He ran monthly charges at the market and the drugstore, I believe. You could verify that, no doubt. Ungley always preferred to withdraw a sufficient sum to take care of everything at once, rather than run to the bank every time he found himself short of pocket money."

Then he'd have run a charge at the college dining room, too, Shandy thought. Mrs. Mouzouka would know if he'd paid up his account that same afternoon before he was killed. It really was typical of Ungley's lazy habits, to run the risk of being robbed every month rather than take the trouble to write a check or stroll around the corner to the bank a little oftener.

That five-hundred-dollar withdrawal also fitted in with the way his apartment had been searched. What could be more easily tucked behind a sofa cushion, for instance, than a roll of bills? And what could be more readily interlarded among the contents of those vanished files than paper money? Suppose somebody had whacked the old man over the head, perhaps only meaning to stun him, and found that unexpected bonanza in his pocket? Risky as it was, might not the thief then think it worthwhile to search the apartment for whatever else Ungley might have stashed away?

Shandy didn't like it. Most particularly, he didn't care for Pommell's readiness to pin the crime on a student.

By and large, the students didn't have much to do with the village anyway. There wasn't much to draw them down here. They had their own student union, bookshop, library, a superb cafeteria, and adequate recreational facilities. They didn't haunt the chic boutiques in which college towns often abound because in the first place, Balaclava Junction didn't have any and in the second, who'd wear designer jeans to muck out a pigpen in? As to banking, the college also had its own credit union. Maybe that was why Pommell was so down on the future farmers.

"I question whether Ungley wanted the money to pay his rent," Shandy said aloud. "Mrs. Lomax claims he always paid on the first of the month, never a day in advance. And you say he told you he was going straight home, so that doesn't sound as if he meant to drop in at the market or the drugstore. Ottermole, why don't you give them a ring and find out if Ungley paid his bill in either place yesterday?"

Ottermole obeyed, after receiving a gracious nod of permission from Pommell. He learned that Ungley hadn't been to either place, and never paid his bills before the first of the month anyway.

"So there we are," Shandy mused. "A man renowned for his indolence walks downtown twice on the same day, the first time to obtain a large sum of money he has no ostensible need for, and the second time to be mugged and robbed."

"The second time to attend the meeting at which he was to speak," Pommell amended.

"I stand corrected. As to this alleged mugging, could you cast any light on the fact that it appears to have taken place behind the museum? According to your wife, all the members left in a group after the meeting. Attorney Hodger says the same. He testifies that he himself walked directly across the street to his own home, without looking back. As we all know, Hodger is constrained by his infirmity to walk very slowly. His hearing seems to be acute enough, though. It would seem reasonable that if Ungley was accosted right after he'd left the museum, there might have been some outcry or disturbance. In that case, Hodger would have turned around to see what was going on, wouldn't he?"

"It would be a natural reaction, I suppose," Pommell admitted.

"Mrs. Pommell said that you and she came to the meeting in your car. Did you go directly to the car after you'd left the museum, or did you—er—hang around a bit? Chatting with one of the other members, or whatever?"

"It was no sort of night for chatting, Professor. There was a heavy frost, as you surely realize. Mrs. Pommell and I merely said good night and went on our way. We'd have been glad to give Ungley a lift, but he always made a point of walking home by himself."

"Inconsistent of him, wasn't it, considering how averse he was to exertion in general, and especially since he'd already had that earlier walk to the bank?"

"I suppose it was, now that you mention it, but he didn't have far to go and we'd offered and been turned down so many times that we'd got out of the habit. I believe I may have said, 'Does anybody want a lift?' or something of that sort, but perhaps I didn't. Anyway, nobody seemed interested and Mrs. Pommell was rather hustling me into the car because I'd forgotten my muffler and she was worried about my catching cold. You know how women are. The long and the short of it is, we drove home by ourselves and I have to say I never gave Ungley another thought until I heard this morning about what had happened after we left."

"How did you hear?"

Pommell spread his fat, mottled hands. "How could I not have heard? Everybody who's come into the bank today has been full of it, and everybody gives you a different version of how it happened. Luckily for me—though I suppose that's hardly the way to put it—Mrs. Pommell happened to have been on the scene shortly after the body was found by Mrs. Lomax who had, as I understand it, gone looking for Ungley because her cat brought in his toupee. Sounds pretty silly to me, but I suppose that's what you call female intuition."

The banker waited for a laugh and didn't get it. "Anyway, he'd apparently tripped and hit his head on that old harrow we've been storing out back for want of space. How he got there is still a mystery to both of us. My wife seemed to think it had something to do with his having left his keys inside the clubhouse. He was perhaps hoping to find the side door open. Who knows? Anyway, my wife says she opened the door with my key, which she had on her ring, and found Ungley's on the table where he'd been exhibiting a collection of penknives during his talk. The knives may be valuable. I don't know. I'm not much up on antiques; though I suppose I ought to be, considering how many people are buying them as hedges against inflation. A chancy way to tie up your money, in my opinion. If you happened to be looking for a genuinely sound investment, you couldn't do much better than the Guaranteed's two-year plan. Let me get you a brochure."

"Never mind," said Ottermole. "What we mainly want

to know is how much money Professor Ungley had in the bank."

"Eh?" Pommell looked as if the police chief had said something dreadfully improper. "Whatever for?"

"Because in case you haven't heard, we've got a long-lost heir in town."

"An heir? To Ungley's estate? Well, well!"

The banker fairly bounced out of his grandiose leather desk chair. "This puts a new complexion on the whole affair, doesn't it. Who is it, or shouldn't I ask?"

"I'm surprised you haven't already heard," sighed Otter-mole. "I've known myself, for almost an hour. His name's Bulfinch."

"Bulfinch? Now, why does that ring a bell? Oh yes, the architect. Professor Ungley mentioned him in one of his talks. Designed the State House, not that we get much good out of Beacon Hill out here in Balaclava County. If it weren't for Congressman Sill, we'd have pretty slim pickings among the cherry sheets,* though the man we've got in now seems to be—" He caught Shandy's look of astonishment, and veered off the subject.

"This would be a different Bulfinch, of course. A descendant, possibly. However, that's none of our concern. You wanted to know about Professor Ungley's bank account. I'm afraid I'd have to check with Henry Hodger before I gave out that kind of information."

"Hodger's not in," said Ottermole. "He had to go over to the county courthouse. We've already seen him and he told us to talk to you."

"That so?" Pommell stuck out his lower lip. "Then I suppose there's no sense in my sending you back to him, is there? I wish you'd got his permission in writing. However —perhaps if Professor Shandy wouldn't mind just stepping outside while I ask my clerk to bring in the information."

"Professor Shandy's working with me," Ottermole replied. "Hodger knows all about it. He talked with us both together, and President Svenson too, for that matter. I don't see why Shandy has to leave."

"Oh well, in that case." Pommell pushed a button, said something into an intercom, replied, "Thank you," and took a folder off his desk.

"My staff's a little too efficient for me sometimes," he remarked, adjusting his reading glasses. "Now let's see what we have here."

He held up the papers from the folder, slid his glasses down to the tip of his fleshy nose, juggled them back and forth until he achieved the correct focus, then scanned the totals.

"Rounding things off, though these figures aren't quite on the button because our computer's been giving us a little trouble the past few days, Ungley's holdings at the Guaranteed amount to approximately six hundred thousand dollars."

"Huh?" Ottermole gaped at him, bug-eyed.

"Five hundred ninety-seven thousand dollars and seven cents is the last total I've got here, but that doesn't include this month's compounding of interest. I'll have the exact figures when the will's filed for probate. As I recall, it's divided into thirds. That means a nice little windfall for your college, Professor Shandy, as well as for your Mr. Bulfinch."

"And for your Balaclavian Society as well, Mr. Pommell," Shandy reminded him.

"Two hundred thousand bucks just for being related to the guy," Ottermole was murmuring. "Jeez! Wait'll the Lomaxes hear this. Where the hell did old Ungley get his mitts on that kind of money?"

"Professor Ungley was a thrifty man and a careful investor, and let that be a lesson to us all."

Pommell put the papers back in the file folder, took off his glasses, and set them down on the desk with a little slap. "Glad I could be of service, Ottermole. Professor Shandy, if you'd care to give some thought to the Guaranteed's special two-year plan—"

"I'll talk it over with my wife."

Shandy took the brochure he was being handed because he could see he had a fat chance of leaving without it. "Thank you for your time, Mr. Pommell."

*In Massachusetts, the so-called cherry sheets list the amounts of state aid given to the individual cities and towns each year. They are printed on cherry-colored paper.

Chapter Eleven

The police chief was still looking stunned when he and Shandy left the bank. "Two hundred thousand dollars!" he exploded. "Jeez, maybe I better go pick up Bulfinch right now."

"What for?" said Shandy. "He hasn't got the money yet. He's not going to leave town without it, is he? Would you?"

Ottermole's face relaxed into a grin. "Hell, no. Okay, Professor, where to next?"

"We have our choice of Congressman Sill, Mr. Lutt, or Mr. Twerks."

"Some choice! Okay, let's head for Twerks. He's nearest. Anyway, Lutt's probably over at the soap factory and Sill's not back from Boston yet."

"How do you know he went?"

"Saw him catching the early bus when I was on my way to the station. He was babbling about some bill coming up for a hearing, I forget what. Chances are Sill did, too, but that won't make no never-mind to him. He'll get up and gas along for as long as the moderator'll let him even if he hasn't got a clue what he's talking about, same as he does at Town Meeting."

Shandy fully understood the cause of Ottermole's rancor. Last session, Sill had managed by sheer volume of words to sabotage the purchase of a new boiler for which Ottermole had put in a request on the perfectly reasonable grounds that the existing one at the station was sixty-two years old and all shot to hell. He himself couldn't have agreed more with Mrs. Elizabeth Lomax's expressed opinion that Sill was nothing but an old gasbag.

That wasn't to say he held any kind regard for Twerks, nor did the greeting they got from the squire of Twerks Hall make him feel any kinder, though it was affable enough. Twerks himself came to the door in what was presumably his leisure garb of slacks in the Buchanan tartan with a peacock-blue pullover stretched across his paunch.

"Well, well," he boomed. "To what do I owe the honor?"

"That's a redundant question, isn't it?" Shandy replied. "You are a member of the Balaclavian Society, are you not?"

"Sure. I get it. So now I'm going to be grilled about Ungley. Poor old duffer, I thought he was retired from the college."

"He was."

"Then how come Svenson's put his tame sleuth on the trail? Watch out, Ottermole. Now that Shandy's muscled in on your territory, he'll be taking over the police station next thing you know. Come in, come in. What'll you have to drink?"

This was Shandy's first time inside Twerks's house. Once, he decided, would be plenty. He didn't like the furniture made of animal horns. There was even a frame of caribou antlers around a steel engraving of President Buchanan and a probably spurious family tree linking the Buchanans with the Twerkses. The carpeting was in the Buchanan tartan, which is among the livelier ones. So were the draperies. Twerks's slacks, which had looked so incandescent on the doorstep, blended into this mélange of colors until he gave the impression of being a peacock-blue floating blob with a shiny pink bobble on top.

Despite his burly physique, Twerks was not a lovesome sight. His face suggested what happens to a wax figure over a slow fire. Swags of half-melted flesh hung from cheekbones and jawline, so hectic a raspberry shade that had Dr. Melchett been of the party, he'd no doubt have upped Twerks's dosage of blood pressure pills on the spot. Even the scalp that showed beneath Twerks's white hair was bright pink. The hair itself was short, flat, and fine, reminding Shandy of a white mouse he'd had to dissect as a youth in biology class. It was that mouse, he'd always felt, which had clinched his decision to stick with plants instead of animals.

Twerks was still offering drinks. Shandy shook his head. "Nothing for me, thanks."

"Me neither," said Ottermole with a touching air of conscious virtue. "We just want to ask you a couple of questions about last night. You were at the meeting, right?"

"Sure. I always go. When I can't think of anything better to do."

"What time did you leave?"

"When the meeting broke up. Quarter of eleven, something like that."

"What did you think of Ungley's talk?" Shandy put in.

Twerks shrugged. "To tell you the truth, I didn't hear much of it. I'd had a few drinks with my dinner and I kind of dozed off for a while. You know how it is. He was talking about cutting up feathers to make pens, I remember that. Didn't make much sense to me. And buckshot in the inkwells, and sand for a blotter. Hell of a mess to go through just to write a letter. Must be why What's-his-name invented the telephone. You sure you won't have a drink?"

"Quite sure," said Shandy. "And how did you feel this morning when you learned Ungley had been killed?"

"Hell, how would anybody feel? You leave a man alive, you go home and hit the sack, you wake up the next morning and he's gone. Makes you stop and think."

"And precisely what did you think, Mr. Twerks?"

With some effort, Twerks managed to raise his eyebrows, causing the festoons of adipose tissue to quiver in a most unappetizing manner. "What did I think? Well, I suppose—oh, *anno domino* and that kind of stuff. You know."

"You didn't wonder what Ungley had been doing behind the museum?"

"Naturally I wondered. But like Ottermole here said, I figured he must have got caught short and couldn't get in to use the john on account of leaving his keys on the table."

"But he could have made it back to his own place in a few minutes."

"A lot can happen in a few minutes, Professor. A man's kidneys aren't what they used to be when he gets to be Ungley's age. Or when he gets to be my age, now that I think of it. Excuse me a second, will you?"

Twerks vanished. Shandy and Ottermole were left alone in the midst of this tartan nightmare, with a stuffed moose glaring down at them. Shandy got the impression the moose would have liked to charge were he not inhibited by the fact that three-quarters of him was missing.

"If you ask me, this is a big, fat waste of time," Ottermole remarked in a low tone, as if not to startle the moose. "What do you bet he's getting himself another drink?"

"I'd be astonished if he isn't," Shandy replied. "Twerks wasn't down at the clubhouse this morning, was he?"

"Not to the best of my recollection."

"He appears to be very accurately informed about what was said there."

"Find me one person in town who isn't, by now."

"M'yes, that is a point to consider. Twerks is a bachelor, is he not?"

"Most of the time, yeah."

"Who keeps house for him?"

"Ethel Purkiser and her husband. Ethel cooks and cleans. Jim cuts the grass and washes the car, stuff like that."

"Purkiser? I don't believe I know them."

"They're not the kind you'd be apt to run into. I mean, Ethel's got sense enough to come in out of the rain if you tell her real slow and careful, but with Jim you sort of have to let it sink in a while."

"Twerks employs them as an act of benevolence, then?"

"Not so's you'd notice it. Jim and Ethel earn their keep and then some. See, people that are kind of slow in the uptake often make better workers than the smart ones. They do what they're told instead of arguing back, and they don't get sick of doing the same things over and over. They don't keep yelling for more money, either. Long as they've got a good roof over their heads and plenty of grub in their bellies, they're satisfied to take what you give 'em. Twerks is cute as a fox, though you'd never think it to look at him."

A fox might have a more innate sense of decency, Shandy thought, than to sweat good work at low wages out of people who weren't equipped to stand up for their rights. He couldn't see a speck of dust on any of those intricately entangled horns and antlers, and he'd already noticed on the way in how clean the yard around Twerks's brown-and-yellow monstrosity was, in contrast to most of the leaf-strewn lawns in town, not excluding his own.

Twerks was not only disgusting, he was rude to keep them standing here so long. Ottermole had consulted his digital watch (another present from his doting wife) five or six times before Twerks at last wandered back into the room carrying, as they'd expected, a half-consumed drink.

"Sorry I took so long," he had the grace to apologize. "I got a phone call. From a friend of mine."

Again something odd happened to the facial flab. Shandy finally realized Twerks was giving them a knowing wink, to signal that the call had been from a willing woman. He was quite sure it hadn't.

"Who do you think killed Ungley?" he asked point-blank.

Twerks slopped a little of his drink, then took a hasty gulp to make sure no more of it got wasted. "What do you mean, who killed him? Ungley cracked his skull falling over that harrow. You said so yourself, Ottermole, and so did Melchett."

"Yeah, well, that was just a preliminary finding," said Ottermole, giving his jacket zipper a fast up-and-down. "I've collected more evidence since then," he didn't look at Shandy, "and it turns out he was bashed over the head with that loaded cane he carried. Either his or Henry Hodger's, that is. We're not sure yet."

"That so?" Twerks gave the police chief a look that was remarkably sober, coming from one who took his drinking so seriously. "Then let me tell you something. You'd better be damned sure before you go around making any more cracks like that one, or Henry Hodger's sure as hell going to slap a lawsuit on you and take you for everything you've got. Including your badge."

And that was about all they got out of Twerks. Not even another chance to turn down a drink, as Ottermole observed bitterly after they'd gone back to the cruiser.

"Damned waste of time," he snarled. "He was slopped to the eyeballs."

"I think not," said Shandy, "and I'm wondering why he tried to make us think he was. I'm also wondering why he didn't ask us for more details about Ungley's murder and—er—succeeding developments. Unless that phone call was, in fact, from one of his fellow members, filling him in. Pommell, for instance. What in Sam Hill is that infernal racket? The car's not blowing up, I hope?"

"It's just the two-way radio," Ottermole explained. "Works a little funny sometimes. They must be trying to get me from the station."

He fiddled with the controls, gave the speaker a few dainty taps, and at last dealt the bottom of the dashboard a lusty kick. At once, transmission became clear as a bell.

"Chief Ottermole. Mayday! Mayday! Hey, Chief, you there?"

"I'm here," Ottermole bellowed into the transmitter. "Can you hear me, Budge? What's up?"

"Congressman Sill just sent in a riot call from the college."

"What the hell's he doing up at the college? And why can't Security take care of whatever the hell's happening?"

"I asked him, Chief. He just kept on bellowing, 'Send a squadron of police.' Heck, we couldn't raise a squadron with a derrick. There's just you and me on duty, and you said if I left the switchboard you'd—"

"I know what I said, and I meant it. You stay right where you are, Budge. I'll go find out what the hell's going on. Any other calls?"

"Yeah, Mrs. Lomax. She can't find her cat."

"Edmund?" cried Ottermole, visibly stricken. "Jeez, maybe the killer—"

"Don't sweat it, Chief. Edmund's right here, flaked out on your chair. He got sick to his stomach after he ate your jelly doughnut, so I thought I'd better let him sleep it off before I sent him home. I'll call her back after a while and tell her we pinched him for loitering with intent over at the Ingrams'. He's got his eye on that cute little white female of theirs with the gray spot over her whiskers."

"She ain't that kind of a girl. They had her fixed."

"So what? The organ may be gone, but the music remains. That's what my great-aunt Mabel used to say after they took out her whatevers."

"Never you mind your great aunt's whatevers. You been reading them girlie magazines on duty again?"

"Who, me? Say, Chief, you want to come back here and take over? I wouldn't mind going to the riot myself."

"Sure you wouldn't. Anything for a laugh. You stay where you are. And get back to Mrs. Lomax before she has a conniption. She probably thinks Edmund's been cat-napped. Better call George in so I can get you up there if I need you."

Ottermole broke the connection, frowning. "Now what the hell?"

"What the hell indeed," Shandy concurred. "It's not like President Svenson to allow rioting on campus. Unless, of course, he started the riot himself."

Chapter Twelve

That Svenson had done so was entirely possible, but what was Congressman Sill doing up there sounding the alarm? Ineffectual old coot though he was, Sill's lobbying efforts had not been of the sort to endear him to the denizens of Balaclava Agricultural College. Or to any farmers anywhere, for that matter. Maybe the students were burning him in effigy as a pre-Halloween prank and he'd been silly enough to take umbrage.

But how could he have found out what they were up to, and what was he doing in Balaclava Junction when he ought to have been coming back from Boston on the five o'clock bus?

Possibly some exasperated statesman had thrown him out of the committee room neck and crop, and shipped him home in a padded van. It would be agreeable to think so. When Ottermole started the engine again, Shandy settled back to enjoy the ride and speculate with pleased interest on what might actually be happening up on campus.

As they started up the hill, though, he felt his brows beginning to knit. "Is that radio of yours acting up again, Ottermole?" he asked.

"What?" the chief shouted over the chugs and rattles. It was high time Town Meeting voted the police a new cruiser as well as a new boiler. Unless this was the boiler they were riding in.

"I said is your radio on?" Shandy roared. "I hear a funny noise. Aside from all the other funny noises, I mean."

"You must have good ears."

"I do." Shandy had unusually acute hearing, as many a student had learned a syllable too late. "Shut off that dratted engine a second, will you?"

Ottermole obliged. The chugging and rattling subsided, but the funny noise continued. Shandy cranked down the window and stuck out his head.

"By George, they are rioting. Listen to that."

A great many voices were doing a great deal of yelling, in any event. As they listened, the random shouts settled into a steady chant.

"We won't flirt with Dirty Bert! We won't flirt with Dirty Bert!"

"Oh, Christ!"

It suddenly occurred to Shandy that he'd been supposed to think of something. He'd got so wrapped up in Professor Ungley's murder he'd temporarily forgotten the potential bombshell parked underneath that misbegotten silo. The students must have found out Bertram Claude was planning to speak on campus, probably from that jackass Sill in person, and were reacting as any sane person might have expected them to. Were Ottermole to go charging up there in the police cruiser, they'd start rotten-egging him. Then the fat would be in the fire for sure.

"Ottermole," he said quietly, "as man to man, I think it would be a sound move for you to go back and—er—make sure Mrs. Lomax's cat gets home safely."

"Huh? What for?"

"Because that call of Sill's was just some more of his usual grandstanding. What's happening up here is nothing you need to get involved with. In a nutshell, Bertram Claude has requested permission to make a campaign speech in our auditorium. The students have got wind of his request and are—er—making their opinions known, that's all."

"You can say that again," said Ottermole as the volume of sound increased. "What the hell would Claude want to speak to the college for? Cripes, they'd tear him apart and stomp on his guts."

"There is that possibility," Shandy conceded. "I must say I don't understand his reasoning myself, assuming that he does in fact reason."

"You going to let him?"

"Me? I don't have anything to say about it. The decision is up to President Svenson."

"Hell, he wouldn't say yes, would he?"

"That," Shandy hedged, "is a question I'm not prepared to answer. The president may feel Claude's as entitled as the next person to air his views."

"They could use some airing," Ottermole grunted. "Claude stinks to high heaven, as far as I'm concerned."

"Hold the thought, Ottermole, and thanks for the ride."

Shandy was getting out of the cruiser when Ottermole's chop-fallen look made him pause in compassion. "If you're going to be around later this evening, I'll try and get Professor Joad to come down to the clubhouse and help us test for bloodstains. That's something else we ought to do as soon as possible. There's always the chance Ungley was killed inside and shoved out a back window or something."

"By who, for instance?"

"At this stage, I'd have to say by almost anybody. What if he didn't forget his keys and did return to the clubhouse after the rest had gone?"

"What for?"

"How do I know? Maybe he forgot his hat, or had to use the bathroom as you suggested earlier. Anyway, he could have dropped his keys back on that table where Mrs. Pommell found them, leaving the door unlocked since he didn't intend to be there long—it's the old-fashioned kind you have to turn yourself, I gather—and somebody followed him in. Or what if the entire Balaclavian Society membership rose up in a body when he'd got to about the fifteenth penknife on his agenda, and slaughtered him to shut him up?"

"That sounds more likely to me," Ottermole grunted. "Cripes, the things people will do to kill time! Okay, Professor, I'll deliver Edmund like you said, then go home and have a bite of supper. We usually eat early so's the kids and I can have a game of Cops and Robbers before they go to bed. You can either call me at the house or check with the station and they'll pass on the message."

"Right. I'll be in touch."

As Ottermole dispersed peaceably, Shandy headed for the shouting. As he'd expected, he soon ran into a seething mass of malcontents, some of them carrying hastily made placards mounted on tomato stakes. He tapped one of the more vocal card carriers on the arm.

"For your future enlightenment, young lady, there's only one 's' in bastard."

"Oh, hi, Professor Shandy. Thanks," she replied politely. "Can you think up any good rhymes for Claude? I'm sick of screaming Dirty Bertie."

"Understandably so." He rubbed his chin. "Maude? Sod?" A vision of Edmund flitted across his mind and he added, "Double-pawed?"

"None of those has the right ring to it, somehow."

"Sorry. The atmosphere around here is not conducive to the poetic mood. How did this fracas get started?"

She shrugged. "It just did, I guess. That old man who's always making speeches came around about half an hour ago and started plastering up posters about Bertram G. Claude and free private enterprise. Some of the kids got sore and then it kind of snowballed. Free private enterprise!" She waggled her sign furiously. "You know what he means by that. Let the rich guys do as they please and to heck with the rest of us."

Despite her righteous dudgeon, the young woman began to giggle. "The old coot brought his girl friend with him."

"Girl friend?" Shandy's eyes narrowed. "She wouldn't be a fluffy little blonde with somewhat prominent blue eyes, by chance?"

"Wearing a bright red coat and a blue-and-white scarf and making a spectacle of herself all over the place. Do you know her?"

"I've seen her around."

Heading the silo drive and digging an elephant trap for Thorkjeld Svenson to fall therein. Ruth Smuth might be short on principles, but she certainly was long on gall. Shandy doubted very seriously that Sill had brought her. Most likely, it was Mrs. Smuth who'd dragged the old halfwit along to help her put on her show. Her object must be to put Svenson at odds with the student body and remind him she had him under her thumb. Or thought she had.

No thought about it. As of now, she did. How in Sam Hill was Svenson to be got out from under?

The young woman student was tugging at his coat-sleeve. "Professor Shandy, I've thought of something. You wouldn't happen to have a Magic Marker on you, by chance?"

"I've got this thing I use for labeling plant sticks."

Shandy produced the pen. The student took it, flipped

over her sign, and scribbled, "Let's Declaw Claude" on the back.

"Thanks, Professor. How's that for a slogan."

"First-rate and congratulations on the spelling. Carry on, and may your efforts be rewarded."

There was no sense in telling her that declawing Ruth Smuth would be more to the point. Without his alleged campaign manager, Claude wouldn't have a talon hold on campus in the first place. As it was, he'd clearly be letting himself in for a rough time up here if he tried to make that speech. But if he got the raspberry, Thorkjeld Svenson would get a lot worse from Ruth Smuth.

Good gad! The dirty work had already begun. Shandy couldn't believe it, but there it was, a little parade of television mobile news units and newspaper reporters in cars, except for one on a motorcycle who had to be Cronkite Swope from the *Balaclava County Weekly Fane and Pennon,* crawling through the mob with the cameramen already shooting film out the car windows.

This was no spontaneous free-for-all, but a carefully orchestrated performance. There was no way those media people could have got out here this fast. According to the student, Sill and Smuth hadn't even arrived until about half an hour ago. It would have taken a while for the students to notice what they were up to, to get hot under the collar, to hunt up their poster boards and plant sticks and get this thing rolling.

Sill hadn't put in his riot call to Ottermole until less than ten minutes ago, but he or his lady friend must have alerted the news services at least an hour before. They wouldn't have done that unless they'd been positive in advance there'd be a demonstration to cover.

Their timing was perfect: late enough for most students to be out of classes, early enough for daylight to take pictures by, and just right for the six o'clock news broadcasts. Who'd touched off the fuse, and how? Shandy looked around for the young woman who was set on declawing Claude, but she'd been sucked into the maelstrom.

Just as the rest of this crowd had got sucked in, including Sill himself, like as not. Shandy could see the ex-Congressman now, beetling toward the television cameras as fast as his dignity and girth would allow, all primed to gas on for as long as they'd let him about anything they wanted him to say. The worst of it was, many people in the audience might not realize they were listening to a blithering idiot. Shandy grabbed another student, one of his own seniors who happened to be a cousin of Ottermole's man Dorkin.

"Who started this clambake?" he roared into young Dorkin's ear.

"I dunno, Professor."

"Then how did you get involved in it?"

"Somebody told me Claude was coming here to speak and it made me sore, so I waded in with the rest of 'em. Say, you're not for Claude?"

"Don't be ridiculous. I'm merely trying to find out who rigged this farce. We've been suckered, in case you hadn't realized it."

Dorkin lowered his placard, clipping the man next to him on the ear. "What do you mean, suckered?"

"Haven't you noticed what's happening up by the Administration Building?"

"Too many signs. Bend over, Fred."

The man who'd got whacked with the sign obliged, rather to Shandy's surprise, and Dorkin climbed up on his back for a clear view.

"Hey, we're on TV!"

"Precisely. To be more precise, Congressman Sill is hogging the cameras, no doubt making an oration about how Balaclava students are trying to deny freedom of speech to the candidate not of their choice. Do you happen to see a small blond woman wearing a red coat and a blue-and-white scarf?"

"Yeah, she's behind Sill."

"She's also behind Bertie Claude. She claims to be his campaign manager."

"But that's Mrs. Smuth!" Dorkin almost fell off Fred in his astonishment. "My mother worked with her on the silo drive. They made me go around on my bike delivering leaflets. She can't be pro-college and pro-Claude, can she?"

"Good question. Now see if you can pick out some demonstrators whom you don't recognize."

"Sure. Hey, Fred, mind turning around slowly?"

Fred minded, but he turned. After he'd completed the circle, Dorkin slid down.

"At ease, Fred. Professor Shandy, I don't know what's going on here but I spotted at least twenty I'll swear I've never set eyes on before. They're all right up there in front of the cameras, putting on a big act, yelling and giving Sill the finger, making us look like a bunch of yahoos. Come on, Fred. Let's go straighten 'em out."

"Don't let them drag you into a fracas," Shandy warned. "Twenty professional agitators, which I suspect is what we've got here, can make plenty of trouble. Your best bet is to put on a better act than theirs. Roll up your pant legs, tie bandanas around your noses, play leapfrog, do any fool thing that comes into your heads, but get those cameras on you instead of them. Round up some of your friends and pass the word. Block the agitators off and herd them back into the crowd as good-naturedly as you can. Above all, no rough stuff. Make it look as if this is all a big joke."

"Right on, Professor."

Cavorting here and there, Dorkin and iron-man Fred began gathering supporters, clowning their way steadily toward the nucleus of the action. Shandy went on with his missionary work. None of the students he buttonholed knew who'd started the demonstration, so he told them.

"You've been manipulated into staging a rally to make you look like a bunch of hicks and roughnecks and gain sympathy for Claude. His people brought in their own goon squad and alerted the media long before this melee got started. You'll be interested to know Congressman Sill phoned a riot alarm to the town police, but Chief Ottermole had better sense than to believe him."

"Sill's a pill," somebody started to scream, but Shandy managed to quell the bedlam.

"You have every right to express your views, but for God's sake keep it light. Claude wants a nasty riot, so give him a Halloween party instead. Get the laugh on him and his plan will fizzle."

"Okay, Professor! Come on, everybody, clown it up. Flirty Bertie had a farm, ee-i-ee-i-o. And on this farm he had a Sill—"

"With a baa-baa here and a baa-baa there!"

They were laughing, singing, capering, painting each other's faces with lipstick, switching clothes, improvising silly costumes from whatever came to hand. Two young geniuses rushed to get a milking bucket and some apples, then charged straight for the cameras.

"Congressman Sill, want to bob for apples? Come on, don't be scared of getting wet. You must be thirsty anyway, after all that talking."

Sill did not want to bob for apples. As the cameramen focused gratefully on the charming, smiling milkmaids, the politician realized he'd been upstaged and turned fretfully to look for Mrs. Smuth. She, however, was already stalking off in the direction of President Svenson's office, tight-lipped as a terrorist who finds out he's been sold a dud bomb. Sill stood around puffing and snorting for a moment, then tried to back off.

"Hey, you're not leaving?" shouted Dorkin, who'd been doing headstands and handsprings with a bunch of other hastily recruited acrobats, screening the imported rough-necks behind a sea of waving boots. "Mr. Sill, wait! What about those guys you brought with you? You're not going to leave them stranded?"

"What guys?" demanded one die-hard reporter who was still trying to make sense out of the chaos.

"This gang right here. The ones with the headbands."

"They're not Balaclava students?"

"Of course not! Couldn't you tell from the way they've been acting? We don't know who they are. They just buzzed along and started yelling Claude's a clod, so we joined in for kicks."

"That's a blanking lie," shouted one of the headbands, to employ a Victorian euphemism for an Elizabethan adjective. "We are too students."

"Not from Balaclava they're not," said Dorkin. "Come on, show us your cafeteria passes."

"Who the hell carries a cafeteria pass?"

This brought general hysteria and a sea of waving cafeteria passes. Mrs. Mouzouka's food being as good as it was, no genuine student would ever run the risk of being deterred from getting at it.

"Shut up, everybody," yelled Dorkin. "Give the poor slobs a chance. Okay, so let's see your calluses."

"Their what?" gasped a young woman reporter.

"Calluses." Dorkin held out his own well-hardened palm. "We all get 'em from doing fieldwork. Come on, you guys, hold out your hands."

"Go to hell." The nearest demonstrator spat at him and jammed his fists into his pockets.

Dorkin turned to the cameras and shrugged. "That's the thanks we get. I was just trying to do these guys a favor. It must be a long walk back to wherever they came from. If they haven't got cars of their own, I think Congressman Sill and Mrs. Smuth ought to be decent enough to take them back to wherever they picked them up, that's all."

"Wait a second," said the oldest and soberest of the out-of-town reporters. "Are you saying this is not a genuine Balaclava student demonstration against Bertram G. Claude?"

"Not so's you'd notice it. This bunch here are the guys running the demonstration. We students are just having kind of a pre-Halloween party. Care to bob for apples?"

"Not now, thanks. You're not really serious about these signs and slogans?"

"That depends on what you mean by serious. See, we already know Claude's not going to get more than four and a half votes in Balaclava County, including his own. It'll be his voting record in the state legislature that defeats him, not a bunch of people yelling and waving signs. Since these outsiders came along and brought up the subject, though, we figured we might as well let Claude find out we don't swallow his line of bull even if we do go to a cow college."

"Then you don't in fact object to Congressman Claude's speaking on campus?"

"Why should we? We love political speeches. Take Congressman Sill, for instance. We could listen to him for hours."

"And often have," piped up one of the apple-bobbers. "Wouldn't you like an apple before you go, Mr. Sill?"

Congressman Sill did not want an apple. He did not, for the first time in history, care to make any further comment. He wanted to go away, and he went. The demonstration was over.

Chapter Thirteen

"Drat!" said Shandy.

"What's the matter?" young Dorkin asked him. "Did I goof up?"

"Far from it. You're going to make a great Secretary of Agriculture one of these days, young man. The—er—expletive was prompted by my recalling that I had a few questions of my own I'd meant to ask Sill. Perhaps this was not an auspicious time, however. Have you seen Mrs. Smuth?"

"She went thataway." Dorkin nodded Svenson-ward. "Don't ask me why. Say, no kidding, Professor, how come she's working for Claude instead of Peters?"

"There you have me," Shandy fudged. "One can only infer that she enjoys being on committees. Claude has lots, and Peters never has any."

"Sam Peters doesn't have a few other things Flirty Bertie does," sniffed the second apple-bobber. "Have an apple, Professor Shandy?"

"Didn't Eve make some such remark to Adam?" Nevertheless, Shandy took the apple. "Thank you, Miss—er—Peters, isn't it?"

"That's right. Sam's my uncle, I'm proud to say. Professor, is President Svenson really going to let that nerd Bertie speak on campus?"

"To the best of my knowledge, the point is still moot. Why don't you ask him yourself?"

"Because I have this thing about not liking to get rent in twain and have the pieces jumped on, I guess. It must be a leftover from the time my brother tore up my paper dolls just because I glued the pages of his *Playboy* magazine together. Men are brutes. Except Uncle Sam. He's an old bunny rabbit, and I'd be sick if that ghastly Bertie so much as nibbled the edge off his majority. Say, you don't suppose we could get Mrs. Mouzouka to schedule a pie-

106

throwing contest as part of the entertainment if he does have the gall to show up?"

"Mrs. Mouzouka takes a dim view of wasting good food on wanton frivolity, as do I and as should you. Anyway, a paper plate full of shaving cream is just as effective. Not that I'm advocating anything so unsubtle, you understand."

"Perish the thought," said Miss Peters's companion. "What I'm trying to figure out is why President Svenson never showed up. Usually if we have a demonstration, he's right out here yelling with the rest of us, only louder."

"One can only assume he had weightier matters on his mind," said Shandy. "I'll go tell him the—er—tumult and the shouting have died, if it will relieve your mind."

"You're a brave man, Professor Shandy," said Miss Peters. "Come on, Angela, we'd better return this bucket to the dairy. Tell the president to be sure and vote for Uncle Sam, won't you?"

"I hardly think he needs any urging."

With those words, Shandy betook himself in the direction Mrs. Smuth had been pursuing when last espied. Why hadn't Svenson so much as poked his head out the window during the entire brouhaha? Was it possible he was actually afraid of that woman?

No, Svenson was not afraid of anything except Sieglinde's displeasure, and he'd even been known to risk that in a pinch. But he was deeply concerned about what Ruth Smuth could do to the college, and if the just-past demonstration was a sample, he had damned good reason to be. This had been genuine kick-in-the-guts stuff, the sort of rotten trick that got labeled professional politics by people who meant professional hooliganism. The real professional politicians were people like Sam Peters, who believed in the vows they took, told their constituents what they aimed to do, did it to the best of their abilities, and weren't ashamed to stand by what they'd done because they had nothing to be ashamed of.

Getting back to Dorkin's question, what was Ruth Smuth mixing herself up in this sort of thing for? Congressman Sill was easy enough to figure. He'd naturally harbor a grudge against Sam Peters for the simple reason that Sam was a winner and he himself a loser. Sam had taken the seat in the state legislature that Sill had got booted out of after that one term in which he'd proved to the voters' full dissatisfaction that he didn't know his hock from his crupper. Sam had been reelected term after term because he'd learned the job and done it right. He'd gone on to national office because he'd earned promotion the hard way.

That wouldn't cut any ice with a man like Sill. He'd never lost his yen for the limelight, and he'd never been averse to jumping on any bandwagon slung low enough to let him get a foot aboard. Mrs. Smuth must have known the sort of character she was dealing with; she'd been around Balaclava County long enough. Dragging Sill up here was in itself an incitement to riot, let alone bringing those headbanded hell-raisers along with him. Was this her own idea, or had Claude put her up to it?

What sort of woman was Ruth Smuth, anyway? Competent enough, she'd proved that during the silo fund raising. Everybody'd been flabbergasted at the way she'd got the money pouring in; amazed at the way unexpected bonanzas kept turning up, like those Chippendale tables some antique expert just happened to recognize at that yard sale and nobly sold for the cause instead of nobbling them for herself as any bona fide antique dealer would be far more likely to do.

Shandy could remember his neighbor Mirelle Feldster sighing in ecstasy, "It just seems as if it was meant to be!" Maybe for once in her life Mirelle had stated an unadorned fact. Maybe Ruth Smuth had orchestrated those dramatic windfalls herself. Had she had this long-term goal even then?

Or had she been what he'd thought her at the time: a clever, energetic woman with a whopping ego drive and too much time on her hands? Had someone used her then, and was someone using her now? Was it Bertram G. Claude in person, or was some master puppeteer manipulating them both from behind a well-camouflaged curtain?

Mrs. Smuth and Claude could be lovers, Shandy supposed. There was a Mr. Smuth floating around in the background, but that didn't cut any ice nowadays, if indeed it ever had. Anyway, to the best of Shandy's recollection from the days of the silo drive, Mr. Smuth had

had neither dimples, wavy chestnut-brown hair, nor lots
of flashing teeth. Shandy couldn't recall if Smuth had any
teeth at all. If it came to that, he wouldn't have known the
man if Smuth had come up and bitten him, though of
course that would have settled the question of teeth.

How the hell had he got himself involved with Ruth
Smuth's husband's hypothetical bridgework? And why
was he deliberately approaching Thorkjeld Svenson's
door?

Well, he was here. Feeling like an especially puny David
with a bad case of hives and a broken slingshot, he
knocked, then stuck his head in.

"Arrgh," said Thorkjeld Svenson.

"Er—quite," Shandy replied. "Were you aware that
we've been having an anti-Claude demonstration?"

"Urrgh!"

"I thought you might want to know it's concluded.
Successfully, I believe, all things considered. Would you
care to consider?"

"No."

"Mrs. Smuth's been here, I gather."

Thorkjeld Svenson picked up a Boston telephone book
that happened to be lying nearby. There is a trick to
making the seemingly impossible feat of tearing a thick
directory in two look easy. Svenson did not employ that
trick, he just ripped. Then he tore the halves into quarters, the quarters into eighths. Then he hurled the resul-
tant confetti in the general direction of his wastebasket
and roared, "Siddown."

Shandy sat.

"You thought of anything yet?"

"Significant progress has been made," Shandy lied.

"Forward or backward?"

"I couldn't say offhand," he had to confess. "Did Mrs.
Smuth tell you how she and Sill fomented the revolution
themselves?"

"Ungh?" Svenson didn't exactly brighten up, but a
momentary rift in the gloom could be discerned by a
trained eye. "How?"

"Alerted the news media in advance and brought in a
gaggle of professional agitators to get the tumult raging
nicely before the reporters showed up. Sill went to Boston

this morning, so we may assume he rounded them up there."

"So?"

"So one of your seniors, whom I intend to recommend for high honors and a Croix de Guerre, pointed out that interesting circumstance for the edification of the media lads and lasses."

Shandy gave a full report of the masterful way in which Dorkin and his cohorts had defused the situation. "As young Lancelot was neatly dropping his bombshell down Sill's throat, I happened to notice Mrs. Smuth heading this way with blood in her eye, so I thought I'd drop over. She's a brave woman, or an extremely foolish one. I wish I knew which."

Svenson reached for another phone book, rolled it into a tube, wrung it in two with one twist of his mammoth forepaws, and flung the remains after the first one.

"Foolish," he said. "Damned foolish."

Chapter Fourteen

"So there you have it, my pearl of the Orient. Any bright ideas?"

"No, but I daresay I'll think of something," said Peter's wife, taking his well-polished dinner plate away. "Might I interest you in a sliver of apple pie?"

"Try me on a hunk. With cheese, if we have any. The extra protein may help to sustain me through the long night watches."

"What long night watches? You're not planning to sit up and brood?"

"No. I'm planning to collect Ottermole after he's finished playing Cops and Robbers with his kiddies, and go down to look for bloodstains at the museum."

"How jolly. Does he really?"

"Look for bloodstains? From time to time, as occasion arises. It goes with the job."

"I meant play Cops and Robbers with his children. It sounds so cozy and parental, and he always goes around scowling and zipping that leather jacket and looking tough. How many does he have?"

"Dozens, no doubt. I never thought to ask. Is the number of Ottermole progeny germane to the issue at hand?"

"Who knows? The most germane thing I can think of is, what happened to Professor Ungley's files?"

"Spoken like a true librarian. By what route did we progress from Cops and Robbers to Ungley's files?"

"Somebody robbed the professor and copped his files, silly. A woman, I should think. Men wouldn't have sense enough to think of plastic bags."

"In October they would. Men—some men of low understanding, that is—have the insane habit of raking dead leaves into trash bags and carting them to the dump instead of dumping them on the compost heap. This is the season for dead leaves, ergo anybody of criminal tenden-

111

cies would naturally be thinking of stuffing things into plastic trash bags."

"Speaking of which," said Helen, "what about our own yard?"

"What, indeed?"

"It needs raking."

"Why do women have this perverse talent for sneaking up on a man and whamming him over the head with some inconsequential chore when he has his mind on weightier issues?"

"Because men have this perverse talent for weaseling out of the chores on the specious grounds that doing a little honest work around the place is less important than playing Cops and Robbers with Fred Ottermole. Do you two honestly expect to find bloodstains on that floor?"

"Not we two, no. We expect Frank Joad to find them if in fact they exist."

"You didn't tell me Professor Joad would be among those present. I do like that man. He's never once asked me to look up a statistic about anything whatsoever. If it's that big a party, why can't I come?"

"No reason, I suppose. We might invite Mrs. Joad and Mrs. Ottermole while we're about it."

"Now you're being snide and cynical. I'm sure it will be a dreadful bore anyway. While you're crawling around getting splinters in your knees, I shall flounce off in a huff and return Mary Enderble's cake plates she left at Iduna Stott's the day we had the party for Grace Porble."

"I suppose that makes sense, but kindly refrain from telling me how. Whatever happened to the pie you mentioned a while back?"

"I'll get it. You sit there and meditate on weighty issues. Such as the effects of eating too much apple pie and cheese."

She gave him a hefty serving nevertheless. He polished it off in pensive mood. Helen was right about those files, damn it. Without that finicking robbery of his flat, Ungley's death would surely have been written off as either an accident or a mugging that resulted from his trip to the bank. And without Betsy Lomax, the robbery would never have been noticed.

But anybody who knew Mrs. Lomax well, and that

included not only her multifarious family and social connections but also faculty people like Shandy for whom she'd worked over the years, would realize what folly it was to think Mrs. Lomax wouldn't notice. Ergo, the robber was either somebody who didn't know Mrs. Lomax well or somebody brash enough to think he could pull off an undetectable burglary right under the sharpest nose in Balaclava County. Somebody, perhaps, cocky enough to beard Thorkjeld Svenson in his own lair. Summing it up in words of one syllable, Ruth Smuth.

Shandy finished his pie, kissed his wife, changed his pants, phoned Ottermole, and walked across the Crescent to collect Frank Joad, who now lived in the house once occupied by the Cadwalls. The Joads were a jolly lot, all science-minded. The little daughter sprouted alfalfa seeds in the kitchen and kept an ant farm in her bedroom. The two sons manufactured rockets in the cellar. Mrs. Joad went around to the local grade schools and gave the children wonderful talks full of smells and fizzes. One of the boys had obligingly skinned a knee and the father was demonstrating how to make sure his offspring was exuding real human blood when Shandy arrived.

"All set, Frank? I told Ottermole we'd be right down. He's going to let us in with Ungley's key. He said Congressman Sill demanded to be present during the investigation, but Ottermole told him nothing doing."

"One might think Sill had hogged enough limelight for one day," said Joad. "Did you happen to see him on the news this evening?"

"I saw him in the flesh, unfortunately. I happened to be on campus while he was spouting."

"What was all that about his allegedly importing a goon squad from Boston to start the fracas?"

"No allegedly about it. I don't know whether Sill or someone else brought them, but they were definitely not Balaclava students. They wouldn't say where they came from, but wherever it was, they've gone back there. I hope to God they stay."

"And to think I left New York for a life of peace and quiet in the country. Well, let's go see about the gore on the floor. Stick a Band-Aid on that knee, Ted, so the bugs won't get in."

Joad bunged a few bottles and test tubes into his pocket and announced he was ready to travel. They walked down to the clubhouse where they found Fred Ottermole already crawling around scanning every crack and cranny through an oversized magnifying glass.

"What ho, Sherlock," was Shandy's first remark. His second was, "Good God, what a moth trap!"

"Oh, hadn't you been in before?" said Joad. "I haven't, mainly because I'd never noticed the place was here. Why don't they get some decent exhibits, for God's sake?"

"Why should they? They've never yet opened the place to the public," Shandy told him. "They're always going to, but so far it's failed to happen. Find anything that looks promising, Ottermole?"

"Maybe." The chief pointed to a biggish stain on what was left of an oriental rug. "What do you think of this?"

Joad did some sleight-of-hand with his phials and philtres, then announced his verdict. "This appears to be where somebody upset the coffeepot. Circa 1937, I'd say offhand. They don't go in much for being finicky, do they?"

"Maybe they equate dust and cobwebs with an aura of antiquity."

Shandy rubbed his chin and took visual inventory. If he hadn't known this was supposed to be an exclusive clubroom, he'd have assumed he was in some old duffer's hayloft that hadn't been redded out in a coon's age.

He saw an old-fashioned hat block, the kind that came apart in sections, propped on a shelf next to some discolored wax flowers under a cracked-glass dome, rusted flatirons and curling-tong holders, mildewed books with their backs peeling and covers hanging askew, a wicker doll carriage in which slumped an eyeless china doll, her kidskin hands and feet chewed off by mice.

There was a hand plow with most of its share rusted away, a few bottomless pots and kettles, a tin candlestick that must have had something heavy dropped on it sometime or other. There wasn't a dratted thing in the entire place, as far as Shandy could see, that was whole or sound or worth a second glance. What the flaming perdition did the Balaclavians think they had a right to be so exclusive about, holding their ill-attended meetings in a dump like this?

Maybe they'd been so snotty about blackballing prospective members because they were ashamed of how little they'd managed to accomplish in all these years. But why hadn't they done more? There couldn't be any dearth of money in that crowd: the banker, the lawyer, Twerks with his inherited wealth and nothing to spend it on but booze and tartan carpets, Lutt the soap-fat man, Ungley with that astonishing dragon's hoard soaked away in Pommell's bank. There was Sill with his alleged connections; why couldn't he have got some halfway decent exhibits on loan from somewhere? Why didn't Mrs. Pommell and her housekeeper go over and dust around a bit, if the men wouldn't bother? She made enough stir in all the other clubs she belonged to. How could she have been coming year after year to sit among this junk and not so much as straighten up the clutter on the shelves?

Yet there was the chair she'd sat in. At least there were six chairs arranged in a formal rank in front of the table behind which Ungley must have stood when he spoke. There were his penknives, still fanned out in a precise semicircle. Ungley had been fussy enough to have done an occasional hand's turn, if it came to that, or at least pay Mrs. Lomax to come in and clean.

Shandy's thoughts went back to that sterile, depressing first-floor flat where nothing apparently had changed position except Ungley's reclining chair, until last night. What was Alonzo Bulfinch making of his new quarters? It mightn't be a bad notion to stop by after they'd got through here, and find out whether Bulfinch had turned up anything of interest among his late uncle's effects. Shandy had a hunch they weren't going to find anything here, and they didn't. After an hour's vain searching, Joad and Ottermole were ready to call it quits.

"I'm afraid we've struck out," Joad was sighing. "Unless they spread a drop cloth before they bopped him, I'd say the man must have been killed somewhere else. You searched the grounds for bloodstains, I suppose?"

"My boys and I were out there the whole morning, just about," Ottermole told him. "It was tough with all those slimy weeds to paw through. What we could do, I suppose, is take a mower and chop down the weeds so you could test 'em at the college laboratory."

"I'm game," said Joad. "I could give the weeds to my freshmen as a lab assignment. They can test for blood, and other things while they're about it. Automotive pollutants, for instance. Let me grow in a field by the side of the road and run afoul of man."

"What I can do," said Ottermole to show he was sparking on all cylinders, "is mow one section at a time, and put the clippings in marked plastic bags. Those big ones, like you dump dead leaves in."

Shandy's lip drew back. He was about to bark his views on dumping dead leaves in anything, most particularly in plastic bags. Then he thought perhaps he wouldn't. Ottermole had been through a rough enough day already. So had he, for that matter. And he still had those test papers to correct. And he'd meant to drop in on Bulfinch. And how the flaming perdition did he keep getting into these messes, anyway?

"Good thinking," he said instead. "Well, Ottermole, I expect you'd like to get home and park your badge. We'll see you tomorrow. Come on, Joad, let's mosey back up the hill."

He'd decided to skip Bulfinch for tonight, but Bulfinch was not to be skipped. As he and Joad started up the side street that led past Mrs. Lomax's house, who should appear but the new security guard in person, charging down Mrs. Lomax's front steps like a man with a mission. As it turned out, he was, and had.

"Evening, Professor. I didn't expect to see you again quite so soon. Clarence just phoned me and asked if I could get up to the campus early. Purvis Mink's wife's gallstones are acting up again, so Purve had to leave before his shift was finished."

"Too bad," Shandy answered. "Did you get a chance to settle in?"

"Oh sure, no problem. Betsy brought down a few plants to make the place look more homey, and Edmund's been in to visit. Say, that cat's a character! He went off on a toot this afternoon and got himself arrested for vagrancy. Fred Ottermole brought him home in the police cruiser. This town sure is a far cry from Detroit, I can tell you. I like it, though, the way everybody knows everybody."

He threw a politely inquiring glance toward Shandy's companion.

"This is Professor Joad from the Chemistry Department," Shandy explained. "Alonzo Bulfinch, our new security guard. He's Ungley's nephew. Joad and I have been down testing for bloodstains at the Balaclavian Society, Bulfinch. We didn't find any and hadn't really expected to, but it was one more thing that needed to be done."

"Nice of you to bother. It's a shame my uncle's causing you all this trouble. As for myself, I don't know what to think about this whole affair. I've been wishing I could have got to meet him before he died, but from what Betsy says—now, there is one wonderful woman. She had me up to supper. Best meal I've thrown a lip over since my wife died. Then we sat and watched the news and—but anyway, Betsy says my uncle was never one for sociability. He mightn't even have liked me."

Bulfinch made the remark in a mildly surprised tone, and Shandy could see why. This chirrupy little chap wouldn't be apt to have much trouble getting himself liked, as a rule. So Mrs. Lomax had asked her new tenant up to supper. Helen would be interested. So was Shandy himself, though he supposed the invitation must have had something to do with Bulfinch's being Silvester Lomax's friend. And possibly a dash of proving Betsy could set as good a table as Maude any day of the week.

All of which didn't get Peter out of correcting that set of test papers. By the time he'd parted from Joad and Bulfinch and gone in to perform his much-postponed task, the hour was well advanced. All in all, he reflected when at last he was free to snuggle down beside his gently slumbering wife, this had been quite a day.

Sleep was welcome, but Shandy didn't manage to enjoy much of it. He'd only just got nicely launched into a dream of cruising down the great, gray-green, greasy Limpopo River in a sternwheeler, searching for the perfect alligator pear and weeping crocodile tears because he couldn't find any, when he felt a jolting and shaking.

"Hard a-starboard," he muttered. "They're mating two points abaft the banyan tree."

"Peter, for goodness' sake!"

"Ungh? Oh, it's you, Helen. Come to me, my little alligatress."

"Stop that, you sex maniac. Thorkjeld's in another swivet."

"Here?"

"No, on the phone a moment ago. He wants you up at Security right away."

"He's out of his mind."

Nevertheless, Shandy sat up and began hurling on the garments he'd too recently taken off. "What time is it?"

"Half-past two. Some woman's been murdered. One of the guards just found her body on the grounds."

"Who was she? Did he say?"

"No, you know Thorkjeld. He just makes noises. It sounded to me like Ruth Smuth, which is ridiculous. Nobody's named Ruth Smuth."

Shandy heaved a mighty sigh. "Not now, maybe, but somebody was this afternoon. Ruth Smuth was the woman who started the shemozzle. I wonder who decided to end it. Would you happen to know what I did with my other shoe?"

Chapter Fifteen

Ruth Smuth had headed her last committee, no doubt about that. The blue-and-white scarf she'd been sporting in front of the television cameras was still around her neck, pulled deep into the flesh and fastened behind with a careful square knot so it wouldn't slip. Someone had wanted to make perfectly sure she died.

"This is exactly how I found her." Alonzo Bulfinch wasn't sounding so chipper now. "I didn't touch a thing, just put out the call on my walkie-talkie and stood by till my partner came."

"As was right and proper," said Clarence Lomax, although nobody had intimated it wasn't. "Well, now that you folks are here, I better go on back to the office and relieve Silvester."

Nobody tried to stop him. They were preoccupied with the shape on the ground. Shandy was shaking his head.

"From the way she's laid out, a person might think Harry Goulson killed her."

He'd come across a surprising number of corpses in recent months, but Ruth Smuth's was the neatest he'd seen yet. Except for the horribly suffused face and the protruding tongue, she might have paused to rest on her way to one of her committee meetings. Her red coat was smoothed down over her knees, all its buttons in order. As far as Shandy could tell by the not inconsiderable light from the large battery lantern Bulfinch was carrying, she didn't even have a run in her stockings.

The white gloves she'd been wearing at the demonstration were still on Mrs. Smuth's hands, still reasonably clean. Her hair was still firmly shellacked into place. There seemed no way this could be a case of rape and robbery. It looked more like a tidy professional assassination, and Shandy had a terrible feeling it was nothing else.

Or was it? Looking down at the body, Shandy found another picture creeping unwanted into his mind, of Thorkjeld Svenson rolling up that thick telephone directory and wringing it in two with his bare hands. *Quod erat absurdem.* Thorkjeld Svenson would never strangle a woman. He'd never strangle anybody. At least not from behind. At least not in cold blood, and that scarf had been most properly tied. Svenson wouldn't have bothered with a scarf, much less a knot. He was a bare-hands fighter.

Just suppose, though, the president had met Ruth Smuth wandering around the grounds here where she'd no business to be any time, much less at this hour. Suppose he'd challenged her, as well he might. Suppose she'd got scared, as she damn well should have. Suppose she'd turned to run away and Svenson had grabbed her by the scarf to pull her back. Suppose Peter Shandy quit supposing. Svenson wouldn't have laid her out so neatly if he did happen by accident to strangle her. He was not a tidy man, as Sieglinde had often been heard to remind him.

Tidiness. It kept cropping up. Shandy thought of Ungley, so tidily propped against that harrow with his hat still in his hand, and of the old man's apartment, so tidily searched. There was no special reason to think of Ungley in connection with Mrs. Smuth. Except that people didn't usually get murdered around Balaclava Junction within so short a distance and during so short a span of time.

And there was a tie of sorts between them, come to think of it. More than one, unfortunately. In the first place, there was Congressman Sill. He'd been associated with them both just before they died, though in different ways. That was the good one. The bad one was the college. Ungley'd been on the faculty here, he'd still taken his meals here, still drawn that oversized pension Svenson was so steamed up about. Ruth Smuth had spent a lot of time here back during the fund drive for the silo, and had been around here the past couple of days trying to collect what she'd claimed as her reward for past services. And Svenson had been more than steamed at Mrs. Smuth.

The hell with that. What about Alonzo Bulfinch? Ungley hadn't been popular with anybody, even some of his alleged confreres at the Balaclavian Society, but he'd doddered on unscathed until his long-lost nephew hove into town. Ruth Smuth had got Svenson's back up, and no doubt a good many other people's as well because she was that kind of woman; but nobody'd done her in until Bulfinch became a security guard on the campus she'd chosen to infest.

Was there any food for thought in the fact that Bulfinch had come on duty early this past evening? He could hardly have orchestrated Purvis Mink's wife's gallstone attack, unless by some wild flight of coincidence Mrs. Mink happened to be an old sweetheart of his and they'd concocted a plot together. However, what if, for the sake of argument, Bulfinch had lied about not having known he had an uncle living in the same small village as his old army buddy, and not having known he was down in the will as one of that surprisingly rich uncle's heirs? Ottermole had accused Bulfinch to his face of lying about that, and Ottermole was turning out to be not quite the blithering idiot Shandy had always thought him.

All right, suppose Alonzo had managed to wangle an invitation out of Silvester Lomax for the express purpose of coming to Balaclava Junction and killing the gander who was going to lay him a fat golden egg. Bulfinch was a fast thinker, a fast mover, and—aha!—a tidy chap by nature. His reaction to Mary Ellen's unexpected tale of woe had shown that. He'd got shaved, combed, and dressed, packed his bags, changed his bed, and been out of Silvester's guest room in roughly five minutes yesterday afternoon. He'd been mighty adroit about overcoming Ottermole's hostility and gaining permission to use his late uncle's apartment, too.

For somebody so efficient and resourceful, would it have been impossible to kill Ungley and not get caught? There were bicycles enough around campus. Suppose Bulfinch had swiped one, pedaled like hell down the hill, slain his uncle, and raced back in time to punch the next clock on his round.

That would have meant knowing exactly where Ungley was going to be at exactly the right moment, but a man boarding with Evelyn Lomax wouldn't have had much trouble finding out anything connected with Betsy's place. Considering the restricted life the old man had led, Evelyn could have told Bulfinch between one breath and the next all he'd have needed to know about Ungley's comings and goings. And forgotten she'd ever said it, like as not.

Judging from the matter-of-fact way Evelyn had been going off to her ladies' tea and leaving Bulfinch asleep in the house, the Lomaxes must have been treating Bulfinch as one of the family, letting him fend for himself a fair amount since he'd started the job at the college. Left alone there, he could even have phoned to arrange a secret rendezvous with Ungley behind the museum after the lecture.

Crazy as it sounded, Bulfinch might have managed to make such a meeting sound plausible to a muddleheaded old coot who went in for theatrical gestures like carrying a cane stuffed with melted lead. Being himself the entertainment of the evening, Ungley could easily have wound up his talk by the appointed time and been out there waiting when Bulfinch swooped in for the kill.

That could account for the disproportionately small amount of blood found on the harrow tine, perhaps. Bulfinch would have been too pressed for time on his first trip to hang around and stage an accident; simply whanged his uncle and left him for dead. Later on, perhaps at his supper break or whatever they called it, he'd have made a second trip.

He'd have had plenty of time then. The guards no doubt staggered their breaks so no two would be off duty at the same time. That would have been when he'd have tidily wiped the cane, and smeared the blood on the harrow peg. There wouldn't be much of it because clots would have formed by then. He'd have set his uncle against the harrow, gone through Ungley's pockets to find his keys and perhaps that five hundred dollars Pommell was so concerned about, then slipped across lots to search the apartment.

That would also explain why the files had been stolen. Bulfinch couldn't have afforded to linger over all those folders in the house. His break would have been running out. He'd still have Ungley's keys to get rid of, hence another trip back to the clubhouse, where he'd most likely have left the bicycle in any case. Putting the keys inside rather than back in the old man's pocket would entail more time and risk, but support the plausibility of Ungley's having locked himself out and having an accident while trying to get back in, just as everybody except Betsy Lomax had been quite willing to believe.

Maybe the risk wouldn't have been so great. Forcing a window in that ramshackle building oughtn't to be any real chore. Why in thunder didn't the Balaclavians, with all their money and pretensions, squander a few dollars on cleaning and repairs?

Never mind that now. Here he had Bulfinch, theoretically, with the uncle's files stuffed into plastic trash bags, as Mrs. Lomax had deduced. They'd be easy enough to carry that way, tied together by their tops and slung over Bulfinch's shoulders as he ran back through the shortcut, across his bicycle carrier when he pedaled back to the college. As to what he'd be hoping to find, one could only guess. Some heirloom he was afraid might be claimed by the Balaclavians if he didn't get to it first? Family letters he could use to prove he was the rightful heir or conceal the fact that he wasn't?

Whoever had taken the risk of searching Ungley's apartment and carrying away those files must have had great hopes, great fears, or feathers where his brain ought to be. Shandy did not think Alonzo Persifer Bulfinch was a stupid man.

Hiding the bags on campus would make sense. Bulfinch could hardly have lugged them back to Silvester's house without letting his driver see them, and then having to think up a lie that would fool a trained security guard. Where could he have hidden them at the Lomaxes'? Evelyn was surely the sort of woman who cleaned under beds and in dark corners. Bulfinch himself had remarked that the campus was the only area around here that he knew really well.

All right, so suppose Bulfinch had put the sacks around here someplace handy? Suppose he'd taken advantage of his early arrival, before the time clocks got turned on for the late shift, to drag them out and settle down for a quiet perusal of their contents? Suppose Mrs. Smuth had come along for no good reason and caught him at it? He'd be apt to recognize her because he'd watched the news with Betsy Lomax. Mrs. Smuth must have been in some of the television pictures and his hostess would have pointed her out to him.

Even if he didn't recognize her, he'd know she meant trouble. Merely being seen with Ungley's files would be enough to brand him as his uncle's murderer, considering the cash value of his motive. If he'd killed to get them and what went with them, why wouldn't he kill again to hang on to what he'd got?

Shandy brought himself up short. He was supposing too damn much these days. Why not try for some facts? "How did you happen to find the body, Bulfinch?" he asked.

"I just looked and there she was. That red coat of hers caught the light from my lantern. First I thought it was fallen leaves, then I realized it couldn't be, so I walked over and took a closer look. Of course I knew right away what had happened. I'd have had to be blind not to. It was awful, I can tell you. She must have been a pretty woman, too."

"Don't you recognize her?"

"Professor, I'd say her own mother would have a heck of a time recognizing her now. Should I?"

"You very likely saw her on the news tonight."

"You mean she was mixed up in that crazy Halloween party, or whatever it was? Doesn't seem the type, somehow. I thought she must have been the school nurse, or a housemother or some such. What in heck was she doing on campus so late? You know who she was, Professor?"

"Ruth Smuth. Does that mean anything to you?"

"Oh sure, now I recognize the coat. Betsy did point her out to me on the news. She was telling me that was the woman who ran a big fund drive for the college some years back and raised the money to build the silo. Gee, this is even worse than I thought. A real friend and benefactor like her."

"Urrgh," said Thorkjeld Svenson. Shandy's heart sank another notch. He was about to ask if the doctor had been sent for and the police station notified when Melchett and Ottermole rushed in tandem toward them.

"Where's the body?" Melchett was demanding testily. "I wish to God you people would space out your corpses a little wider. Two murders within twenty-four hours is too damn many for my taste."

President Svenson gave the doctor a look. "Why ours?"

Melchett flinched. "I'm sorry, President. I just meant—Professor Ungley—"

"Emeritus. Means retired. Happened in the village."

"Er—so it did. Puts a different—and this—good Lord! Can that be Mrs. Smuth?"

"Same coat."

"That's right," Ottermole put in. "I saw her wearing it on the news. I was wondering how come she got mixed up in that nutty demonstration."

"So were we," Shandy said before Svenson could erupt. "We're hoping Congressman Sill will be able to cast some light on the matter. If he'll shut up long enough for us to ask him a few questions," he added, for by now he was feeling pretty vicious. "Ottermole, would you have something we can spread on the ground so Dr. Melchett can get to the body without destroying any clues that might be lying around?"

"Sure." Ottermole ambled over to his cruiser and came back with a smallish cardboard box in his hand. "Plastic trash bags," he explained. "Never know when they'll come in handy."

He laid a sort of processional carpet corpseward. Melchett stepped gingerly over the slippery plastic and knelt to exercise the mysteries of his calling. The other members of the party stood around trying not to watch and wondering if their companions felt as sick as they did.

"Was she—you know—attacked, Doctor?" Ottermole asked when he couldn't stand it any longer.

"I can see no outward sign of rape or other physical assault, though of course something may show up in the autopsy. It appears to have been a quick, clean strangling from behind. Apparently she didn't even have a chance to struggle. Her fingernails are intact, and she wore them long."

"Any idea how long she's been dead?"

"I wouldn't want to be pinned down, but offhand I'd say between five and seven hours. Not much more, and almost certainly not less."

"That's interesting," Shandy remarked. "We were all under the impression she'd left the campus along with the other—er—outsiders. Didn't you think so, President?"

"Saw her. Drove off. Too fast. From a no-parking zone." Svenson fumed in sulphur-laden silence for a moment, then added, "Husband."

"What?" yelped Ottermole.

"What President Svenson means is that we ought to contact Mr. Smuth and see whether he can enlighten us as to his wife's subsequent movements," Shandy translated.

"Oh sure. She'd have had to go home and cook his supper, wouldn't she?" Clearly Ottermole took it for granted the rest of Balaclava County existed in the same state of contented atavism as his own household. "He'll have to be told anyway. I suppose I better bust the news myself. Okay if I use the phone in the security office, Lonz?"

"Go right ahead," said the chief suspect. "Silvester won't mind."

"I thought Silvester was off duty."

"He came back to cover for Clarence. We can't leave the office unmanned, no matter what, on account of the signal board. I ought to be out doing rounds, myself. You folks don't need me here any longer, do you?"

Ottermole glanced at Shandy, got a shrug for an answer, and shook his head. "Stick around a few minutes. How long you been on duty, Lonz?"

"Since twenty-three minutes to nine." Bulfinch explained yet again about Purvis Mink's wife's gallstones. "So the way it works out, this was my second trip along here. There wasn't any body the first time."

"You sure?"

"Being sure's what I get paid for, Fred. Anyway, she'd have been hard to miss, wouldn't she?"

That was true enough. The killer hadn't made any great effort to hide Mrs. Smuth's body, though that would have been simple enough to do. He could have dragged her farther into the shrubbery, removed that red coat and stuffed it away somewhere, and strewn dead leaves or branches over the corpse as camouflage. It was almost as if he—or she, since a reasonably strong woman could have handled that petite form easily enough—had wanted the body found right away.

No, not right away. She must have been dead some while before she'd been laid out so neatly beside the path;

unless Melchett was far out on the time span during which she'd been killed or Alonzo Bulfinch was lying about her not having been there when he'd made his first round.

"Could you tell us exactly when you passed here before?" he asked the guard.

"Six minutes to eleven on the dot. I finished Purve's last round, see, before I started my own. Then Clarence decided I'd better keep the same route, though he arranged it a little differently."

"According to Dr. Melchett, Mrs. Smuth must have been dead well before eleven," Shandy reminded him.

"I never said she wasn't dead. I only said she wasn't here. Which means," Bulfinch wrapped it up in his orderly fashion, "she must have been someplace else."

"But why should anybody kill her someplace else and bring the body here?" Ottermole wondered. "That doesn't make sense."

"It might if you strangled the woman out of exasperation, then realized it wouldn't be smart for you to get caught with a corpse on your hands," Melchett snapped. "There's nothing more I can do here. I'm going home to bed, and God help the person who wakes me up for anything less serious than a typhoid epidemic."

He stormed off into the night. His headlights flashed on and his car zoomed away.

"Speeding in a restricted zone," Ottermole noted. "I better not write him a ticket, though. Guess I'll go give Harry Goulson a buzz."

"No," said Thorkjeld Svenson. "Daylight."

"The President's right," Shandy agreed. "We'd better leave her just as she is until we have daylight enough to examine the ground by. These lanterns can be deceptive, casting shadows and making you think you've seen something you haven't. Or vice versa."

"Okay. In the morning we look for gum wrappers and cigarette stubs the killer might have thrown away. Then we find out if he likes Camels and Juicy Fruit. So what do we do in the meantime?" Ottermole asked unhappily.

"I'm afraid we sit it out. Why don't you send up a man to take your place here, Ottermole? You still have to notify Mr. Smuth, and the sooner the better. I'd go with you, if—"

"Go," barked Svenson. He glanced around, selected a

particularly rugged-looking oak tree, and settled his own massive bole against its trunk. "I'll stay."

"What about me?" inquired Bulfinch.

"You may as well go on and finish your rounds," said Shandy. "Er—and make radio contact with the office at each checkpoint."

"So they'll know I haven't skipped out on 'em, eh?"

"So they'll know you haven't been bopped over the head or garroted like Mrs. Smuth," Shandy amended. "Since we have no idea how recently her body was parked here, we don't know whether her killer might still be lurking on campus."

"Gee, that's right." Bulfinch sounded more interested than alarmed. "We don't, do we? Okay, Professor, I'll keep calling in."

"Do," Svenson grunted. "Damn nuisance, breaking in new guards."

Bulfinch trotted off. Ottermole turned to go. "I'll rouse Budge Dorkin. He'll think it's a barrel of fun climbing out of a warm bed to come up here and baby-sit a stiff."

"Blanket," Svenson ordered. "Cover her up. Couldn't stand the sight of her alive. Can't stand it now."

Shandy could only hope Chief Ottermole had got out of earshot before President Svenson finished that thought-provoking utterance.

Chapter Sixteen

"Whoever it was, I'd like to shake his hand."

The remark was not what one might normally have expected from a new-made widower. When Ruth Smuth's husband said it, though, Peter Shandy found it reasonable enough.

Smuth probably wouldn't have been quite so forthright if Ottermole hadn't wakened him from a stupor that appeared to have been induced by several stiff nightcaps. The man was still half-slopped, though he showed none of the usual symptoms of an habitual drunkard. He wasn't tall, dark, and handsome, and he didn't have a dimple in his chin. In fact, he didn't look like anything in particular except the potato men Shandy's late mother had carved sometimes for her young son's amusement. He'd be fairly low down on somebody's totem pole, no doubt; and probably hadn't stood all that high with Ruth, despite the rather lavish house he'd provided for her.

Ottermole was clearly pleased to find somebody he could bully. "Oh yeah? Maybe you know the guy a damn sight better than you're letting on. Where you been these past few hours?"

"On a goddamn plane from Detroit, that's where. First we're an hour late taking off. Then they serve a lousy dinner that's supposed to be hot but isn't. And the meat was all fat. I hate fat."

Smuth brooded awhile on the faults of the airline, then went on with his jeremiad. "So I didn't eat it and I'm sitting there starving to death, so the engine starts acting up again. So instead of flying direct to Boston they have to shuttle us in from Newark, so it's another goddamn couple of hours. So I get into the parking garage and find out some jerk's swiped the goddamn wheels off my car. So I call the airport cops and futz around there till they finish

telling me how deeply they regret the unfortunate inci-
dent."

Smuth paused to burp, but held up his hand as a signal
that he hadn't finished his tale of woe. "Then some guy
offers me a lift, but it turns out he's only going as far as
Leominster. So it costs me another forty-seven bucks cab
fare to get home. So I get in the house with my belly
flapping against my backbone and I can't find so much as a
hunk of cheese and some crackers to chew on because my
goddamn wife's too goddamn busy with her civic service to
shop for the goddamn groceries. I know what kind of
service she's been getting from Ol' Dimplepuss, and you
needn't think I don't."

Smuth burped again. "So I say the hell with it and pour
myself a few slugs of Bourbon and turn in, and now you
come along and wake me up to tell me she's gone and got
herself killed. Christ, what a day!"

"You expect us to swallow a yarn like that?" snarled
Ottermole, reaching for his longest jacket zipper.

"I think we might as well," Shandy interposed. "Mr.
Smuth would doubtless be able to have it witnessed by a
few dozen airline personnel, not to mention the airport
police, the chap who drove him to Leominster, and the cab
driver who brought him the rest of the way. Were you
surprised not to find your wife at home when you got here,
Mr. Smuth?"

"Hell, no. Ruth hasn't been home since the day after we
got back from our honeymoon. And then she only dropped
in to ask me for money. By the way, what happened to
her?"

"She was strangled."

"Huh?" At last Smuth was giving Ottermole his full and
undivided attention. "What do you mean, strangled?"

"I mean like somebody snuck up behind her and yanked
at the ends of her scarf till she was dead. That kind of
strangled."

"Oh my God! Mugged and raped. What'll J.B. say?"

"As far as we know, she wasn't molested. She was
merely killed."

"You say somebody just plain walked up and strangled
her? Christ, that's even worse. Means it was a personal
grudge. More damaging to the corporate image."

"How do you yourself feel about strangling, Mr. Smuth?" Shandy asked out of curiosity.

"Listen, whoever you are, what difference does it make how I feel about it? What counts is how the guy three rungs above me on the corporate ladder feels about it. Wise up to the facts of life, buddy. J.B.'s going to blow his stack. I think I'll have another drink."

"I think you better throw on some clothes and come down to make a formal identification," said Ottermole. "We've got coffee and doughnuts at the station," he added more compassionately.

Even a tough cop couldn't help feeling a little sorry for a man whose wife prowled around dark places getting herself killed instead of staying home and doing nice, uxorious things like replacing the worn-out zippers on his jacket or fetching him another beer while he watched reruns of "Barney Miller" for professional instruction.

"Doughnuts? Okay. Just a second."

For coffee and crullers, Mr. Smuth would be only too willing to cooperate. He got dressed, more or less, and accompanied Ottermole and Shandy to the police station, where they baled enough refreshment into him to ease the pangs and sober him up a little. Having then obtained a reasonably coherent statement and a list of people who might be able to corroborate his complicated alibi, they took him along to make a formal identification of his wife.

Ruth Smuth was still where they'd left her, covered by the same ratty gray blanket that had shrouded Ungley's corpse the previous morning, Shandy noted with a small frisson. President Svenson and Officer Dorkin had been whiling away the tedium of guardianship playing mumblety-peg by the light of Budge's battery lantern. As Ottermole and his entourage hove into sight, Svenson whipped the jackknife into his pocket and assumed a demeanor of terrifying dignity. Dorkin stood smartly at attention, thumbs pressed against where the seams of his uniform trousers would have been if he'd thought to put them on instead of the emerald green running pants his mother had bought him on her last expedition to Filene's Basement.

Ottermole reached down and pulled away the blanket. Smuth nodded perfunctorily.

"That's Ruth. Damn it, why couldn't she have been killed in a plane crash? Plane crashes are okay PR-wise. Besides, I could have sued the airline for damages. Cover her up again, can't you? I feel queasy."

So Mr. Smuth was capable of human feeling after all, Shandy thought. Of course, it could have been the three honey-dipped chocolate doughnuts on top of all that whiskey. On the other hand, that purple face and protruding tongue weren't doing much for his own stomach, either. Young Dorkin was looking as green as his running pants, and Ottermole was having to work his pocket zippers for all they were worth. Svenson was retaining his Augustan demeanor by the simple expedient of not looking.

"Okay, Smuth," Ottermole told him. "I'll run you home. Don't get any ideas about leaving town."

"How the hell can I?" Smuth pointed out reasonably enough. "I haven't got a car to drive me as far as the all-night diner, even. I wish to Christ we had a halfway decent hotel around here. I wish we had an indecent one, even."

"So do I," said Dorkin wistfully.

Ottermole gave his subordinate a look. "Cover her up, Budge. Mr. Smuth, if you want to give Dorkin here a few bucks, he can pick you up a few groceries after the stores open. Coffee, doughnuts, you know, the basic necessities."

"Sure." Smuth forked over a twenty-dollar bill. "Get me a fifth of Old Factory Whistle while you're about it, hey, kid?"

Dorkin magnanimously ignored the "hey, kid," in view of the grave situation, and said he would.

"Okay, then," barked Ottermole. "Let's get this show back on the road. You coming, Professor?"

Shandy did not want to go with Ottermole and Smuth. He wanted to go back to the little red-brick house on the Crescent and climb back into bed beside a wife who would not have charged off to head a committee but stayed to share a decent breakfast with him when he woke up. He sighed and climbed back into the cruiser.

Slumped in the back seat, Shandy wondered why Smuth and Mrs. Smuth had stayed married all these years. On account of the corporate image, probably. Maddening as she must have been to live with, Ruth would have known how to cut the right kind of figure at company dinners. Her charitable activities would have provided ways for the husband to funnel off excess profits into deductible donations real or alleged. Maybe they hadn't been two hearts that beat as one, but the chances were they'd marched to the same drum. What in Sam Hill were a pair like that doing in Balaclava County?

"How did you happen to settle around these parts, Mr. Smuth?" he asked.

"What the hell, we had to live somewhere, didn't we? Ruth's got folks around here, so I figured what the hell? Hoddersville's not quite such a hick town as the rest of 'em around here, and it's a damn sight cheaper than Weston or Dover. Not bad for the corporate image, either. Nice big house in the country, away from the hurly-burly and all that garbage. Doesn't matter to me where I hang my hat, I'm on the road most of the time anyway."

He yawned and stretched. "Ruth was okay out here. For Hoddersville she had class. For Wellesley or Concord she had class but not the right kind of class. But hell, if she'd had that kind of class, she wouldn't have married a no-class guy like me. See, I'm not on the class end, I'm on the production end."

"Really?" Shandy yawned, too. "What do you produce?"

"Nothing. I'm not on the producing production end, I'm on the talking production end. Walk into a sales meeting with an armload of blueprints, start waving 'em in everybody's face, give 'em the facts straight from the shoulder, figures, technical stuff, that kind of garbage. Doesn't matter if you get it right side up or ass-backwards. They don't know what you're talking about anyway, but they're all too scared to say so, just in case the guy next to 'em happens to know. You get the picture. Hoddersville fits my image. If I tried to get too classy, I'd class myself right out of the production end. Then where'd I be?"

"On the class end?"

"Nah, we're already overloaded on the class end. Princeton, Dartmouth, Valparaiso, you know. The Dry Sack and Chivas Regal crowd. I couldn't hack it. With those guys you not only have to know where you're going, you have to know where you're coming from. Right?"

"If you say so."

Shandy mulled the corporate image over in silence for a while. This night had been so unreal anyway that he decided what Smuth had been telling him might even make sense. However, it was hardly germane to the problem at hand. He thought of another question.

"How did your wife get tied up with Bertram Claude?"

"Huh?" Smuth must have been dozing. "Who?"

"I was asking why Mrs. Smuth became active in the Claude campaign."

"Because it was there, I suppose. How the hell do I know?"

"You—er—made no objections?"

"Me object to anything Ruth had set her mind on doing? You got to be kidding, mister. Anyway, Claude's okay, isn't he? PR-wise, I mean."

"I wouldn't know about PR. As to wise, Claude has never impressed me as showing anything beyond a particularly low form of cunning."

"So who needs a pol with brains? All we want is one who's got what it takes to get elected and vote the way he's told to, right?"

"Wrong. I'd rather have one who's more interested in doing his job right than in keeping it at any cost."

"Me, too," said Ottermole. "Heck, I haven't got time to run the government even if I knew how, which I sure don't," he added with surprising candor, "but it's a cop's job to know an honest guy from a phony. That's why I'm voting for Sam Peters like I always do. How did we get started on politics, anyway?"

"We were trying to get at the facts about Mrs. Smuth's relationship to Bertram Claude," Shandy told him.

"Yeah?" Smuth yawned again. "If you mean was she screwing around with him, I've got two pieces of information for you. I don't know, and I don't give a damn. Wake me up when we get to the house."

Chapter Seventeen

"Sheesh!"

Ottermole gunned the cruiser, spraying gravel from the Smuths' well-raked drive all over their expensive landscaping. "Am I glad to unload that bird! You know something, though? In a way, I kind of feel sorry for him. At least when I get home, if I ever do, I'll know who my missus has been keeping the bed warm for. Want me to drop you off at the Crescent?"

"Yea, but nay," Shandy told him. "I'm afraid our night's work isn't over quite yet. Would you happen to know where Bertram Claude lives? I have a hunch it's not far from here."

"Professor, you're not planning to go and wake up a congressman?"

"Why not? I'd like to wake up a few more of them, if it comes to that. We have a responsibility to let Claude know his campaign manager's been murdered, haven't we?"

"No, but I guess we could use that as an excuse. Okay, I think I know the house. It's just a few streets over, with an eagle on the mailbox. Why didn't I think to swallow another cup of coffee back at the station?"

"Perhaps Claude will offer us some. It would be good politics and he's supposed to be a smart politician. Roll down your window if you're getting sleepy. The fresh air will pep you up."

"The hell it will."

Nevertheless, Ottermole let in a frosty blast. They drove on a little farther, turned down another of the well-paved roads in what the snobby folk of Hoddersville considered to be Balaclava County's most exclusive residential section, and found the house with the eagle on the mailbox. Shandy climbed out of the cruiser, stretched to limber up his muscles, and thumped at the second eagle, this one of brass, that served the Claudes for a door knocker.

"You know, Ottermole," he murmured while they were waiting for somebody to respond, "I just happened to think. You don't really have any jurisdiction over here, do you?"

"Nope," the chief admitted, "but we don't have to tell him that, do we? Anyway, us chiefs in the Association have kind of a—oh, oh. Here comes somebody."

The somebody turned out to be a smallish, blondish woman who looked enough like the late Ruth Smuth to give Shandy a jolt. She was clutching an over-elaborate negligee around her thin body as she opened the door on its chain and peered nervously out at them through the narrowest possible crack.

"Who is it?"

"We're police officers," said Ottermole, projecting a combination of toughness and reassurance, and keeping his hands off his zippers for the moment. "Are you Mrs. Bertram Claude?"

"Yes. Yes, I am."

"Is your husband home?"

"He's asleep. What do you want him for?"

"We'd like to talk to him a minute, that's all. Would you mind getting him down here?"

"He doesn't like being waked up."

"Neither do I, Mrs. Claude, but things are tough all over. Could you hurry it up, please?"

Ottermole's left hand began to creep ominously toward his topmost pocket zipper. She went, trying to shut the door behind her but prevented by the chief's fast footwork. The two outside heard the click-click of her high-heeled slippers, then some dialogue that indicated Claude didn't waste his charm in places where it wouldn't enhance his public image.

"They said they were police officers." Mrs. Claude's voice was pitched even higher and whinier now.

"Anybody can say that, stupid. For all you know, they may be political assassins."

"Who'd bother assassinating you?" Mrs. Claude retorted with discernible regret. "They only go after important people."

"Thank you, sweetheart. I'll remember that."

"You try any more funny business and I'll file for divorce. Right before the election. How'd you like that, Bertie dear?"

"Shut up, they might hear you. Did you have sense enough to shut the door?"

"I couldn't. He stuck his boot in the crack."

"Jesus, now you tell me! Look, go on back to bed. Let me handle this."

"With pleasure."

The two men on the doorstep heard a door slam. Some moments later, Claude's mellifluous locution floated through the crack.

"Would you identify yourselves, please?"

"Ottermole. Chief of police, Balaclava Junction. And—uh—Detective Shandy."

"Could I see your credentials?"

"Sure." Ottermole held his badge and his Balaclava County Police Chiefs' Association membership card up to the crack. "Okay?"

Shandy had got out his faculty dining room pass in lieu of anything more official, but Claude didn't ask him to show it. He was revving up to bluster.

"And what do you want of me at this hour? I warn you, Ottermole, it had better be important."

"Don't sweat it, Claude, it's important. We thought maybe you'd want to know your campaign manager's been murdered."

"What?" That stopped Claude cold. At last he choked out, "You—ah—did say murdered?"

"Strangled," Ottermole amplified. "With her own scarf."

"Her scarf? Who did you say this was?"

"Your campaign manager. Ruth Smuth."

That was when Claude released the chain and swung open the door, revealing himself in the effulgence of a Sulka lounging robe, silk pajamas, and a full set of dimples.

"Ruth Smuth? Now, who could—oh yes, Mrs. Smuth. I'm afraid there's been some mistake, Chief Ottermole. Mrs. Smuth was one of our willing workers on a, so to speak, local basis. We have a large and zealous group of volunteers helping with our campaign, you know. It's sometimes difficult to recall precisely what responsibilities we've given each and every individual, but," he laughed lightly, "I'm quite sure I'd remember having named someone my campaign manager."

"Shove it, Claude."

That was Shandy butting in, borrowing tone and cadence from Ottermole and wishing he had a more appropriately situated zipper to yank. "Ruth Smuth was nobody's willing worker. If she hadn't been running the show, she wouldn't have been in it. Okay, we understand it's rotten PR for you, her getting bumped off right after she'd bitched up that phony demonstration at the college yesterday afternoon, but it's what happened and there's not much you can do about it now so never mind trying to give us the baloney. Where were you between about seven o'clock last night and two this morning?"

Bertram Claude flared his Grecian nostrils and bared his superbly capped teeth. "I don't have to stand for this. Do you realize to whom you're talking?"

"Yeah," said Ottermole. "That's why we're here instead of someplace else. How about answering Shandy's question?"

He whipped out his gold-plated ball-point pen to prove Claude wasn't dealing with a couple of country bumpkins, and poised it over his notebook. Either the pen or the realization that his dimples weren't going to get him anywhere with this pair prompted Claude to utter.

"Certainly. I have nothing to hide. For the record, then, I attended a reception given in my honor by some of my loyal constituents. It was held at the home of Mr. Lot Lutt in Lumpkin Upper Mills. Mr. Lutt is chairman of the board at the—"

"Former chairman," Ottermole corrected. "At the soapworks. His sister-in-law that keeps house for him is an aunt of Ruth Smuth. Was Lutt himself there?"

"For a time."

"How long a time?"

Claude essayed another genteel snicker. "I'm afraid I didn't have my stopwatch with me. You know how it is at these affairs. People come and go."

"Yeah. They come because they feel sorry for the neighbor that got sucked into giving the shindig, and go when they can't stand it any longer. Get much of a crowd?"

"We had a lively meeting," the politician sidestepped. "The guests asked a number of stimulating questions."

"I'll bet they did, both of 'em. I'm surprised anybody at all bothered to come. That's pretty solid Peters country around there. So when did you get to Lutt's place and when did you leave? And you can skip the stopwatch routine this time. I'll double-check with Edna Jean later on."

"Edna Jean?"

"Sure. That's your loyal constituent's name, in case you didn't know. Edna Jean Bugleford. She's my wife's aunt, too, but only by marriage. My wife's mother was a Bugleford, but I never held it against her. Okay, the time."

Ottermole waggled his gold-plated pen impatiently. Claude sighed and managed to dredge up the more-or-less straight facts.

"I arrived at approximately seven forty, and left a little before nine."

"Stuck it out for a whole hour, did they? Not bad, Claude. Then what did you do?"

"I went on to another meeting."

"Where?"

"It was an informal gathering at a club called, I believe, the Bursting Bubble."

"Beer joint over behind the soap factory," Ottermole explained to Shandy. "Figured he might catch a few of the night shift when they snuck out for a brew. Any luck, Claude?"

You had to hand it to Ol' Dimplepuss, Shandy thought. Bertram Claude must have the hide of a walrus. He actually managed to answer Ottermole's rude interrogation with another of those rippling laughs and another deft evasion.

"I thought you were the one who knew all the answers, Chief Ottermole. As for myself, I'm afraid I'll just have to wait till election day and find out."

"What is there to be afraid of? It's not as if you were going to be faced with having to pull up stakes and leave this nice, comfortable house for some high-priced dump in Washington." Ottermole was really quite a card when you got to know him. "What time did you get to the Bubble, and when did you leave? Bearing in mind that I also know the bartender."

"I'm sure you do." Chalk one up for Claude. "I went there directly from the Lutt house, so I suppose it must have been about five minutes past nine when I arrived. I stayed until closing time. According to local regulations which you must also know, that would have been midnight. Naturally your friend the bartender wouldn't flout the law by staying open a moment longer."

Ottermole could take needling, too. "Then what?" was his only response.

"Having received considerable encouragement from the factory workers I'd met at the Bubble, as you call it, I decided it mightn't be a bad idea to drop by the factory and shake a few hands there. Mr. Lutt's name gave me an entree. The night watchman can no doubt tell you the exact times of my arrival and departure, but I do know it was exactly two o'clock when I got home because we have a grandfather clock that strikes the hours. For corroboration on that point, you'll have to rely on my wife and any neighbors who might have been looking out their windows."

"Yeah, there's always somebody, isn't there? Even in a ritzy neighborhood like this. How'd you come?"

"In my car, Chief Ottermole."

"I mean, what road did you take?"

"I came through Lumpkinton Center and picked up the highway as far as the Hoddersville exit."

"At that hour of the night you'd have made better time cutting across through Balaclava Junction."

"Perhaps, but as it happens, I didn't. Come to think of it, I do have an alibi of sorts, for what it may be worth to you. My car started making strange noises, so I stopped at that turnout just before you go on to the highway, and put up the hood. A Lumpkinton police cruiser came along and the men in it very kindly stopped and asked if I needed help. Not being all that clever about engines, I said yes. So they got out and found the cause of the trouble, which happened to be a twig that had somehow worked its way through the grille and was hitting against the fanbelt. I never thought to ask their names, but I did shake hands and give them each one of my pamphlets. They'll remember me, no doubt."

"No doubt," said Ottermole. "If you spent all that time at the Bubble, I'm surprised they didn't make you take a breathalyzer test."

"Perhaps because I didn't drink anything but ginger ale," Claude replied urbanely. "I never do when I'm campaigning. Unlike my worthy opponent, they tell me."

It was well-known around his district that Sam Peters never left for Washington without a jug of home-squeezed and home-hardened cider. His loyal constituents considered this yet one more proof of Sam's Yankee thrift and sound common sense. Shandy's hackles rose.

"Did they tell you your worthy opponent doesn't hang around beer joints buying drinks for barflies, as you must have been doing or you'd have been laughed out of the Bubble before your second ginger ale? Right, Chief?"

"Right," said Ottermole. "Okay, Claude, go on back upstairs and finish your beauty sleep. And don't get any notions about taking a quick trip out of state."

"Should I take that as a threat, Chief Ottermole? It can't be an official warning, since you have no authority in Hoddersville."

"No, I don't, but your chief of police is a lodge buddy of mine. How about if we call it a friendly hint?"

Ottermole had sense enough not to spoil a good exit line by hanging around any longer. Besides, as he explained to Shandy when they were back in the cruiser, he'd run out of things to say.

"Any more bright ideas, Professor? That was one fat waste of time, I guess."

"On the contrary, Ottermole. You've performed a masterful stroke of investigative work."

"I have?"

"Masterful," Shandy replied firmly. "You made Claude admit he had a beautiful alibi all lined up for the entire evening."

"Yeah, well, what could you expect? Everybody else has one."

"That's precisely what I mean. I might grant you

Bulfinch, since his alibi depends largely on the Lomaxes and we both know there's no way anybody alive could get one of them to deviate a hair's-breadth from the truth. I suppose I more or less have to grant you Smuth because his tale of woe was based on a string of calamities he'd have had one hell of a time trying to arrange in advance. But three in a row is stretching things pretty far, don't you think?"

"Well, yeah. That's why I kept pounding at him," Ottermole replied with understandable mendacity. "What do you make of his so-called alibi, Professor? Comparing notes, as you might say."

"M'yes. Now, I don't say Bertram Claude sneaked over to Balaclava Junction between meetings and bumped off Mrs. Smuth, who he's trying to make us believe was not his campaign manager after all. That, I expect we're going to find, is another sample of his approach to politics. It does occur to me that Claude wasn't actually all that far from our campus at any time during his peregrinations since the college lies about halfway between Hoddersville and Lumpkinton. What if he'd picked up Mrs. Smuth either at her own place or over here somewhere after the demonstration, and they'd started out together to attend that reception she'd bullied her aunt into giving? They could have quarreled on the way."

"Yeah, specially if they had something going on the side like Smuth and Mrs. Claude claimed. Claude's wife was threatening to wreck his campaign if he didn't cut out the funny business. We heard her, remember?"

"True enough. Clandestine relationships do tend to give rise to—er—emotional difficulties"—Shandy had experienced one or two himself during his long bachelorhood—"and Mrs. Smuth was by all accounts an exasperating woman. Claude might very possibly have lost his temper and strangled her with that scarf she was so conveniently wearing. He's under a lot of pressure with the election coming up, and he's obviously not the sunshine kid he makes himself out to be in the first place."

"You can say that again."

"So then he'd be faced with the problem of what to do with the body. He could hardly dump it beside the road because somebody might have seen them drive off together. My guess is that Claude would have stowed his late lady friend in his car trunk, gone on to his reception, and been innocently surprised when she didn't show up. He'd have told the aunt he was expecting Mrs. Smuth to meet him there because she'd said she was going on ahead to help with the refreshments or whatever."

"How come Edna Jean didn't push the panic button when her niece never showed up, I wonder?"

"Good question. Perhaps she wasn't all that fond of her niece. I expect Mrs. Smuth had broken earlier engagements with her and made excuses afterward about having to cope with some desperate emergency or other. Claude could have made noises about things being hectic at campaign headquarters, as they no doubt are. Luckily for him the affair was a flop, so he'd have been able to escape before Mrs. Bugleford really got the wind up. He could then have gone to a pay phone and arranged for another of his henchpersons to meet him with a second car in some lonely spot, and deal with the corpse while he made himself conspicuously present elsewhere. Since Mrs. Smuth had been involved in that much-publicized shemozzle at the college earlier, the campus was the logical place to leave her. They could count on her being found pretty soon because everybody knows we maintain tight security."

"Jeez, Professor, that would take moxie. And money. I can't see any campaign worker taking on a job like that without a hefty payoff."

"After what they pulled yesterday, I'd say that crowd have gall enough for anything. As to money, there seems to be plenty. Claude's been spending a fortune in the media, and political advertising always has to be paid for in advance."

"Okay, but how'd the guy dump the body without being spotted?"

"If Bulfinch is telling the truth, it must have happened sometime around eleven o'clock, about the time the night shift comes on. Until then, there'd be security guards on duty, but they wouldn't bother anyone who wasn't acting suspiciously. People are still around as a rule, coming back from meetings or whatever. Suppose someone drove up that path where Bulfinch found the body. He's got Mrs.

Smuth down on the floor behind him, covered with a blanket. The door opens, somebody says, 'This is fine. I'll cut across the yard. Just let me get my books out of the back seat,' or some such innocent-sounding remark. He then drags the body out where it can be seen easily but not too easily, slips back into the car, and the car drives off before anybody who might be nearby realizes what's happened."

Ottermole nodded. "I get you. Like down in the village, people are always dropping their kids or their friends off. You don't think anything of it because why should you? Okay, so where do we go from there?"

"Home to bed," Shandy told him. "I don't know about you, Chief, but I'm beat to the socks."

Chapter Eighteen

"I do wish you didn't have classes this morning," Helen sighed. "What time did you come in, for goodness' sake?"

"Who knows?" Shandy held out his cup for more tea. "Sometime around three or half-past, I think."

"Which means you may possibly have got as much as four hours' sleep, counting what little you had before that fiend Thorkjeld woke you. Darling, I hate to remind you, but you're not an undergraduate any more."

"Thank you, my love, I'm rather pleased to be reminded. Just think, I shan't have to sit passive the next hour listening to some yawning old josser drivel on about some damn thing or other. You wouldn't happen to recall which subject I'm supposed to be teaching?"

"It will come to you. Might I suggest you try to keep your tie out of your coffee? That will save having to change your shirt."

"Why?"

"Because if your tie gets wet and slops on your shirt, everybody in college will start whispering around that I neglect you, and Dr. Porble's dubious about me already."

"What right has Porble to be dubious about you, prithee?"

"He's my boss, after all. We have a sort of love-hate relationship."

"The hell you do. Remind me to stop by the library and hurl my gauntlet in his face sometime when I have a spare moment."

"It's not that kind of love-hate, silly. It's because Dr. Porble secretly thinks woman's place is in the home."

"Especially women with doctorates in library science. Porble weeps with delight when you give him a smile, and trembles with fear at your frown."

"He does no such thing."

"He damn well should. Get off my briefcase, Jane. Daddy's got to go out in the cold, cruel world and earn you the price of a new catnip mouse. Good gad, I wonder if Jane's related to Edmund?"

"Fourth cousin six times removed," Helen answered promptly, lifting the young tiger cat off Peter's lecture notes. "Mrs. Lomax worked out a complete genealogy the day we got her. I can give you a synopsis, if you like."

"Some other time, perhaps. Duty calls and I must obey."

"Better duty than Thorkjeld, I suppose. What time do you think you might be home?"

"I'm past thinking. I can only hope."

Shandy started up the familiar path to his classroom. He hadn't got twenty steps from his own front walk, though, when Mirelle Feldster burst forth from the house next door.

"Peter! Peter, wait. Is it true?"

"I can't wait. I have a class. It probably isn't," he called over his shoulder and kept on going.

That was hardly enough to discourage Mirelle. She slip-slopped after him in slippers and housecoat.

"I heard it on the news just now. That Smuth woman who threw her weight around so much during the silo drive." Mirelle stopped to pant, but only for a moment. "Who did it, Peter?"

"I didn't. That's all I know. Why don't you go home and get dressed? Jim may take a dim view of your chasing me in your nightgown."

Jim wouldn't notice or give a hoot if he did, but that was beside the point. Shandy stepped up the pace. Mirelle cast a slipper and he managed to put a safe distance between them while she was hopping around on one foot trying to get it back on. She'd hardly follow him into the classroom. More likely she'd go over and pester Helen, who'd be trying to straighten up the kitchen and get off to work.

It occurred to Shandy that he'd told his wife nothing about Mrs. Smuth's all too timely demise, having been too preoccupied trying to keep the lids propped up above his eyeballs. Helen might be a trifle put out at hearing the no doubt erroneous details from Mirelle instead of the horse's mouth. What had they been saying on the broadcast, and how had they found out? Had any of those reporters who'd appeared with such mysterious promptitude yesterday afternoon been hanging around last night to see what else was going to happen? Had they again been tipped off in advance? If so, for the cat's sake, by whom?

Yesterday, Shandy would have been willing to swear Ruth Smuth herself and her corpulent cohort Sill were responsible for getting the media people out here. It was hardly to be credited, though, that she'd have invited them to her own murder. Shandy couldn't believe Sill would have been so totally fatheaded as to mix himself up in something this crazy. Did that mean somebody else had been using both Sill and Smuth as expendable tools? And was or was not Bertram Claude that somebody?

Shandy could see why Bertram Claude had denied Ruth Smuth was his campaign manager if in fact she was. Whether or not he'd had anything to do with her death, his well-developed political reflexes would recoil automatically from involvement in anything that sticky so close to an election in which he must surely know he was the underdog. But if by some chance Claude was right and she wasn't, then why would she have told Svenson she was? Had she been trying to pull off a coup that would elevate her in Claude's esteem? Had she been entertaining some unrealistic hope of a pork-barrel appointment? Had she not in fact been on beddable terms with Ol' Dimplepuss but wanted to be?

Maybe she hadn't been working with Bertram Claude but against him. That was a crazy notion. Sam Peters didn't need any dirty tricks squad. He'd throw a fit if he found out somebody was trying anything underhanded on his alleged behalf. He might conceivably even withdraw his name from the ballot.

Was that the idea? Could Ruth Smuth have been trying some kind of fancy triple play to finesse Sam out of the race? If so, she'd been taking one hell of a chance with Bertram Claude's future. Though Sam Peters would never try anything funny himself, he'd been around politics long enough to realize other people might. What if he didn't quit? He'd be apt as not to call a press conference, rat on himself, stand on his record and take his chances, and win in a landslide as usual.

There was, Shandy reminded himself, also the chance

Ruth Smuth had been killed by somebody else for some reason that had nothing whatever to do with politics. At least nothing political per se. For instance, that husband of hers had acted awfully offhand about how his wife was spending the money he must be making via his anxiety-ridden climb up the corporate ladder. Smuth had been more convincing when he was fretting about how Ruth's private pastimes might affect his public relations.

Shandy didn't see how Smuth could have hexed that plane into developing engine trouble, but he did wonder why Smuth had been so conveniently out of town the night his wife got killed. If the plane hadn't been late, would he have contrived to miss it? If some crook hadn't been obliging enough to swipe the wheels off his car, might he have found some other excuse to delay his return to Hoddersville? Smuth might not be so great on the producing production end, but it wouldn't take a mechanical genius to yank a fistful of wires loose, then go bitching to the airport police about vandalism in the garage.

And was it yet another coincidence that Smuth had been coming back from Detroit, the erstwhile home of Alonzo Persifer Bulfinch? Granted, Bulfinch was hardly your prototype hit man, but wouldn't that make him more rather than less eligible for the job?

Shandy couldn't envision any circumstance that would provoke him personally to hire someone to kill his wife, but then he hadn't been married to Ruth Smuth. Assuming he had, and assuming J.B. would approve death over divorce, wouldn't it be smarter to employ a jolly type like Bulfinch than a beady-eyed waxwork with a sawed-off shotgun stuck down his pant leg?

Suppose, for the sake of argument, Smuth had known Bulfinch back in Detroit, and that Bulfinch had done a few of those hard-headed, no-class jobs for him in the past? Shandy was no authority about corporate infighting; but he'd heard a few tales of industrial accidents that happened conveniently to inconvenient people, of sabotage and car bombs, and prominent executives gunned down by midnight intruders. Maybe this sort of thing was inspired by individual initiative rather than company policy, but the individuals involved would be the running-scared ones like Smuth. Fear, ambition, and money enough to hire somebody else to do your dirty work could be a deadly combination.

All right, so Smuth had the qualifications. Bulfinch, as an ex-MP and a professional security guard, would have the training and perhaps the inclination. If they'd worked out their deal in Detroit, who'd ever think to discover any connection between them in Balaclava County?

Bulfinch mightn't have been planning to kill Ruth Smuth so soon after his arrival, but if he'd happened to find her hanging around the college when he'd got that emergency call to finish Purvis Mink's shift, he'd have had a chance too good to miss. Her own scarf was as handy a weapon as any. Better than most, in fact, because it was silent, effective, wouldn't take fingerprints, and couldn't be traced to anybody except the victim herself. They had only Bulfinch's own word that Mrs. Smuth's corpse hadn't been there when he made his first round. Maybe she hadn't been dead until after he'd gone by.

What good were all these ifs and maybes? Shandy realized he was floundering, trying to pin the murder on somebody or other. He didn't much care whom, apparently, so long as it wasn't the one person who'd had motive, opportunity, provocation, and God knew strength enough to have slaughtered Ruth Smuth. Let it be anybody but Thorkjeld Svenson. He'd confess himself if he had to. But then he'd have to implicate Fred Ottermole. Then who'd play Cops and Robbers with Fred's kids every evening?

It was in no amiable mood that Professor Shandy entered his classroom. Nor was he better pleased, when he'd got out his notes, reminded himself of what this session was all about, and buckled down to sharing the knowledge, to be interrupted by a student rushing in late and breathless, dropping her books as she tried to slip unnoticed into a rear seat. He stopped talking, and glared. Students craned their necks. The young woman responsible for the flurry turned red and began to sniffle.

"I'm sorry, Professor Shandy. The reporters outside recognized me and wouldn't let me get away. I kept saying I didn't know anything, but they pestered and pestered. If Uncle Sam—" she broke down into sobs.

"Damnation!" Shandy exploded, to his students' delight. "Don't apologize, Miss Peters. It wasn't your fault those bas—er—that is to say, I deeply regret the harassment. I'll try to see that it doesn't happen again."

"You're not going out there yourself, Professor? You're the one they're really laying for."

After that, one could hardly expect normal lecture-room decorum to prevail. It was either talk or quell a mutiny, so Shandy talked, as briefly as they'd let him.

"President Svenson is relying on every student," he wound up, "to keep on showing the same intelligence and resourcefulness you demonstrated so ably yesterday afternoon. We're at war, in case you hadn't realized it. Congressman Peters is being made the target of a smear campaign. The fact that his opponents are trying to discredit us in order to defeat him shows how much our support means toward keeping him in office. And you damn well ought to realize what Sam Peters means to small farmers everywhere. We don't know yet who's running the dirty tricks, but we'll find out. In the meantime, let's keep our eyes open, our mouths shut, do what we can to protect Miss Peters, and get on with what you're paying me to teach you."

Thus ended the first lesson. The next was much the same, except that Miss Peters wasn't present. She'd found sanctuary at the infirmary with a "Measles" sign on the door, her textbooks for diversion, and a basket of goodies packed by Sieglinde Svenson to keep up her spirits.

By half-past nine, the Lomax boys had called in most of the off-duty security guards and organized the Varsity Horsemen's Team to patrol the campus on Thor, Freya, Hoenir, Heimdallr, Loki, Tyr, and Balder. President Svenson himself led the mounted troops on Odin, greatest of all the Balaclava Blacks. The haphazard influx of media people and ill-advised trespassers was transformed to a disciplined but rapid efflux.

Students and faculty tried to carry on as usual amid the hubbub, but this became more of a struggle as reports filtered in via radio and television, and newspapers began to get passed around. This, as Shandy remarked to Joad when they met in the dining room for coffee and pie, was turning into one hell of a day.

"Cheer up," said Joad, with one of his insufferable

chuckles. "It'll be worse before it gets better. How does that grab you?"

Shandy took the handful of fresh newsprint and moaned. "Oh, Christ on a crutch!"

CLAUDE MANAGER SLAIN IN AFTERMATH OF DEMON-
STRATION. WE NEVER DONE IT, CLAIM STUDENT PROTEST-
ERS. PRESIDENT SVENSON DENIES COLLEGE INVOLVE-
MENT, ALLEGES FRAME-UP. MEDIA GETS HORSELAUGH
AS BALACLAVA CALLS OUT THE CAVALRY. ANOTHER
KENT STATE? WHATEVER THEY TEACH, IT CAN'T BE
RESPECT FOR FREEDOM OF PRESS, SAYS REPORTER HA-
RASSED BY GUARDS.

"Blah!"

He wadded up the papers and hurled them at a trash basket. "Why in Sam Hill should we respect morons who churn out this kind of hogwash? What about that wretched Peters girl a gang of them were hassling this morning?"

"They only count it as harassment when somebody else is doing it." Joad stuffed a large piece of piecrust into his mouth and chewed happily. "We never had this kind of excitement at CCNY. Here's one that ought to soothe your jangled nerves."

"By George, the *Fane and Pennon*'s put out an extra." Shandy re-adjusted the reading glasses to which time and presbyopia had at last driven him. "And Cronkite Swope's come through like a toe in a cheap sock."

OUTSIDE AGITATORS BRING TROUBLE, DEATH, IN UNSUC-
CESSFUL ATTEMPT TO SMEAR COLLEGE AND BOOST FAL-
TERING CLAUDE CAMPAIGN. PRESIDENT SVENSON LAUDS
LOCAL POLICE. CONGRESSMAN PETERS LAUDS COLLEGE,
TRUSTS CONSTITUENTS.

Asked what he thought of yesterday's dramatic events, Peters replied, "How many dang fools do they think we've got in our district?" Asked his views on the murder of Mrs. Ruth Smuth, he replied, "Dang shame." Asked if he intended to take any personal action in the affair, he replied, "Not my job. Svenson can handle it."

Asked whether he intended to do any last-minute campaigning in response to Claude's stepped-up effort, he replied, "Nope." Asked about his immediate plans, he replied, "I got to nail up some loose slats in the corncrib, then get back to Washington and vote against the poll tax on stud bulls that dang artificial insemination lobby's trying to push through. Too little fun left in farming as it is."

Asked about the demonstration at Balaclava Agricultural College yesterday, Congressman Peters pointed out this was one of the fringe benefits of turning agriculture into agribusiness. "Dang so-called labor-saving machines out there ruining good soil, bankrupting farmers, putting farmhands out of work. Any idea how many thousands of jobs have been lost because a few big manufacturers managed to sell this country a bill of goods about how it's demeaning to get your hands dirty? All I say is, if that crowd yesterday could have hired on for a respectable day's pay instead of having to pick up a few bucks doing somebody's dirty work, we and they would all have been a dang sight better off." He was referring to a group of outside agitators found stranded on the highway last evening and given transport to the county line in a Department of Sanitation dump truck.

"Now, there, by gad, is responsible journalism. I wonder if the poor buggers ever got paid?"

"Half in advance and whistle for the rest, I shouldn't be surprised," said Joad. "Now there's a thought. Maybe they snuck back and slew Mrs. Smuth because she wouldn't cough up the outstanding balance."

"It would be great if they had," said Shandy, "but I doubt whether any of that lot would dare put in a return appearance after the bum's rush they got. They were a puny bunch compared to our braw lads and lasses, and Security would have been on the lookout for them. I expect sending that Sanitation Department truck to take them away was the Lomax boys' idea, and a careful head count would have been made to be sure they were all aboard. No flies on Clarence and Silvester."

There were indeed no flies on Clarence and Silvester, so how would they have let themselves be hoodwinked by an old army buddy? Shandy stared bleakly into his coffee cup, watching his chain of suppositions about Alonzo Bulfinch start to come unlinked.

After all, he argued with himself, Clarence and Silvester were country born and bred. They wouldn't know big-city ways. Bulfinch had come from a big city. Smuth was a big-city man, too, even if he did park his corporate image out here in the boondocks. Big-city people thought big was always better. Big-city promoters talked farmers into buying big machines to work it and bigger bank loans to buy them with. Big-city people made big money out of those big machines and big loans and also out of forcing small farmers to sell out to big conglomerates after they'd had their last nickel's worth squeezed out of them.

Big money was being spent on Bertram Claude's political campaign. The only logical reason was that Balaclava County still had a good many small farms. These could be bought up and turned into big business, too, if only subversive elements like Congressman Sam Peters and his allies at Balaclava Agricultural College could be swept from the path of what big-money people were pleased to call progress.

It was an oversimplification to label the big-money people as being inevitably big-city people, though. The good guys and the bad guys were far more unevenly distributed than that. So were goodness and badness, if it came to that. It was a matter of how you personally felt about things, he supposed. One person's virtue might be another's anathema, and both could be sincere according to their lights. And the crime he was supposed to be investigating here and now could be something far different from a simple case of Mr. Smuth wanting to get rid of Mrs. Smuth, but exactly what was it? And why in Sam Hill was Inspiration never around when you needed her most?

Chapter Nineteen

If one couldn't find the missing muse, one might at least obtain brief surcease from worry by dropping in on Helen at the library. Peter thought of a secluded nook among the pork statistics where a man and his wife might snatch a moment of conjugality, provided it hadn't already been nabbed by a pair of lovesick undergraduates. As he was leaving the dining room, though, he bumped into Fred Ottermole. The chief looked tired and disheveled, but withal self-satisfied.

"I've brought those weeds from the clubhouse yard, Professor. What we did, see, we took strings and divided the yard off into blocks. Then we numbered the blocks, mowed each one separately, and put the clippings in different trash bags, like I said last night. We numbered the bags, too," Ottermole added with justifiable pride.

"Nice work, Ottermole."

Shandy had in truth forgotten all about the weeds around the clubhouse. He thought the chances of finding anything significant among them were just about nil, but he was not about to say so after what Balaclava Junction's brave boys in blue must have gone through cutting them down.

"Joad's still in the dining room," he said. "Why don't you pop in and ask him where he wants the weeds delivered? Have something to eat while you're there. Tell them to put it on my bill. I'd go back in with you myself, but I have—er—other business on hand."

"Oh, sure. Thanks, I will. You checked on when Claude left Mr. Lutt's place yet, or should I do it after I've dumped the bags?"

"No, I was planning to go there now," Shandy lied, grateful for the reminder. "I've been tied up with classes. And reading the papers. I suppose you've seen what they're printing."

"Yeah. Say, that was a nice piece Cronk had in the *Fane and Pennon* about me being in charge of the investigation."

"You deserve a slap on the back, Ottermole. Keep it up. Try the pumpkin pie."

That was the least Shandy could say, and the least was enough to send Chief Ottermole happily pieward. Shandy himself directed one long look of yearning toward the library, and went to get his car.

It occurred to him when he'd got about halfway to Lumpkin Upper Mills that he should have called to see if anybody would be at home. According to Ottermole, the Edna Jean Bugleford who kept house for Lutt was an aunt of Ruth Smuth. Mrs. Bugleford might be out buying black stockings to wear to the funeral, if people did that sort of thing any more, or at the undertaking parlor weeping over the remains. Unless they were still at the morgue being autopsied. He should also have asked Ottermole if a report had come in from the county coroner.

Probably not, or the chief would have told him. Anyway, he wasn't going back now. It was a relief to be away from the confusion on campus. He was tired. Damn tired. Maybe he'd have been smarter to go home and take a nap than be driving out here on what might well turn out to be a fool's errand.

But if he'd done that, some reporter would have been leaning on the doorbell to wake him up, no doubt. If the reporter happened to be Cronkite Swope, as it well might, he wouldn't even have the heart to pour a pot of boiling oil over his head from the upstairs window. Anyway, pots of boiling oil, like inspiration, never seemed ready to hand when most needed. He smothered a yawn and kept driving.

He found Edna Jean Bugleford at home and in good voice.

"I told Ruth no good would come of it. Putting me to all that work, and nobody even bothered to show up except a few of the girls from the whist club that I practically had to beg on my hands and knees. And old Mrs. Mawe, naturally. She'd go anywhere if she thought there'd be a cup of tea and a piece of cake in it for her. And that young Cronkite Swope from the paper, who didn't do a thing but pester poor Mr. Claude with embarrassing questions till I thought I'd sink straight through the floor into the cellar. And Ruth not here to help, after she'd promised me faithfully. I'd have given her an earful, I can tell you, if she hadn't gone off and got herself murdered."

"M'yes, I daresay you would." Shandy was not prepared to consider the possibility Ruth Smuth had opted for strangling in preference to a scolding from her aunt. "Would you happen to remember what time Mr. Claude got here?"

"Of course I remember. I had to put the water on for the tea then, didn't I? My brother-in-law won't have a hired girl to live in, though goodness knows he could well afford one. Mr. Claude—Congressman Claude, I suppose I should say—anyway, he rang the bell at a quarter to eight on the dot. He was right on time, I will say that, though it's no more than he should have been, after putting me to all that trouble."

"I should say not," Shandy agreed diplomatically. "And what time did he leave?"

"Five minutes to nine. I looked at the clock while he was putting on his coat, and it was almost a shock to realize such a short time had taken so long to go by. Mrs. Mawe was the only one left by then, and she hadn't even had the courtesy to make believe she was paying attention to anything Mr. Claude said. She just kept stuffing her face with whatever she could lay her hands on. I packed up a basket of leftovers, finally, and asked if she wouldn't like to take them home with her. If I hadn't, she'd be sitting there yet, lapping up every last crumb on the table."

"There's always one like that, isn't there? Mrs. Bugleford, you haven't mentioned your brother-in-law. I was given to understand Mr. Lutt was also at the—er—gathering."

"Just long enough to shake hands and drink a cup of tea. Lot never takes coffee at night."

"Wise man. He didn't wait to hear what Claude had to say?"

"Oh, no, Lot wouldn't be bothered. He always says it's not what a politician says but how he votes that matters."

"Then Mr. Lutt is supporting Sam Peters?"

"Well, hardly. After that dreadful mess Peters got Lot

into over a few measly little soap bubbles in the drinking
water? Pollution, Peters called it, simply because a bunch
of silly young mothers who had nothing better to do and
wanted an excuse to get out of the house began picketing
the factory, claiming the soap in the water was making
their children sick to their stomachs. Why couldn't they
drink bottled water? That's what we did. Furthermore,
the language you hear around the schoolyard these days,
it wouldn't hurt those brats to get their mouths washed
out with soap. That's what I said, and I'd have said it to
their faces, only Lot told me to stay out of it. He said he'd
handle the whole business himself. Lot isn't one to back
down from anybody, you know. So then some of the fathers
that worked at the factory started siding in with their
wives. They came complaining to Lot, and he fired every
single one of them right on the spot."

"Good Lord!" said Shandy.

Mrs. Bugleford appeared to find his response satisfacto-
ry. "That's just what he did. Told them to put on their
coats and go, and they went. That was before they got the
union in, of course. They'd all march out on strike if you
tried such a thing nowadays. Pack of communists, if you
ask me. And then didn't the board of directors get down on
Lot and blame him for giving the union an excuse to come
in and organize. They wanted him to resign, if you can
believe it, after all those years. So Lot threw up his hands.
He said if a man couldn't run a business to suit himself, he
wasn't going to have any part of it. Lot's very strong on
principle, you know."

"He must be," Shandy managed to reply. "Er—where
did Bertram Claude go after he left here last night, do you
know?"

"She does not know. Why should she?"

A man who looked enough like Henry Hodger to be his
cousin, and quite possibly was, stalked into the room.
"Who are you?"

"My name is Shandy."

"Well, well!" This must be the deposed soap king in
person. "The great Professor Shandy, as I live and
breathe, deigning to grace my humble abode. Edna Jean,
you damn fool, why didn't you have brains enough to slam
the door in his face?"

"Shandy?" Mrs. Bugleford couldn't see what her brother-in-law was so upset about. "You mean that man who was so nice to the Horsefalls last summer?"

"That man who did my good friend Gunder Gaffson out of the only decent piece of development property left in Lumpkin Corners. For your information, Professor Shandy, Gunder Gaffson's brought more tax dollars into this community than all the Horsefalls ever hatched. Apparently they don't teach the simple facts of life at that highbrow college of yours."

"On the contrary, Mr. Lutt, we're rather big on the simple facts of life. How do you personally like your tax dollars, for instance? Fried, boiled, or fricasseed? The simple fact of life is, people don't eat tax dollars. They eat food, and you can't buy food unless you have land to grow it on." Shandy was losing the struggle to keep his temper, and didn't care. "How do you think anybody's going to stay alive when the farmland's all developed out of existence and there's no clean water to drink or air fit to breathe?"

"I won't have that filthy, un-American environmentalist talk in my house!"

Lutt was a really amazing shade of magenta now, deepening to blue-purple around the jowls. Rather like a sunset over Mount Agamenticus on a hazy evening in July, Shandy thought. He bowed slightly to Mrs. Bugleford.

"Then I'll take my leave. Might I just ask one or two non-environmental questions before I go, Mr. Lutt?"

"No."

Shandy went on regardless. "You attended the Balaclavian Society meeting this past Wednesday night, did you not?"

"Get out before I call the police."

"I am the police, Mr. Lutt. That is, I'm on—er— temporary assignment to Chief Ottermole of Balaclava Junction for the purpose of investigating Professor Ungley's murder and—er—subsequent events. Ottermole has a reciprocal assistance agreement with your Chief Olson, as you can easily verify by picking up the telephone and calling the police station."

Shandy hoped Lutt wouldn't do it. He had not been on cordial terms with Olson during the Horsefalls' troubles, and had no reason to believe time had yet healed the breach. He didn't even know if Ottermole had been exercising his sense of humor with that Detective Shandy routine they'd fed Bertram Claude last night. In any event, he'd managed to bring Lutt up short.

"Why didn't you say so in the first place?" the former bubble baron was growling.

Edna Jean Bugleford snatched at the chance to save her own face.

"There you are, Lot. Why didn't you give me a chance to speak up before you started biting my head off? What makes you think I'd have stood here talking to him if Edna Mae Ottermole wasn't my own late husband's brother's daughter?"

The housekeeper's reasoning might have been a tad obscure, but her words appeared to carry some weight. Perhaps Lutt was remembering the soapsuds fiasco during which he'd blustered himself out of a job. His color began to fade, though his eyeballs continued to bulge.

"In answer to your question, Shandy," he snapped, "I did attend the meeting Wednesday night. Will that be all?"

"Not quite. When did you leave?"

"When the rest did."

"Who went first?"

"I don't recall. We left in a group."

"What did you do then?"

"Got into my car and drove home."

"Where was your car?"

"In front of the post office."

"Did you offer Ungley a lift?"

"No. He preferred to walk."

"When did he last tell you he preferred to walk?"

"I don't remember. We all knew Ungley preferred to walk."

"Then none of you offered him a ride?"

"Not to my knowledge."

"Did you see Ungley start walking back to his flat?"

"No."

"But he'd have had to pass the post office, in front of which you say your car was parked."

"He may have. I didn't notice. I was hunting for my car keys."

"Ungley was an old man. He walked slowly."

A flicker of a grin flitted across Lutt's doughlike face. "I'm no spring chicken, either. Maybe I hunt slowly."

Shandy let that pass. "Can you tell me what order you drove off in?"

"Order? I don't understand you."

"Yours wasn't the only member's car on the street, was it? I understand the Pommells had theirs, for one. Did they start off before you did?"

"I couldn't tell you."

"What about Twerks and Sill? Did they ride or walk?"

Lutt stuck out his lower lip, thought that one over for a while, then shook his head. "I don't remember. Sometimes they ride, sometimes they walk. Hodger walked, I believe. He lives just across from the clubhouse and can't drive anyway on account of his arthritis. Yes, I'm quite sure Hodger walked home. He was crossing the street, I think, when I drove off. Or maybe he was just getting ready to. He moves very slowly. What difference does all this make? I told you we left at the same time, near enough as makes no difference."

"So you did. And what did you think of Ungley's speech?"

"What the hell—" Lutt pulled himself up short. "I should hardly care to express my ignorant opinion in front of an educated man like you."

"Hodger tells me he spoke about inkwells," Shandy said with calculated guile.

Lutt didn't answer for a moment. Then he said noncommittally, "Professor Ungley had a fund of knowledge on many subjects. His death is a great loss to the Balaclavian Society."

"No doubt." Had Lutt slept through Ungley's talk, as Twerks apparently had done, or was he playing stupid for some other reason? "You'll have to start casting about for someone to replace him," Shandy remarked. "Getting rather shy on members, aren't you?"

"Oh, we always have applicants. Edna Jean, is my dark gray suit pressed? I'll need it for the funeral. Call Goulson and find out if they've set a time yet. Are we through here, Shandy? I have other calls on my time, in case that hadn't occurred to you."

"My brother-in-law's a very busy man," Edna Jean recited as if she'd had plenty of practice telling people so.

"Then I'll thank you for your—er—courtesy," Shandy said, and left.

He must be even sleepier than he'd thought. It didn't occur to him until he was out on the Balaclava Road that Lutt had in fact not told him one damn thing about what happened after the club meeting, or where he'd gone after he'd left that abortive Claude reception last night.

Chapter Twenty

Shandy knew better than to go back for another try. He'd made himself about as *persona non grata* at Lutt's as he could have without committing a nuisance on the carpet. Maybe Ottermole would be able to get Edna Jean Bugleford alone and pry something more out of her on the strength of his family connection.

Anyway, and Shandy winced at the prospect, there was still one member of the Balaclavian Society to be called upon. At least he shouldn't have much trouble getting Congressman Sill to talk. That old blowfish might not be so quick to recognize the apparently notorious Professor Shandy, either. Sill had always been too full of himself to bother much about anybody else. The big question was whether he'd be at home or out recruiting another goon squad to storm the college.

There was something to be said for interviewing a pack of septuagenarians. They were more apt to be at home than college students. Congressman Sill was. He came to the door himself, with a pair of pince-nez as worn by Woodrow Wilson dangling from a black cord in one hand and a badly dog-eared copy of the *Congressional Record* for March 1957 in the other. It was about time he got himself some new props.

Shandy made due obeisance. "Good afternoon, Congressman. I hope I haven't interrupted you in the midst of something important."

"You have, but no matter. We public servants are used to being interrupted." Sill flourished the *Congressional Record* with a great fluttering of pages. "Press, I take it. Which paper do you represent?"

The old walrus must be blind as a bat without those pince-nez. With them, too, like as not. That was a stroke of luck. "I'm with an independent news service," Shandy improvised.

"Ah yes, to be sure. Too bad you missed my press conference this morning."

Good God, had Sill actually called one? He must be even loopier than popular opinion made him out to be. Shandy essayed another fast prevarication.

"Transportation problems. You know how it is. Now that I'm here, maybe you wouldn't mind giving me a short private interview? I understand you've been right at the heart of everything that's happened around here during the past couple of days."

Sill tapped lightly with the pince-nez on one of his chins. "Well, now, I'm not sure I'd say right at the heart, exactly. Finger on the pulse is how I like to think of it. My fellow citizens depend on me to keep a finger on the pulse of government for them, as you've no doubt been aware. But come in, come in. Mustn't keep you standing in the cold. Loula! Loula! Drat the woman, where is she?"

"Up here in the bedroom, where I'm paid to be," shrilled a voice from over the stairs. "What do you want now?"

"We need some drinks down here."

"No, really," Shandy protested.

Sill waved his objection aside. "Nonsense, my dear fellow. I know what it's like, in and out of airports, rushing to meet deadlines, rushing back to meetings, rushing here, rushing there, grabbing a sandwich on the run, catching a nap when you can. How much sleep did you get last night?"

"Not much." Shandy welcomed the chance to tell the truth for a change.

"Then sit down and rest yourself, my boy. Loula!"

"Quit pestering me, can't you?" came the shriek from above. "It's on the sideboard, as you ought to know better'n anybody else. I'm changing her bed, for the cat's sake! Should have done it this morning, but you kept me standing around down there waiting for that crowd of reporters who never showed up."

Sill faked his indulgent chuckle rather well. "You'll have to make allowances for Loula. She likes to think of herself as a character. Faithful old servant, you know. A vanishing breed. Yes sir, a vanishing breed. My wife's an invalid and needs a lot of care. We have another woman who comes in at night, but Loula does most of the nursing.

Loula knows her work. Yes, Loula's good to my wife. So I forgive and forget."

Sill waddled over to get the drinks himself, pouring a long time from the bottle and not bothering with fripperies like ice or water. "There you are, sir." He handed Shandy one of the almost-full glasses. "That's how we take it in Balaclava Junction."

The hell it is, Shandy thought. He went through sipping motions, then found himself a chair next to an overgrown rubber plant. It looked healthy enough and didn't have a liver to worry about.

While Sill was laving his tonsils for the interview, Shandy slopped whiskey into the plant pot and looked around. The Balaclavians were a well-heeled organization, that was for sure. Lutt's house had been the very model of a soap magnate's turn-of-the-century mansion. Twerks's endless yards of Buchanan tartan carpeting must have been woven to order and cost a mint. Pommell clearly wasn't one to stint. Ungley, although he'd lived modestly enough, had left that astounding legacy.

Shandy couldn't recall whether Warren G. Harding and his Duchess had done any major redecorating during their brief stay in the White House. If they had, he thought, the result might have come out somewhat like Sill's place, only in better taste and not so flossy. All this parlor needed were a few gold-plated cuspidors.

And that was interesting. Sill neither toiled nor span. In fact, he hadn't done a damn thing for over thirty years, as far as anybody around Balaclava Junction, including Mrs. Lomax, had been able to find out. Yet here he was, living like one of the Teapot Dome financiers, running up travel expenses, shelling out for round-the-clock nurses and expensive liquor. Those newspapermen who hadn't been here this morning would slit their throats if they ever found out what they'd missed. Shandy ran his eye over the labels displayed in such profusion on the sideboard and wondered if perhaps he'd been a trifle precipitate in treating that rubber plant to so much of this superb Bourbon.

Either the Sill family fortune or that of the invalid wife must have been pretty darn lavish, or else the ex-congressman was less of an idiot than he appeared. Maybe he'd been hauling down substantial fees as a lobbyist all these years. Being a professional pest oughtn't to be beyond his talents when he did it so well for nothing. Maybe he was on the payroll of the CIA or the FBI. That was an interesting conjecture. Shandy essayed another sip of his Bourbon.

"Now," said his host, the amenities observed and the preliminaries taken care of, "what did you want to ask me?"

The Bourbon it was that spoke. "I don't suppose you'd care to tell me who strangled Ruth Smuth."

Sill put on the pince-nez and glared over their tops. "If I knew, young man, I assure you I wouldn't be sitting here chatting. I'd be taking prompt, effective action to bring the malefactor to swift and certain justice."

Well, he'd brought it on himself, Shandy reflected as Sill continued to assure him, according to the late James Michael Curley's formula for successful public speaking. First, Sill told him what he was going to tell him. Then he told him. Then he told him what he'd already told him. All told, it took quite a while. Sorted out, it boiled down to the conclusion that Sill in fact had nothing of importance to tell.

Knowing he'd hate himself for doing it, Shandy risked another question. "Could you tell me what was the last time you saw Mrs. Smuth after that demonstration at the college broke up?"

"Let me pause a moment to refresh my memory." Sill refreshed his drink while he was about it. "Ready for a refill?"

"I'm still working on this, thanks." Shandy decided he'd better give the rubber plant another nip in the interest of lucidity. How in thunder did the old soak manage to keep it up like this? Practice, no doubt.

"Now, you asked me when I last saw Mrs. Smuth."

Sill resettled himself in an armchair that had bobbles the size of Ping-Pong balls depending from its skirt. "First let me say Mrs. Smuth was a woman of impeccable character, highly respected throughout Balaclava County, and dedicated to the lofty principles for which we all stand."

Having so recently been given a sample of the principles

Lot Lutt stood for, Shandy thought of asking Sill to explain what he'd meant by lofty. Then he thought of not asking, which was surely the wiser course. He merely nodded and made an attempt to nudge the interview along. "Was that why she managed to get you involved in the Claude campaign?"

"Perhaps we might explore precisely what we mean here by involvement."

Great Caesar, was there no stopping this old windbag? Shandy found himself drifting off on the whiskey fumes, back to the time his Uncle Charlie had taken him to the County Fair. He'd been six going on seven then. Uncle Charlie had bought him a red balloon fastened to a thin stick of whippy rattan.

Later on, Uncle Charlie had bought him a great, globby cone of pink cotton candy. While trying to deal with the candy, Peter had let go of the stick and the balloon had got away. Instead of sailing off to infinity, though, the toy had bounced along the midway, staying just out of his reach while he ran after it making sticky, futile grabs. At last, outside the India-rubber Man's tent, he'd managed to get a sticky hand on the rattan and yank down the balloon. Was there any stick to yank Sill by, and how in Sam Hill did one get hold of it?

"So what you're saying basically is that you yourself were more interested in the principle of freedom of speech than in getting Bertram Claude elected to the House," he interrupted, when he'd run out of patience.

What Sill was actually saying, as far as Shandy could make out, was that any chance to get up and spout off in public was better than no chance at all, but he'd have a fat chance of making the old blowhard admit that. Balked in the midst of a subordinate clause, Sill blinked and paused to reflect. Before he could get launched again, Shandy pressed his advantage.

"Mrs. Smuth, however, was already actively involved as Bertram Claude's campaign manager. You knew what her position was before you agreed to participate in the demonstration, didn't you?"

"I—hm—that is, Mrs. Smuth gave me to understand she'd been pressed into service, so to speak, as a neighbor of Congressman Claude. We stand by our own out here, sir."

"But if you stand by your own, why wasn't Mrs. Smuth working for Sam Peters instead of Bertram Claude?" Shandy had the floor now, and he intended to keep it.

"Peters was born and bred right here in Balaclava County and has supported this district faithfully and efficiently at both state and federal levels for a good many years. Claude rolled in from God knows where about five years ago, managed to get himself elected to a vacant seat on a platform of dimples and snake oil, and has already piled up the second-worst voting record in the history of the Massachusetts House of Representatives. According to a poll taken by the League of Women Voters," Shandy hastened to add.

He should have remembered sooner that it was Sam Peters who'd once booted Sill out of the seat now held by Bertram Claude, and that Sill himself still held the never-disputed record of first worst. While the ex-congressman was seeking inspiration in the bottom of his glass, Shandy tried a quick change of subject.

"Getting away from Mrs. Smuth for a moment, what's your opinion on the murder of Professor Ungley? You belong to the Balaclavian Society, according to my information. Could you say something about that last meeting? Would you say Ungley was in good spirits, or did he act worried about something?"

"I'd say Ungley was in his usual spirits," Sill replied cautiously. "Of course, he may have been worried. I couldn't say. As a gentleman and a scholar, he naturally maintained a certain reserve of manner."

Sill liked the sound of this. He said it again, rolling it around his tongue and washing down the savory taste with another belt of whiskey. "Yes, that was it, a certain reserve of manner."

Shandy wasn't letting him get away on another flight of rhetoric. "You were the last to see Ungley alive, right? You stayed to talk with him after the rest were gone, didn't you?"

"No, I did not." For once in his life, Congressman Sill managed to give a simple, direct answer. "We all left together. I didn't know Ungley had stayed behind. I can't tell you why he did."

"You never once looked back to see whether he'd started walking home?"

"Why should I?" Sill was weaving an uncertain course between truculence and his usual bland pomposity. "Advanced in years though he indubitably was, Professor Ungley prided himself on his vigor and cherished his independence. We all respected his dislike of being, as he himself would have put it, fussed over."

Shandy thought of the times he'd seen Ungley at the faculty dining room, brandishing his cane and snapping at the student waiters for extra service. Was all that pestering due to the former professor's dislike of being fussed over? He wasn't about to ask. What he really wanted to find out from Sill, though he didn't quite know why, was, "Did you yourself walk to the meeting, or did you drive?"

"Living so close to the clubhouse"—Sill's ornate barracks was in fact only the second house down from Harry Goulson's—"I walked to the meeting. Our distinguished industrialist, Mr. Lutt, dropped me off on his way home. At least I think he did. He often does. Now that I mention it, I honestly can't recall whether he did or not. He might have and he might not. And that, young man, is the best I can do. Ah, me. *Anno domini* is catching up with me, I fear."

"Happens to all of us sooner or later," said Shandy. "Was Mr. Lutt the only member who brought a car?"

"No, the Pommells had theirs, I believe. They always drive. I'm inclined to believe Mr. Twerks drove, too, though I can't say for sure."

Sill's speech was slurred by now. Considering how much he'd drunk in the space of this meeting, aside from whatever amount he might have had before, Shandy marveled that he was able to talk at all. Any more questions had better be asked fast, or Sill wouldn't be conscious to answer them.

"Which of the cars drove away first?"

Sill belched, then put a hand genteelly to his mouth. "Par'n me. I don't remember. What difference does it make?"

None, most likely, but why couldn't a single one of this

bunch give him a straight answer to such a simple question? Were they all blind drunk by the time they left the meeting? Recalling what the inside of that so-called clubhouse looked like, Shandy wondered if maybe they smoked peyote or something. You could probably grow hallucinogenic mushrooms easily enough in those dusty corners.

"Could you tell me what refreshments were served at the meeting, Congressman Sill?" he asked, just for the heck of it.

"Hah! Got you there. None. We never have refreshmentsh. Ushed to, but not any more. Too busy. Important business. Excuse me, young man. I have important business. Be sure to shend me the clippingsh."

Sill took hold of the arms of his chair and managed to pull himself more or less upright. He then essayed a step forward, swaying in a seventy-degree arc. Shandy decided it might not be a bad idea to clear out before the crash.

Chapter Twenty-one

The afternoon was just about gone now. It would be dark soon and Shandy was more than ready to quit. While he was down here in the village, though, he supposed he might as well pay a short call on Mrs. Pommell. She was the only one of the Balaclavians he hadn't spoken to yet. Ottermole had given him a report on what she'd said and done the morning Ungley's body was discovered, and he ought to be concentrating on Ruth Smuth instead of the old professor, but what the hell? The Pommell house wasn't far away and he couldn't think what to do about Mrs. Smuth anyway.

He might as well have obeyed his inclinations instead of his by now no doubt addled brain. Mrs. Pommell was not at home. At least that was what the maid told him when she came to the door. Shandy supposed she must be the maid because the uniform she had on was much too classy for a mere hired girl. He'd never noticed her around the village before and decided she must be a recent import from some exotic foreign clime. She didn't seem to know any English except, "Nobody here."

And why in Sam Hill wasn't somebody here? This was a strange time for a Balaclava Junction housewife not to be in her own kitchen. It was odd Pommell himself wasn't around, for that matter, since the bank closed at half-past three.

"Did the Pommells go out to dinner?" he asked.

All he got was another shake of the head and another, "Nobody here."

Shandy gave up. He'd started walking away from the house when he happened to glance back. There in the Pommells' garage sat their big blue Lincoln, looking smug and self-satisfied like the Pommells themselves. The car was getting on in years, but the Pommells wouldn't dream of doing anything so vulgar as to trade it in for a less opulent and more fuel-efficient model.

They'd gussied it up with a new set of lambswool seat covers, though. Shandy wondered why. The velvet upholstery was still in perfect condition, or had been a couple of days ago when he'd last seen the car down at Charlie Ross's garage. Charlie'd been vacuuming it when he'd stopped by for his own car, and he'd had to pause to admire because Charlie took pride in his work and liked his customers to notice. The Pommells must be expecting another cold winter. Considering the combined breadth of their beams, one might have thought they already had padding enough.

That was unkind, but Shandy was miffed. If the Pommells hadn't taken their car, they couldn't be far away. Then where were they? There wasn't a restaurant around town fit to eat in. Nobody gave dinner parties during the week except Shandy's own wife, Helen, and she surely wouldn't have invited them without telling Peter. "Nobody here" must mean simply nobody who cared to speak with Peter Shandy.

The hell with it. Shandy gave up and went home. To his astonishment, he found the house devoid of cooking smells and Helen slouched in a living room chair with her feet up on the fireplace fender and a Balaclava Boomerang in her hand.

"Good gad, woman," he exclaimed. "What's the matter?"

"Hello, Peter," she replied languidly. "I'll start dinner sooner or later. Just give me time to pull myself together. It's been the most ghastly day at the library. All hands to the pumps and never a letup since the moment our newspapers started coming in. Can you believe the stuff they're printing? And we had the radio going in Dr. Porble's office to get the news, and that was even worse."

"What are they blethering on the tube?"

Peter went to turn on the television set, but Helen moaned.

"Don't, please! Whatever it is, I don't want to hear it. The demonstration yesterday was bad enough, but this Ruth Smuth strangling is the absolute end. Poor Sieglinde dropped in just before I left work, and she was actually in tears, Peter. Thorkjeld's positively beside himself, she says. That makes an awful lot of Thorkjeld even for her to handle. She wants him to call in the state police, but he's turned balky. He says he started out relying on you and Fred Ottermole, and he's not about to change horses in midstream. Peter darling, that's putting a terrible responsibility on your shoulders. Couldn't you possibly—"

"No, I couldn't."

That was the first time Peter had snapped at Helen since their marriage. "Drat it, Helen, this is the biggest thing that's ever happened to Ottermole. I can't take it away from him. If Svenson trusts me, why can't you?"

Her face stiffened. "I'm sorry, Peter."

"So am I." He knelt and buried his face in her skirt. "Don't worry, Helen. Please."

Why should she, after all? Wasn't he worried enough for both of them?

After a while, Helen lifted his face to hers and gave it a few therapeutic kisses. "I'm not worried, Peter. I just hate to see you wearing yourself out like this. Why don't you stretch out on the couch while I throw a few eggs and things into the frying pan? Want me to mix you a Boomerang?"

"Better not, thanks. I had a bucketful of straight Bourbon with Congressman Sill a while back."

"Getting rather unselective about your drinking buddies, aren't you? I should have thought Sill would flee at the sight of you, after what you did to him yesterday."

"He doesn't know I did it, I don't suppose. Besides, he mistook me for a newspaperman. My God, that old blowhard can put it away! Actually, I only had one drink and I poured most of that into a convenient *ficus elastica*. They bounce back pretty quickly. Maybe I could trifle with a smallish, weakish Bourbon and water, at that. And perhaps a morsel of cheese, if you feel up to fetching it?"

"Oh, I think I can stagger as far as the kitchen and back. I ought to have got something to nibble on for myself. Drinking without eating gives me a headache, and goodness knows I've had enough of those today already."

Helen got Peter his drink and snack. When she came back to the living room, he was asleep on the couch. She postponed supper again, put more wood on the fire, and settled back in the easy chair with a handful of crackers and the remains of her Boomerang. Before she'd finished the crackers, she too was asleep.

When she woke, the fire was down to a bed of coals, the couch and the cracker plate were empty. Peter was out in the front hall talking on the phone, softly because she was still asleep, urgently because what he was saying must be important.

"That's right, Ottermole. I confirmed it with Mrs. Lomax. Yes, I understand your position, but it's a risk we have to take. Svenson will—naturally, he'd slaughter us both if we left him out. Get hold of Cronkite Swope and call the—no, I understand you'd rather handle the whole thing yourself, but how—oh, I see. By all means, if you're sure they can manage. Right. Give me five minutes."

When he hung up, Helen was at his elbow. "Peter, what's this about risk? Where are you going?"

"My love, what were we talking about just before you deserted me for the arms of Morpheus?"

"You deserted me first. We were talking about cheese, I think. Good heavens, I still haven't started dinner. What time is it?"

"Half-past ten."

"You must be starved."

"Not really. I ate some cheese."

Helen had her eyes open now. She took a closer look at him. "I must say it's certainly perked you up."

"Oh yes. Great stuff, cheese. Stimulates the brain cells. Well, *au revoir, ma chérie.* I'm off to the wars again."

"Peter Shandy, if you think I'm going to let you go cavorting around all night on an empty stomach—"

"A physical impossibility, my love. Unless of course the stomach belongs to somebody else."

"You know who did it, don't you?"

"Let's say I have a theory. In a little while, I hope, I'm going to have a big, fat, juicy clue."

The doorbell rang. It was Professor Joad and his test tubes.

"All set, Shandy?"

"All set. *En avant!*"

"*En avant* where?" Helen insisted.

"To a game of Cops and Robbers, where else? Keep the home fires burning, and pray Fred Ottermole doesn't bust a zipper."

Shandy gave her a quick but efficient kiss, grabbed his old mackinaw jacket, and vanished into the night. Helen sighed and went to poach herself an egg.

Chapter Twenty-two

"He's there."

That was Fred Ottermole, breathing hot and heavy into Shandy's ear. Shandy had an impulse to retort, "I had a feeling he might be," but didn't. Ottermole was laying his job on the line here. Who could blame him for acting a trifle jittery? "Right," Shandy answered. "Let's move in."

"Okay." Ottermole gave one last, nervous tug to a zipper tab and charged up the front steps.

It was the law clerk who came to the door, looking frazzled and a little bit scared. "Yes, sirs? I'm sorry, but Mr. Hodger was just going to bed."

"That's what he thinks." Ottermole unzipped a pocket in his most official manner and pulled out a printed form with some words inked in. "Know what this is?"

"A—a search warrant?"

"Yup."

The chief regarded the warrant fondly. He must have been yearning for years to wave one of these under some miscreant's nose. Too bad the law clerk was already so browbeaten that he didn't do anything except cringe away from the door.

"C—come in. I guess. Mr. Hodger—"

"Go tell Hodger I want him in his office. Pronto, savvy? Deputy Joad will go with you, so don't take a notion to try anything funny."

"I wouldn't dream of it," the law clerk assured Ottermole with pathetic sincerity.

He slunk off down the hallway, Joad at his elbows grinning like a catfish. Chemistry professors probably didn't have all that many chances to get deputized at CCNY. As Cronkite Swope pussyfooted after them, notebook in hand and pencil at the ready, Shandy and Ottermole started pawing through Hodger's filing cabinets. It didn't take them long to find what they were looking for.

"Aha!" Shandy hauled out a handful of folders.

His cry brought Cronkite Swope haring back. "What is it, Professor?"

"Ungley's writing. Ergo, these are his missing files. Looks as if the old lizard wasn't lounging all those years after all. Great Caesar's ghost!"

"Holy cow!" added Cronkite Swope, reading over Shandy's shoulder.

"Cripes," Fred Ottermole contributed from behind the other shoulder. "Does that say what I think it does?"

"M'yes, I expect it does. Ungley appears to have been a veritable Boswell to the Balaclavians. As soon as he was let in on their important business, he began keeping a complete record. Here, hold this while I find the rest."

Shandy thrust the folders at Swope and was rooting through Hodger's files like a terrier who's found a rat i' the arras when the lawyer himself limped in, escorted by Joad and the terrified clerk.

"What's the meaning of this outrage?" he was roaring. "Whitney, get Judge Jeffreys on the phone."

"Don't bother, Whitney," Shandy told the clerk. "Mr. Hodger will be seeing a judge himself sometime tomorrow morning, I expect. It won't be Jeffreys, though. I notice Ungley has mentioned him a number of times in—er—most appreciative terms. It must have given the Balaclavians quite a jolt Wednesday night, Mr. Hodger, when Ungley revealed the wonderful surprise he'd been preparing for you over so many years."

"I have nothing to say," Hodger snarled, "except that you're going to pay dearly for this, all of you. I have friends in high places."

"So you have, and it's fascinating to see who they are," said Shandy, still flipping pages. "And how helpful they've been, and what they've been helpful about, and how much their assistance cost your esteemed society. Why the flaming perdition didn't you burn this stuff as soon as you got your hands on it, Hodger?"

Hodger did not care to offer an explanation.

"Wow, I'll say this is hot stuff all right!" Cronkite Swope raced through the files, picking out scraps and ticking them off for future reference. "Care to tell us how this material fell into your hands, Mr. Hodger? Mr. Whitney, would you care to make a statement for the press?"

"If you got anything to say, Whitney, you better spill it fast," Ottermole growled.

"I—all I know is, I heard them down here that night."

"What night?"

"Wednesday, after the meeting."

"Who's them?"

"I couldn't say for sure. I didn't come down. I sleep upstairs, see, and Mr. Hodger has this bell he rings when he wants help in the night. If he doesn't ring, I'm not supposed to come downstairs till breakfast time, when the housekeeper comes in. He didn't ring Wednesday night, so I didn't come. I thought some of his friends from the club must have brought him home."

"What time was this?"

"Pretty late, I know that. Seems to me I heard the church clock strike two while they were here."

"Did your boss usually stay that late at the club?"

"I wouldn't know, sir. I mean, Chief. This was the first meeting he'd been to since I came. Mr. Hodger only hired me three weeks ago."

"That so? Well, you just lost your job, in case you don't realize it yet. Your boss is going to be away for quite a while. What are we charging him with, Professor?" Ottermole muttered in a frenzied aside.

"Would receiving stolen property do to start with? You might tack on bribery and conspiracy if that sounds too thin. Rack your memory, Mr. Whitney. Are you sure you didn't hear a voice you could recognize?"

"I did sort of think it might be that Mr. Twerks who lives in the big brown-and-yellow house with all the antlers," Whitney admitted. "I had to take some papers over there for him to sign one day last week. He's got this kind of honking way he talks, and he laughs a lot."

"Was he laughing that night?"

"Yes, some. Mr. Hodger told him to keep quiet." With nothing left to lose, young Whitney threw caution to the winds. "I remember now. He said, 'Shut up, Twerks. That blasted young ninny upstairs might hear you.' He didn't have to call me a ninny. But it couldn't have been Mr.

Hodger who killed Professor Ungley, could it? He can barely manage to scratch himself, let alone swing hard enough to bash anybody's skull in."

"No, it wasn't Hodger," Shandy agreed amiably.

"Then who killed Ungley, Professor?" Cronkite Swope pleaded. "Was it Twerks?"

"All will be revealed, Swope. First let's get Mr. Hodger stowed comfortably in the lockup at the station. Were you planning to read him his rights, Ottermole?"

Ottermole read them with verve and panache. Then he telephoned the police station and asked temporary Deputy Chief Silvester Lomax to send over temporary officer Purvis Mink. Then he deputized Whitney to help Mink take the prisoner and the impounded files down to the lockup.

Shandy was impressed. "Gad, Ottermole," he remarked, "I didn't realize you were such a leader of men."

"Neither did I," the chief admitted. "Maybe that's because I never had this many to lead before. You want to get deputized, Cronk?"

"Thanks, Fred, but I'm supposed to remain detached, objective, and personally uninvolved. Anyhow, that's what it says in the course." Cronkite Swope now had his diploma, *magna cum laude,* from the Great Journalists' Correspondence School framed and hung in his mother's vestibule for all to see and admire.

"Okay, if you say so. Let's go then. Professor Joad, you better come, too. I guess this'll be where Professor Shandy wants you to do your stuff. Provided there's anything to do."

Even as he watched deputies Mink and Whitney departing with the prisoner, Ottermole didn't sound as if he quite believed he'd just put the arm on one of Balaclava Junction's hitherto most respected citizens and was about to jug another.

"Fear not, Ottermole," Shandy exhorted him. *"L'audace, l'audace, toujours l'audace."*

"Who's he? Somebody I've got to pinch or somebody I ought to deputize?"

"Neither. It's just a piece of advice Napoleon once gave somebody or other. Onward and upward is the gist. We've been right so far, haven't we?"

"Yeah, but I'm not sure why."

"Simple logic, man. Hodger lived closer to Ungley than any of the other Balaclavians. Hodger has an office. Offices have filing cabinets. Ungley's files had to be got out of the house in a hurry, for reasons we now understand. Hodger's office was the easiest place to hide them. Ergo, that's where we found them."

Ottermole jabbed the ignition key at the lock. "You mean to say that big moose Twerks, who can't take three steps without falling over his own feet, managed to search Ungley's apartment without waking up Betsy Lomax?"

"Far from it. Twerks didn't do any searching, he was just the caddy. Another exercise in logic. Twerks is the only one of that flaccid flock who's strong enough to have carried all Ungley's files at once. We must assume the person who found them in the house was not. Otherwise the person wouldn't have had to use four of those plastic trash bags instead of just one or two."

"But why couldn't the person who took them away have made four separate trips?" asked Swope.

"Because, I expect, that would have quadrupled the chance of being spotted with the swag. Being respectable citizens, the Balaclavians couldn't afford that big a risk. That's why Whitney heard Twerks in Hodger's office, instead of somebody else."

"So now you're going after Twerks, right?"

"Our lockup's only ten feet square, and Twerks is a big guy," Ottermole worried. "Maybe we should leave him till later."

"Excellent suggestion," said Shandy.

"Then who are you going to arrest next?" Swope persisted. "Whom, I mean." He didn't want another of Shandy's lectures on literate reportage just now.

"Good question." Ottermole popped his lower lip in and out a few times to show he was deep in thought. "Kind of hard to make a decision. You got to approach these crackdowns scientifically."

Shandy handed him a nickel. "It's late, Ottermole. Make a decision. Heads we get Sill, tails it's Lutt."

"Huh? Call that scientific?" Nevertheless, Ottermole spun the coin. "Tails. Okay, so what are we tagging Lutt for? According to your theory, I mean. Just comparing notes, Cronk. Professor Shandy's been a lot of help to me in my investigation. He ought to get some of the credit, too."

"Big of you, Ottermole," said Shandy, "but I'd be willing to eschew the glory in exchange for an occasional uninterrupted night's sleep. Let's see. About Lutt. Oh, the usual, I suppose. Bribery, conspiracy, and abetting murder in the first degree."

"How the heck did the Balaclavians ever think they could get away with it?" Swope marveled.

Shandy shrugged. "Why shouldn't they? They always had before. This is going to be rather a lengthy story, Swope. You'll have a chance to go into the—er—ramifications tomorrow when Ottermole holds his press conference. We decided to give you a scoop tonight because you're the only reporter so far who hasn't been willing to make the college look like a hideout for a gang of cutthroats."

And because somebody had to publish the straight story before Sam Peters came up against Bertram Claude, and Balaclava County readers were the ones who'd be voting, and Swope could be trusted to tell it the way it had to be told. Shandy didn't feel this was the time to go into all that.

At the rate Fred Ottermole was pushing his beat-up cruiser along, coherent exposition would have been a chancy business anyway. The official pothole season hadn't yet been declared in Balaclava County, but there were enough bumps and dips in the road, not to mention broken springs and wornout shock absorbers in the car, to freight lengthy conversation with serious risks of a badly bitten tongue.

Rather to Shandy's surprise, they got to Lumpkin Upper Mills without mishap and parked a short way from the house that soap had built. As they climbed out, he asked, "Who's guarding Lutt's place, Ottermole?"

"Clarence Lomax's boy Frank. Officer Frank Lomax, I mean. Officer trainee anyway, kind of. On the nights he doesn't have to work at the apple warehouse. I'd like to put Frank on the force full-time, but Town Meeting won't vote me the money."

"M'well, now that you've exposed a seething hotbed of

crime in our midst, maybe our tightfisted taxpayers will think better of their pestiferous penury."

"Huh! Probably fire me for not having exposed it sooner." The chief was having another attack of apprehension. "Aunt Edna Jean's going to be madder'n a wet hornet when I arrest Uncle Lot. She thinks he's God Almighty. She had my wife down for a nice little something in her will, too."

"Say, that'll make a terrific headline, Fred," cried the inestimable Swope. "'NO SACRIFICE TOO GREAT IN LINE OF DUTY, SAYS OTTERMOLE.'" Don't sweat it. By the time this story breaks, you're going to be such a hero you might even wind up with a new set of shocks for the cruiser. Mind waiting a second till I reload my camera? I want to get a shot of you making the collar."

"That ought to put me in real good with the Buglefords." Nevertheless, Ottermole made sure his cap was on straight and his zippers all in order. "Come on, let's get it over with."

He rang the doorbell. After a while, Edna Jean Bugleford came down. Sure enough, she was mad as a wet hornet.

"Fred Ottermole, are you out of your mind? What in the name of tarnation do you think you're playing at, waking decent people up at this hour? Does Edna Mae know where you are? And the kind of company you're keeping?" she added when she'd caught sight of Shandy. "That's the bird who got Lot all upset. I haven't seen him so put out since the day they made him resign from the board at the soap factory. He wouldn't even eat his supper, and I'd made my special meat loaf."

"He should have eaten it while he had the chance." Mrs. Bugleford's nephew by marriage had got his courage back. "Next meat loaf you bake him, you'll have to put a file in it. Which way is his room, Aunt Edna Jean?"

"What do you mean which way is his room? And don't you Aunt Edna Jean me, Fred Ottermole. I told Edna Mae right from the start she was foolish to throw herself away on you when she could have had William Twerks. Just because you looked so dashing and romantic in your uniform and William was a few years older—what was that about a file in it?"

Ottermole hadn't waited to explain. He was already up the stairs. Lot Lutt met him on the landing.

"Fred Ottermole, you blasted fool, what are you doing in my house at this ungodly hour? Is this another of your silly games of Cops and Robbers?"

"Yeah, and I'm the cop and you're the robber. I'm charging you with conspiracy, being an accessory to first-degree murder, and what was that other charge, Professor?"

"Bribery, I believe, was the word we had in mind."

"That's right, Bribery. Had it right on the tip of my tongue. Stand still, Uncle Lot. I mean—what the hell do I mean? Mr. Lutt, I guess. Anyway, I got to read you your rights, so quit bellowing and pay attention. Hey, Frank," he yelled down over the banisters, "you happen to have a pair of handcuffs on you?"

"No, but there's some in the cruiser, Chief. Shall I go get 'em?"

"I'll need those for Sill. Get a hunk of rope or something. For crying out loud, Cronk, see if you can work in a plug for a few extra bucks in the supply account, can't you? How the heck does the town expect me to run a major crackdown with two lousy pairs of handcuffs? Okay, this'll have to do."

Ottermole accepted the length of clothesline his part-time assistant brought him and began securing his new prisoner.

"Untie me, you oaf," Lutt shouted. "I demand the right to telephone my lawyer."

"Take it easy," said his nephew-by-marriage just removed. "You'll be seeing him soon enough. We've got Hodger in the lockup already. And we'll be collecting some of your other pals before the night's out."

"How dare you?"

"Oh, we dare. See, we nabbed Professor Ungley's secret files, too. I don't know why you're so down on the Ottermoles, Aunt Edna Jean. Look what your own sister married into. Cripes, after this, Edna Mae'll be ashamed to show her face at the Policemen's Ball. And you nagged her into blowing half my week's pay on a new dress so she wouldn't disgrace her high-toned connections."

Leaving Edna Jean Bugleford speechless, Chief Ottermole stalked out of the house with the soap magnate under close custody.

"Okay," he said when he'd got Lutt stowed in the back seat next to Frank Lomax, "let's go get Sill."

Ottermole hadn't even bothered to post a guard on the ex-congressman. He'd known the old man's habits too well. Arresting Sill was mostly a matter of getting him down the stairs and into the cruiser. When Sill got his eyes far enough open to observe his distinguished fellow Balaclavian trussed up beside him, he did manage to start a drunken harangue about something or other. Lutt snarled, "Shut up," and for a wonder, Sill shut.

Chapter Twenty-three

The lockup was getting crowded by the time Ottermole and his assorted deputies had crammed Sill and Lutt in with Hodger. Cronkite Swope was entranced by the visual effect.

"Wow, let me get a shot of this. Move in closer and sort of put your hands on the bars, Fred. HERO OTTERMOLE CITES NEED FOR BIGGER LOCKUP OR HIGHER MORAL STANDARD IN COMMUNITY."

"Look, I don't want to hog all the glory," Ottermole protested, neatly elbowing Frank Lomax out of the way and grinning straight into the camera lens. "Frank, how about you calling Solly Swain over at the apple warehouse? Ask him if he'd mind lending us a closed van to transport some prisoners over to the county jail. They got real cells with beds in 'em over there. Want one of my profile, Cronk?"

"Why not?"

Swope didn't, particularly, but he thought perhaps Edna Mae Ottermole might like it to hang over her mantelpiece. The *Fane and Pennon* was going to have to get out another extra after tonight's work. They might as well convert to a daily and be done with it.

Shandy gave Ottermole a couple more minutes' vanity-sating time, then he urged, "Come on, let's get Twerks."

"But what about Pommell, and Smuth, and—and who-ever?" Swope finished lamely.

"All things in good order. We have to proceed scientifically. Ask Ottermole."

"Yeah," said the chief. "Okay, Professor. Frank, you stay here and help your uncle Silvester guard the prisoners. Or go get the van if Solly says we can have it."

"Why can't we ask President Svenson to let us borrow one from the college?" put in deputy Joad, who was beginning to feel rather out of it.

Shandy smiled enigmatically. "President Svenson has other things on his mind just now. Ready, Ottermole?"

"Yeah. Say, Silvester, if Edna Mae calls, tell her everything's under control, but for Pete's sake don't mention about me arresting her uncle. I got to figure out some way to break the news easy so's she won't bean me with the frying pan. Not that he's really her uncle, you understand, only her aunt's brother-in-law by marriage. But you know how it is."

Silvester Lomax, being after all a Lomax, said he knew just how it was and not to sweat it, Fred. It happened even in the best of families.

Shandy cleared his throat. Ottermole said he was ready. "You ready too, Cronk?"

"You bet!" Swope finished putting a fresh film pack into his Polaroid and headed for the station door, a steely glint in one eye and a gleam of pure delight in the other. For him, the ride in the cruiser couldn't go fast enough, though Shandy was relieved to be out in the night air, away from the unsociable atmosphere around the lockup.

As they approached Twerks's mustard-and-chocolate pile, a vast, ominous hulk loomed up from the murk like the last of the dinosaurs. "Yesus, what took you so long?" whispered Thorkjeld Svenson.

At least he'd probably meant to whisper. To the strung-up senses of Cronkite Swope, the noise suggested the distant roaring of maddened trolls, deep within some mountain cavern. Peter Shandy, on the other hand, thought the president sounded rather cheerful. He always did when he sensed a fight in the offing.

"Now?" Svenson growled.

"Now," Shandy agreed. "Go get him, President."

Thorkjeld Svenson strode up to William Twerks's front door and thumped. The wood was solid walnut, four inches thick. It began to buckle. Fred Ottermole winced.

"Say, President, could you knock a little softer? He'll be accusing me of police brutality."

"Arrgh," said the great scholar, and thumped again.

That fetched Twerks, his sparse, light hair sticking up in little stiff quills around his cannonball head, his Buchanan tartan bathrobe imperfectly clasped around a frame almost as big as Svenson's.

"What the hell's going on here?" he bellowed.

With so distinguished an audience, Chief Ottermole couldn't resist the urge to ham it up a little. "You're what's going on, Twerks. You're going on down to the station and join the gang. I'm arresting you for being an accessory to the murder of Professor Ungley and the robbery of his flat. Anything else, Professor Shandy?"

"You might put in the premeditated murder of Ruth Smuth," Shandy suggested.

"Huh? Honest, no kidding?"

"No kidding," Shandy assured him. "Go ahead, Ottermole. Stick it to the bastard good and proper."

"Well, okay, if you say so. And for the—uh—you sure it was premeditated?"

"I couldn't be surer. Isn't that right, Mr. Twerks?"

"I don't know what you're talking about," snarled the biggest Balaclavian.

"I'm sure you do. Moreover, I shouldn't be surprised if you got a fair amount of enjoyment out of strangling Mrs. Smuth. Though I expect you were rather galled at having to take your orders from the person who gave them. You like to think you're high man on the totem pole, don't you?"

"You're talking through your hat, Shandy. I don't take orders from anybody. Except—"

"Go on," said Thorkjeld Svenson in his gentlest, hence most dangerous, tone. "Who?"

"Don't bother trying to get a confession out of him, President," said Shandy. "The people who've been using him as their one-man goon squad had Mrs. Smuth's death planned well in advance. I found the particulars of their plot neatly documented in the files Ungley kept so scrupulously all those years when we thought he was just sitting around gathering dust. Ruth Smuth was getting too swollen with her own importance. Wasn't that your problem, Twerks? The group you work for had found her useful enough a few years ago when they organized that misbegotten silo fund for the purpose of getting a hold on the college. Lately, though, she'd been getting too chummy with their other puppet, Claude, and too uppish about trying to run the show her own way. And she'd have taken over, because most of your crowd were getting old and running out of steam. You're not the man you used to be. Are you, Mr. Twerks?"

"Like hell I'm not!" Twerks reached up and snatched a set of seven-pronged antlers off the wall. "Get out of here or I'll kill you all."

Stabbing and thrusting like a maddened water buffalo, he began herding them back toward the door. In one mighty leap, Thorkjeld Svenson had grabbed a four-foot elephant tusk and stood before him, waving the tusk like a Viking broadsword.

"En garde, you bastard."

Tusk clashed upon antler as the two human behemoths lunged together. Shards of broken horn filled the air. Twerks hurled the shattered antlers from him and heaved up a staghorn hatrack.

"Holy cow," yelled Ottermole. "It's the Battle of the Titans."

"Fred, can't you stop them?" Cronkite Swope shouted.

"You crazy? I'm just kicking myself because I didn't bring the kids. They're nuts about monster movies." Ottermole dodged an oncoming corneous prong and found a reasonably safe perch atop a pile of woven cowhorns that was probably meant to be a sofa. "Too bad we haven't got some popcorn. Attaboy, President!"

"OTTERMOLE COMES OUT SQUARELY ON SIDE OF LAW AND ORDER." Swope had built himself a barricade of ottomans upholstered in the Buchanan tartan and was pursuing his journalistic calling more or less unscathed by flying chitin. "Darn it, why didn't I bring a movie camera? Nobody's going to believe this if I write it up the way it's happening."

To Ottermole's loudly voiced regret, it didn't keep happening long. Twerks caught his foot on the head of a tiger skin rug, suffered a bitten instep, and crashed to the floor howling, "Foul!"

"No foul. Tiger." Thorkjeld Svenson wiped sweat out of his eyes with the tail of his shirt, cast an expert eye over the chipped end of his elephant tusk, flung it aside, and balled his fists. "Get up and fight, you yellow yackal."

Ottermole sighed, disentangled his breeches from the cowhorns, and reached for the handcuffs he'd salvaged from Congressman Sill. "Sorry, President Svenson, but I guess I better run him in before you damage the evidence any more."

Fred was getting to be a deft hand with the manacles. Thanks to that assist from the tiger, he made the arrest in record time.

"Ow," whined the fallen Twerks. "Those damn things are pinching my wrists."

"Sorry," said the chief, who didn't sound as if he meant it. "I can't adjust 'em any bigger. Quit bellyaching and stand up, you yackal. I bet you never cared how much you hurt Mrs. Smuth when you were twisting that scarf around her neck."

"It didn't hurt at all," Twerks protested. "I know my stuff. She didn't even squeak. Just twitched a couple of—"

"Thanks. You made a note of that, Cronk?"

"You betcha, Fred. Gee whiz, wait'll the Great Journalists' Correspondence School gets a load of this."

"How about United Press International?" Shandy suggested.

"Oh, them." Swope shrugged and slapped the lens cover back on his camera. "They can read all about it in the *Fane and Pennon*. Say, Mr. Twerks, is it okay if I use your phone to call my editor?"

Chapter Twenty-four

"All in good time, Swope," said Shandy. "We're not through our night's work yet. We'd better get Twerks into the lockup and collect Joad. We're going to need him on our next stop."

"The chemist? How come? Aren't you going to pull in Mr. Pommell? Gosh, come to think of it, he's still holding the note on my motorcycle."

"Yeah, and the mortgage on my house." Fred Ottermole tried to smile, but managed only a grimace. "Ah, the hell with it. Get in back, Twerks. One false move and I'll bust your head."

"You and whose army?" snarled the still-defiant prisoner.

"I'm the army," said Thorkjeld Svenson. "In, Twerks."

Twerks got in. The next-to-last leaf on the cruiser's rear spring parted with a noticeable crack. Fred Ottermole winced and held his breath, but the much-tried vehicle consented, after some alarming creaks and rattles, to move.

At the station, Twerks put up only token resistance. Svenson offered sweetly to stay and guard him, in the hope that he'd perk up enough for another round after he'd had a chance to rest. As Twerks was complaining about his tiger bite and seemed indisposed to attempt a jail break, Ottermole consented. It was as well Svenson didn't choose to come, anyway. Those springs weren't going to take much more punishment.

This time, at least, they hadn't far to go. Cronkite Swope, who'd elected to sprint the distance, was there to meet them when Ottermole pulled up to the curb.

The chief got out first, fiddling with the cuffs of his black leather jacket. "Cripes, I haven't been this nervous since the day I got married," he muttered. "Why the hell didn't you give me a little more advance notice so's I could rent a tux, Professor?"

"Sorry about that, Chief. Here, don't forget your car keys. It would be a shame if some playful soul took a notion to swipe the cruiser while you were in the midst of the biggest crackdown in the history of Balaclava County. Dorkin, is that you?" Shandy added in a low murmur as a shadow drifted away from one of the clipped cedars on the well-raked lawn.

"Yeah, it's me. I mean it's I. Okay, Chief. All aboard and ready for the bomb to drop."

"Then come on," said Ottermole with a wild, desperate laugh. He rushed ahead as if he were storming a barricade, and thumped on the elegantly molded brass knocker.

It was the foreign maid who answered, still wearing her uniform but looking as if she'd been asleep in it. "Nobody here," she told them, and tried to shut the door.

"The hell there isn't." Ottermole had exceptionally large feet and was a fast man in a door jamb. "Steppo asideo, sister. Either they come down or we go up. And never mind trying to escape by the back way, Pommell," he yelled up the stairway. "We've got a cordon around the house."

The cordon was Ottermole's brother-in-law, Joe Bugleford, with a baseball bat, but the Pommells didn't have to know that.

"You tell 'em, Chief," cried Budge Dorkin.

"Never mind me." Ottermole was again a leader of men. "Show Professor—I mean Deputy Joad where to go. He knows what he's supposed to do."

"You bet!"

Joad took a firmer grip on his test tubes, and hastened after Dorkin. Mr. and Mrs. Pommell, both in green wool bathrobes over green-and-white striped his-and-hers pajamas, stormed downstairs.

"What's the meaning of this outrage?" Pommell was demanding. That must be the Balaclavians' stock reaction to late-night police raids. Like "We all left in a group." Something they'd got together and agreed upon in case they happened to need a suitable remark in a hurry. The sort of remark that showed how used they were to working as a group. And perhaps not a terribly bright remark, and not so bright a group as they'd thought they were.

"What's the meaning of it is that your friend Hodger's under arrest and so are—"

Shandy dug an elbow into Ottermole's ribs. "Not him," he whispered.

"Oh yeah. And so is she. Mrs. Pommell, I'm arresting you for the murder of Professor Ungley, and anything you say may be used against you so you better not get started. You neither, Mr. Pommell. I'm arresting you as an accessory. Mind if I read you both your rights at the same time? We're in kind of a hurry. Professor Shandy, you know how to work these handcuffs?"

"I think I can manage. And I must warn you, Mrs. Pommell, that I have no compunction against striking ladies who themselves go around whanging old men over the heads with silver foxes, so you may as well quit trying to scratch my eyes out in the presence of witnesses."

Despite his admonition, Shandy had a struggle securing the deadlier of the species. Budge Dorkin finally had to snap the cuffs on while Shandy held Mrs. Pommell's clawing hands behind her ample back. The husband was no problem. He acted like a man in shock, which he no doubt was, submitting to be manacled with no more than another feeble, "This is an outrage."

The maid looked terrified but held out her own hands with a resigned meekness that wrung Shandy's heart. He shook his head.

"That's quite all right, miss. You're not under arrest. I expect the main reason they hired her was that they figured she couldn't understand what they were up to. Don't you think so, Ottermole? We'll have to get an interpreter and question her, assuming we ever find out what language she speaks."

"That's up to you guys at the college. Come on, we better see what Joad's come up with," the chief replied.

"I cannot imagine what you imbeciles think you're talking about." Mrs. Pommell wasn't giving up the struggle yet.

"Oh, I daresay you can," Shandy answered cheerfully enough. "Those new sheepskin covers on your car seats don't exactly harmonize with your—er—lifestyle, you know. I expect they were the best you could manage under the circumstances."

"What circumstances?"

"Let's just step around to the garage and get that report from our staff chemist. After you, Mrs. Pommell, and don't—er—try any funny business. Did I phrase that correctly, Ottermole?"

"Fine."

Ottermole also appeared to be fighting the effects of shock. Arresting the banker who held your mortgage could have that sort of effect, Shandy supposed. Still, he'd done it. Ottermole might not be the world's greatest intellect, but by gad, the man had guts. Shandy only hoped to God Joad had found what he'd been sent to look for.

Nor did he hope in vain. When they got to the garage, the chemistry professor rushed to meet them, grinning from stem to gudgeon.

"In a word, my dear colleague, eureka! All over the front seat, just as you predicted. They'd obviously tried hard to wash out the stains, but no go. Bled like a stuck pig when you beaned him with Hodger's cane, didn't he, Mrs. Pommell?"

"Who is this person?" she demanded. "How dare he speak to me like that? Is he trying to claim Professor Ungley was murdered in our car?"

"He's Professor Joad, a highly qualified chemist," Shandy told her, "and he's not implying. He's completed blood tests that prove beyond any possibility of doubt that Ungley was in fact killed in your car."

"That's impossible! Professor Ungley never accepted rides after our meetings. Everybody in the club knew that."

"Correction, Mrs. Pommell. Everybody in the club said that, after Ungley was dead and you'd agreed on the yarn you were going to spin. The truth is, Ungley was a very lazy man. The notion of his insisting on asserting his independence by walking home alone on a dark, frosty night is so much horsefeathers. Ungley would have leaped at a chance to be chauffeured in style, as in fact he did.

"Being a knave of the old school, he doffed his hat before

he climbed into the car. He wouldn't have bothered to do that if there hadn't been a lady present, and you were the only woman in the group. You didn't anticipate his hand would close in that unusual cadaveric spasm on the hat, naturally. Nor, we must further assume, did Ungley expect his affable hostess to dash his brains out after he'd delivered such an eloquent address.

"It was not about penknives, as you tried to make us believe, but about how he, unbeknownst to you all, had kept a full record of your exploits with which to dazzle posterity. Mass approbation would have been more the ticket from his point of view, I expect. No doubt you did manage a spot of backslapping and a few discreet huzzahs while you were thinking up the most expeditious way to get rid of him. I can't think why it didn't dawn on any of you years ago that Ungley was soft as a grape."

That raised the question of whether Ungley's associates were much saner, but Peter thought he wouldn't pursue it.

"So then," he went on, "I presume the pair of you beat it the hell out of there while somebody else—Twerks, no doubt, on account of his superior strength and his lame-brained failure to wrest the hat out of Ungley's hand or smear enough blood on that harrow peg to be convincing—lugged the body around back and set the stage for the alleged accident. You came back home, thought up that silly lie about Ungley's having been robbed of five hundred mythical dollars, cleaned up the car, and changed out of the blood-spattered clothes Ottermole will doubtless discover hidden in the house."

"What if they dumped 'em somewhere?" the chief suggested.

"They won't have had a chance. Mrs. Pommell could hardly waltz their duds down to the dry cleaner's, or burn them in front of the maid. If they threw them away, the clothes might be salvaged and recognized as theirs. Their most sensible course would have been simply to sponge out the stains as best they could and hang the garments back in their closets, which I expect you'll find is what they did. We must congratulate you also, Mrs. Pommell, for your presence of mind in taking Ungley's keys so you could search his flat for those precious memoirs he'd told you about. You did a magnificent job of searching. No doubt you insisted on carrying it out yourself, on the grounds that no mere man could be so thorough or so tidy. Right, Mrs. Pommell?"

Her lip curled. Shandy kept pounding at her.

"You weren't expecting anything so—er—copious, of course. Knowing Ungley's cloak-and-dagger propensities, you perhaps envisioned something more in the nature of a strip of microfilm rolled up inside a hollow turkey quill. You should have remembered Ungley was once a teacher of the old school. Er—no pun intended. I meant that he'd have been habituated to preparing his notes in longhand on ordinary writing paper, large enough to be read easily in the classroom. Since he owned a filing cabinet, that must have been where he always used to file his notes. Now, Ungley was a man of rigidly fixed habits. Faced with what he no doubt considered a scholarly task, he'd have handled it the same way he'd prepared his papers and lectures. I doubt whether it would ever have occurred to him there might be another way."

Budge Dorkin wasn't all that interested in the late Professor Ungley's scholarly methods. "What beats me is why she didn't get one of the men to bump him off," he wondered.

"I expect none of the men was ready to take the initiative," Shandy told him. "From the evidence, it would appear that while the rest were dithering on the sidewalk, Mrs. Pommell simply grabbed Hodger's cane, slid into the back seat of her car, and invited Ungley to ride in front with her husband. As the old man was getting in, she slugged him with the loaded handle of Hodger's cane, told Hodger to take Ungley's and pretend it was his, and gave Twerks the bloodstained one to put beside the body. It wasn't bloodstained by then, of course. She'd have wiped it as clean as she could on a tissue or something. The cane had to be found with the body but the blood had to be on the harrow peg to make Ungley's death look convincingly like an accident."

"She didn't wipe the cane shaft," Joad objected. "I fingerprinted it just for the heck of it, and found a fair number of smudged prints. None of them looked like a woman's."

"No, they wouldn't have been Mrs. Pommell's. She'd have been wearing her kid gloves. Mrs. Lomax says so, anyway, and she'd know. As to the other prints, some of them must be Twerks's, but that could have been got around. Any of the Balaclavians could say Ungley'd dropped his cane and they'd picked it up for him, or something of the sort, and the rest would back him up. Not that they expected to be questioned."

"Jeez, they're a cocky lot," said Ottermole. "Finding Ungley's blood on the cane that was supposed to be his wouldn't give you anything to hang on them, either."

"True enough," said Shandy. "Finding the bloodstained cane in Hodger's possession, of course, would have been a very different matter."

"How did you know the canes had been switched, Professor?" Budge Dorkin asked. "They're just alike, aren't they?"

"Not if you examine them closely. The ferrule of the cane Mrs. Lomax found beside Ungley was worn down by hard use, and there were a number of nicks and scratches on the shaft. The one we got from Hodger on Thursday is in much better condition."

"But Hodger's is newer," Ottermole objected. "Remember he told us Ungley gave it to him as a present after he'd been admiring the one Ungley got for himself?"

"Yes, but he didn't say how long ago he received it. Anyway, carried is the operable word here. Bear in mind Hodger is badly crippled. He really uses a cane, leaning on it heavily for support when he walks and poking it ahead of him to test for a firm footing. Ungley was just a vain old coot with a theatrical streak that was gratified by carrying a dangerous weapon in such an elegant guise. He used to flourish his cane around a lot, but I can't recall ever watching him use it to shore up his faltering footsteps. I may remind you that I'd seen Ungley around campus off and on ever since I came to Balaclava."

"Yeah, and I've seen him around the village a lot ever since I can remember," Ottermole corroborated. "I remember him waving that cane at us kids when he got sore at us, but now that you mention it, I don't think I ever saw him leaning on it the way Hodger does. Hey, I just thought of something else. You know those keys of his? I'll bet Mrs. Pommell never found them inside the clubhouse like she claimed. I bet she had 'em in her pocketbook all the time."

"Perspicacious of you, Chief. Swope, you'd better make a note for posterity that Chief Ottermole has done an impressive job of unraveling this tangle of evasions and obfuscations."

"I got a picture of me examining Ungley's corpse," Ottermole added with becoming modesty. "The wife wants to frame it for over the mantelpiece, but you can borrow it first to put in the paper if you want."

"Gee, thanks, Chief," said the reporter. "So can I say you've got the case wrapped up now?"

"Cripes, I hope so, Cronk. I feel as if I'm running the Black Hole of Calcutta already. Dorkin, how'd you like to take Mr. and Mrs. Pommell down to the station and book 'em. Joe—I mean, Deputy Bugleford here can help you stuff 'em into the lockup."

"Deputy Joad may as well go along, too, in case the—er —prisoners take a notion to become unruly," Shandy suggested. He meant Mrs. Pommell. The banker had no more fight in him than a wet sock. "We shan't be needing a staff chemist any longer, Joad. I expect you'd like to go home and get some sleep."

"Who, me?" The chemist chortled. "I'm fresh as a daisy. Fresher. But I'd be delighted to help Dorkin cage your birds. Form up, folks. This way to the hoosegow. Hi-ho, hi-ho, it's off to clink we go."

"Really!" sniffed Mrs. Pommell. With surprising dignity, all things considered, she gathered her green bathrobe around her striped pajamas and decided to come quietly.

Chapter Twenty-five

It had been a long night. Now it was past daybreak. Still nobody felt like going to bed. When Shandy and Svenson said they supposed they might as well mosey on back up the hill, Fred Ottermole and Cronkite Swope offered to walk them home. When the four of them met Alonzo Bulfinch coming off the night shift and he offered them coffee at his place, they went.

When Betsy Lomax came downstairs with a plate of coffee cake because she thought she'd heard Lonz bringing some friends home and knew he didn't have anything in the house to feed them, they welcomed her company. When Edmund sauntered in behind her, they welcomed him, too. When Fred offered Edmund a piece of his coffee cake from force of habit, Mrs. Lomax said Edmund was welcome to have it if Fred was fool enough to part with it, though she couldn't see why four grown men were making such a time over one little cat all of a sudden.

"Edmund's not so little," said Cronkite Swope. "Besides, he's a great detective. SMARTEST CAT ON FORCE DUE FOR PROMOTION, SAYS OTTERMOLE."

He took off his lens cap and snapped a picture of Edmund eating coffee cake for the special edition of the *Balaclava County Weekly Fane and Pennon,* for which type was even then being set. "Now how about a full statement for the press, Fred? There are still a few things I don't quite understand."

"You and me both, Cronk," Ottermole answered, with his mouth full. "Come on, Edmund, quit hogging the cake."

He settled the cat more cozily on his lap. Edna Mae would have one heck of a time getting the hairs off his pant legs, no doubt, but she wouldn't mind. She'd be thinking about that impressive montage of photographs and headlines she was going to make for over the mantelpiece after the extra came out. Which reminded him he ought to be thinking about his public image.

"What I mean is, I'm more a man of action than a man of words." Edna Mae had told Fred that some months before she'd presented him with the fourth member of his Cops and Robbers team, and he'd liked the sound of it. "I'll let Professor Shandy fill you in on the details. Talking's what he gets paid for."

"The hell it is," Svenson mumbled, though in an amiable and non-threatening manner. "Talk, Shandy."

"M'well, since you insist. Thank you, Bulfinch." Shandy took a sip from his freshly refilled coffee cup, and talked.

"I haven't yet had time to read everything we found in those files of Ungley's, but I did manage to skim through some of the more—er—informative portions while Ottermole and you others were packing the prisoners off to jail. The gist of his minstrelsy is that the Balaclavian Society has been a far more active organization all these years than any outsider ever suspected. They've been supporting the spirit of free private enterprise in a fairly big way. I took a partial list of businesses with which the members have been involved at various times in their—er—fundraising ventures."

"Can I see?" Cronkite Swope took Shandy's list and his eyes, as Betsy Lomax remarked later to her cousin Evelyn, bugged out like a bullfrog's. "Erroneous Enterprises, Profits by Proxy, Fabricated Fiscal Fund—wowie! They sure knew how to pick 'em. Every single one of these companies has been in big trouble for one thing or another."

"Yes," said Shandy, "and every single one of them made a great deal of money for a few principal shareholders before its sins found it out. A hefty chunk of the money made for the Balaclavians has been spent by them to further the cause of high-mindedness in government, of which Bertram Claude is such a sterling exponent. It was they who bought Claude his seat in the state legislature and also they who've been throwing such great wads of cash around trying to shove Claude into Sam Peters's seat so they'd have a tame puppy instead of an irresistible force to deal with at the national level."

"Holy cats!"

"Precisely. Their *folie de grandeur* appears to have increased in direct ratio to their years of successful covert operations. I can't think why else they'd have hung on to that history Ungley wrote, even though they did have wits enough left to get it out of his highly unreliable hands as soon as they found out it existed. No doubt they were cocky enough to believe nobody would ever dare to go snooping around Hodger's office for clues to a murder that wasn't supposed to have been taken for anything more than an unfortunate accident. They thought they'd covered their tracks perfectly, and they were, after all, leading citizens of Balaclava County."

"I don't know who ever gave 'em that idea but themselves," Mrs. Lomax sniffed. "Not but what the Ungleys used to be a well-thought-of family in years past, or so I've always heard. I daresay your uncle would have been all right, Alonzo, if that crowd hadn't got their hooks into him. If you want my humble opinion, he was just a fussy old coot who'd have been well enough pleased to spend the rest of his life puttering around with his books and snoozing in his easy chair. But I suppose Pommell and Hodger and the rest got to flattering him and shoveling money into his pockets, and he got carried away. Puffing himself up with his own importance while they were calling him a fool behind his back. Right in my own house, and I didn't even know it."

"Now, Betsy." Alonzo Bulfinch reached out a comforting hand to pat her on the arm. "A decent woman like you couldn't be expected to realize what a gang of thieves and cutthroats like them were up to. What I can't figure out is why they rung my uncle in on it, if he was the kind of fool he sounds like to me."

"I'm surprised at you, Alonzo. Why, Edmund here could tell you the answer to that one, if cats could talk. No, Fred, don't you dare give him any more of that cake. He's fat enough already. Where was I? Oh, yes. In the first place, Alonzo, you ought to remember your uncle had an in at the college. Naturally, they were out to get Sam Peters because he must have been putting a spoke in their wheels from the word go, so naturally they'd want a spy up at the college because it's the college that's done more than anybody else but Sam himself to keep him in office."

"Huh!" Thorkjeld Svenson was too great a man to snicker, but he was emitting noises suggestive of mirth. The idea of Ungley's being a spy appeared to have been too much for his sense of gravity.

Mrs. Lomax wasn't to be flustered by having a mere college president make noises at her. She patted her neatly combed gray hair and swept up some crumbs with a paper napkin.

"That's my story and I'm sticking to it. They'd figure they had to keep tabs on what you folks were up to, wouldn't they? And if you'll pardon me for saying so, President Svenson, I don't think Professor Ungley ever forgave you for making him retire the way you did. Not that he wanted the work, Lord knows, but that's neither here nor there. He was mad at you and ready to do you a bad turn if he could, is what I'm driving at.

"The other thing to remember is that having a professor in the club sort of dressed up their membership list and made them look more high-toned and intellectual, which would give them an excuse for never getting anything practical accomplished. They wouldn't have let in any of the real brainy professors, but I daresay they figured poor old Ungley was safe enough. They must have known they could twist him around their fingers any way they wanted to. He was too lazy to go stirring up trouble like that Smuth woman."

"An astute analysis, Mrs. Lomax," Shandy approved. "Ungley came in handy as window dressing in a good many ways, I expect. For instance, if anybody had the effrontery to ask what in Sam Hill went on at those monthly meetings of theirs, the Balaclavians could always say, 'Professor Ungley gave us a most erudite lecture on toothpick cases,' or whatever. I wonder if he ever did get around to delivering one of his discourses."

"If he did, I don't suppose they listened," Mrs. Lomax sniffed. "Not but what he'd go on talking whether anybody was paying attention or not. Once he got wound up, you'd just have to stand there and let him wind down, like an old-fashioned gramophone."

"True enough. I don't suppose they'd reckoned on his being such an everlasting bore. Or on that exaggerated sense of the theatrical which prompted him to pen his dramatic secret history of their doings. No doubt they thought he was working off his—er—cloak-and-dagger proclivities in relatively harmless ways, such as carrying that loaded cane on his perilous espionage missions to and from the faculty dining room."

Ottermole was stretched back in one of Ungley's armchairs, tickling Edmund over the eyebrows. "I wonder why he gave a cane like his to Hodger and not to the others?"

"I suppose because Hodger needed a cane and the rest didn't," Shandy replied. "Ungley liked money too well to fling it about on presents that would be stuck in a closet and forgotten. Also, I expect he had wits enough about him to realize Hodger was the real leader among them. Hodger, Lutt, and perhaps Mrs. Pommell would have been the executive committee. Pommell was the money man. He'd evidently developed some ingenious ways of laundering funds through the Guaranteed for political payoffs as well as for the members' personal coffers. There was a note among Ungley's papers reminding him to have Pommell clarify those methods for the club records after Ungley'd revealed the joyful tidings about their existence."

"Funny," said Thorkjeld Svenson. "Records. Only work Ungley ever did without being driven to it. And they killed him for keeping them."

"Let that be a lesson to us all," chirped Alonzo Bulfinch. "Sill was the bagman, I suppose, and Twerks the muscle. He's an ex-commando, Clarence tells me. Not a bad little organization for a place like Balaclava Junction. Did they ever pull off anything really big, I wonder?"

Shandy set down his empty cup. "They were pretty agile at getting state contracts awarded to firms they had dealings with, since they gave lavish support to certain people they believed they could count on to deliver the goods. Not all their candidates got elected or appointed, thank God. Some took the money and then disappointed them by turning honest. Claude was their biggest success to date, from their point of view. They were confident they could snag Peters's seat for him. The campaign wasn't going anywhere near so well as they'd hoped, despite the immense sums of money they'd poured into it, but they still had an ace up their collective sleeve."

"Goddamn silo," growled Thorkjeld Svenson.

"Yes, that was their well-laid plan that went agley. They'd had it cooking on the back burner for years, as we now know. They hadn't originally planned to murder Mrs. Smuth after she'd done her stunt, but they did have a contingency plan all drawn up in case it fizzled. I'm afraid we—er—hastened her demise by causing that demonstration to backfire. If their propaganda ploy had succeeded—"

"Couldn't," barked Svenson. "Not enough morons in our district. Take a major scandal to budge Peters. Created one. Dumped it in my lap. Meant to set me up as the killer. Preserving their heritage. Urrgh!"

He emitted a few low rumbles, then went on in a more civilized tone. "Don't waste your sympathy on the Smuth woman, Shandy. She didn't know she was putting her head on the block, but she must have realized she was playing a dirty game. Chose to. Ambitious. Grievous fault."

"And grievously hath Mrs. Caesar answered it," Ottermole put in most unexpectedly. "We had to learn Shakespeare in school. Not the 'Mrs. Caesar'—I made that up myself."

"You're a man of unexpected parts, Ottermole," said Shandy. "President, I hope you're right about Mrs. Smuth."

"I am. Wrong once. Not twice. Who picked her?"

"Mrs. Pommell, according to Ungley's report. They were in some women's club together, and Mrs. Pommell—er—saw the potential. She appears to have handled a good many of the practical details. Hodger and Lutt were the resident Machiavellis. Even before they started grooming Claude to be a state representative, they'd already made their plan for him to be the long-range gun they'd fire against Peters."

"I wonder how they managed to get hold of him?" Bulfinch remarked.

"Sill ran into him at the State House. Fetching sandwiches for one of the people Sill was—er—doing business with at the time. Ungley makes Claude sound like one of those movie starlets who get discovered in drugstores. Anyway, the members checked Claude out pretty thoroughly and decided he had winning ways, so they greased a few palms, hired an advertising agency, and managed to buy him his chance to put a few more blots on our escutcheon. Once he was in office, of course, Claude belonged to the Balaclavians. They'd bought him: curls, dimples, and all. Ungley even put down how much they paid to get his teeth capped."

"That doesn't surprise me any," said Mrs. Lomax, starting to gather coffee cups. "I wondered who was forking out for his television commercials. Those things cost an awful lot of money, Alonzo tells me."

"They do indeed," Shandy confirmed. "Ungley himself, who was no doubt the least affluent of the Balaclavians, claimed he'd already contributed almost fifty thousand dollars to the campaign."

"Our money," Svenson growled.

"Oh yes. You'll be charmed to know, President, that the college financed Ungley's entry into the Balaclavian Society. Back when he was still teaching, if such it could have been called, Hodger and Pommell managed to get then-president Trunk over some kind of fiscal barrel. They then set up a touching melodrama in which Ungley was made to appear the hero who saved the college from bankruptcy."

"Trunk," sighed Svenson. "Good farmer. Lousy administrator."

Shandy nodded. "One gathers Trunk was an excellent college president in many respects, but none too swift at reading the fine print on a contract. Being rock-bottom honest himself, he must never have paused to consider that maybe the other chap wasn't. At any rate, he let Ungley pull the fat out of the fire for him. A few days later, when Ungley trotted into his office with a shiny new contract Hodger had drawn up for him to sign, Trunk bombed again. Perhaps he felt so deeply obligated to Ungley that he couldn't refuse. More likely, he didn't realize how much all those incremental percentages would add up to as time went on. That's where a good part of your inheritance came from, Bulfinch."

"Thanks for telling me, Professor. I figured it had to be something like that. So I guess I'd better go ahead with what I've been thinking about. What I'd like to do is keep maybe ten thousand dollars for each of my five grandchildren to give 'em a little nestegg, and turn the rest over to your Endowment Fund. If that's all right with you, Mr. President."

"Hell, yes. Decent of you, Bulfinch. Call it the Bulfinch Grant."

"Shucks, I wouldn't want you to do that. You could call it the Ungley Grant, I suppose. After my mother," Bulfinch added quickly as he saw the thunderclouds gathering around Svenson's brow. "See, I don't have any use for that kind of money. I've got my pension from the plant, and my job here with Security. And a good home with Betsy, if she'll let me stay on."

Edmund yawned, stretched, crouched, took off from Fred Ottermole's left thigh, and made a neat landing on Bulfinch's lap. Mrs. Lomax gave her cat a nod of perfect understanding.

"Oh, I daresay we can put up with you awhile longer. Come along, Edmund, you can't stay down here pestering. I'll have your dinner on the table at twelve o'clock sharp, Alonzo. In the meantime, you go to bed and get some sleep. I'm going to call Silvester right this minute and tell him he'd better put you on the day shift for a while or I'll know the reason why. A man your age, traipsing around in the cold all night long. Land's sake, you're beginning to look like something the cat dragged in."

CHARLOTTE MACLEOD

"Suspense reigns supreme" <u>Booklist</u>

THE BILBAO LOOKING GLASS   67454-8/$2.95

Sleuth Sarah Kelling and her friend, art detective Max Bittersohn are on vacation at her family estate on the Massachusetts coast, when a nasty string of robberies, arson and murders send Sarah off on the trail of a mystery with danger a little too close for comfort.

WRACK AND RUNE   61911-3/$2.75

When a hired hand "accidentally" dies by quicklime, the local townsfolk blame an allegedly cursed Viking runestone. But when Professor Peter Shandy is called to the scene, he's sure it's murder. His list of suspects—all with possible motives—includes a sharp-eyed antique dealer, a disreputable realtor, and a gaggle of kin thirsty for the farm's sale!

THE PALACE GUARD   59857-4/$2.50

While attending a recital at a fashionable Boston art museum, recently widowed Sarah Kelling and her ardent lodger Max Bittersohn witness the disposal of a corpse from an upper-story balcony to the garden below. A life-threatening hunt for the murderer exposes and international art scandal and unveils yet another museum murder!

"Mystery with wit and style" <u>Washington Post</u>

Also by Charlotte MacLeod:
THE WITHDRAWING ROOM   56743-4/$2.25
LUCK RUNS OUT   54171-8/$2.25
THE FAMILY VAULT   62679-9/$2.50
REST YOU MERRY   61903-2/$2.50

AVON PAPERBACKS

COLLECTIONS OF TALES FROM THE MASTERS OF MYSTERY, HORROR AND SUSPENSE

Edited by Carol-Lynn Rössel Waugh, Martin Harry Greenberg and Isaac Asimov

Each volume boasts a list of celebrated authors such as Isaac Asimov, Ray Bradbury, Ron Goulart, Ellery Queen, Dorothy Sayers, Rex Stout and Julian Symons, with an introduction by Isaac Asimov.

MURDER ON THE MENU
86918-7/$3.50

This gourmet selection offers a fabulous feast of sixteen deliciously wicked tales, sure to please the palate of everyone with a taste for mystery, menace and murder.

SHOW BUSINESS IS MURDER
81554-0/$2.75

Get the best seat in the house for the most entertaining detective fiction from Hollywood to Broadway. The curtain's going up on murders that ought to be in pictures, and crimes that take center stage for excitement.

THIRTEEN HORRORS OF HALLOWEEN
84814-7/$2.95

Here are a devil's dozen ghoulish delights, filled with bewitching tales of murder and the macabre.

THE BIG APPLE MYSTERIES
80150-7/$2.75

An anthology of thirteen detective stories set in the vibrant, electric—and sometimes dangerous—city of New York.

THE TWELVE CRIMES OF CHRISTMAS
78931-0/$2.50

When twelve masters get into the holiday spirit, it's time to trim the tree, deck the halls...and bury the bodies. Here are a dozen baffling tales of murder and mischief committed during the so-called merry season.

AVON Paperbacks